THESE PUCKING BOYS

THIS PUCKING LOVE
BOOK 1

MICHELLE HERCULES

INFINITE SKY PUBLISHING

These Pucking Boys © 2024 by Michelle Hercules

This book is a work of fiction. Names, characters, places, and incidents either are products of the author's imagination or are used fictitiously. Any resemblance to actual persons, living or dead, events, or locales is entirely coincidental.

Model Edition
ISBN: 978-1-959167-79-2

CHAPTER 1
JUNE

'm grading the last English test when I glance at the clock and panic. Shit. It's already past four on a Thursday. The Titans game starts at seven. Thanks to LA traffic, if I don't hurry, I won't make it to the arena in time.

Hastily, I collect all my things and, in true *me* fashion, I bump the desk and send the pile of already graded tests cascading to the floor, spreading everywhere.

"*Fork* my life!" I drop to my knees to pick them up.

"Tssk. What kind of language is that, coming from a sixth-grade teacher?"

I lift my gaze and find Katrina, my work bestie, leaning against the classroom doorframe and sporting a smug grin.

"I said fork. Stop judging and help me, please. I'm late."

"That you are. Hence why I stopped by." She walks over in her five-inch heels with a grace I don't have. She's five-foot-nothing and claims she needs the added height. I think she's insane. As I collect the papers, my hands are shaking, and Katrina notices with her hawk eyes. "What's wrong with you? It's just an off-season hockey game. Big deal if you miss the beginning."

I sigh, meeting her gaze. "It *is* a big deal. I'm proposing to Bill on the Jumbotron tonight."

Her brown eyes widen. "What? Where's that coming from?"

"From a deal I made with him in high school. During our senior year, we got into an argument about feminism."

"That doesn't surprise me."

I ignore Katrina's comment. She isn't Bill's biggest fan, even though she's friendly with him. I don't blame her. Bill is an acquired taste, and most people dislike him immensely until they get to know him better. He's abrasive, but he can also be kind. And he's supportive of my dream of becoming a screenwriter. Most of my family thinks I'm delusional.

"Anyway, he said that if I truly believed in feminism, then when the time came, I should be the one to propose to him."

Katrina grimaces. "I can't believe you agreed to that. You're the most romantic person I know. I thought for sure you'd want to be swept off your feet."

"I do... I mean, I did, but Bill has a point. Expecting the guy to propose goes against my belief that men and women should have equal roles in society. Why should we wait for the guy to decide when to get married?"

"What does your bestie think about that?"

"Oh, I didn't tell Danika about my plan."

Katrina quirks an eyebrow. "Why not?"

I sigh. "She'd probably convince me it was a bad idea. Besides, she's also close to Bill, and they work together. I didn't want her to accidentally spill the beans."

Katrina collects more papers from the floor and sets them on my battered desk. "Call me old-fashioned, but I'd never have proposed to my husband. He knew from the start that if he wanted to put a ring on my finger, he had to earn it."

My chest feels tight. I'd have loved it if Bill had forgotten about our agreement and proposed already. But every time I hinted about us taking the next step, he looked at me and pointedly said that the ball was in my court.

After dating Bill for nearly nine years and living with him for two, I decided to bite the bullet and propose during the game tonight. Bill is a major Titans fan, and I figured asking him to marry me during the game would be super romantic. Booking the Jumbotron wasn't cheap, but Bill's worth it.

Thanks to Katrina's help, all my papers are back on

my desk. I put them in the top drawer and lock it. "I'd better hurry, or I won't have time to change."

"Yeah, you need to look stunning tonight if you're going to show your face on the Jumbotron."

I tilt my head, squinting. "Are you saying I don't look good?"

She arches an eyebrow. "Do you want an honest answer?"

I shake my head, laughing. "Nope."

Katrina isn't trying to be mean. We just spent the whole day at school dealing with students. No middle-school teacher looks good at the end of the day.

I grab my purse and head for the door but stop when my phone rings. It's Bill. "Hey, babe."

"Are you home yet?" he asks in a curt tone. He must be stressed about something at the office.

"No. I'm about to leave work. Why?"

"Can you pick up my dry cleaning? I need my lucky suit for tomorrow."

Shit. "I don't know if I have time. I'm already running late."

"June, come on. You know I won't get off work for another hour. And it was already a big deal for me to leave an hour early. I'm a lawyer. I don't have your easy, breezy work hours."

I sigh. "All right. I'll stop by the dry cleaner."

"Thanks, babe. You're the best."

"I love you," I say, but he's already ended the call.

Katrina is watching me with a stern expression. "Did you seriously agree to run an errand for your lazy boyfriend when you're already late?"

"It's Bill's lucky suit—he needs it for court tomorrow. It's an important case."

She rolls her eyes. "If he expects you to propose, then you should expect him to pick up his own dry cleaning."

"I don't mind," I lie. I *do* mind, but I don't want anything to go wrong tonight. If I told Bill I couldn't pick up his dry cleaning, he'd be in a foul mood at the game. I don't want to propose to him when he's aggravated over something minor. "I'd better go."

"Good luck tonight. I'll tune in to the game to watch your proposal."

Her comment makes me queasy. I knew all along that the game would be on TV, but I've been trying to ignore that detail. I'm more nervous than ever as I rush out of the classroom, hoping traffic won't be too terrible.

It's LA, June. Not even all the mighty gods combined could fix the damn traffic in this town.

CHAPTER 2
JAKE

I hear Mrs. Carpenter's voice in the living room and rush out of my bedroom, hoping I can prevent her from spilling the beans to whoever answered the door. I made her a promise that I'd rather my roommates not find out about it.

She's talking to Lachlan, and the are-you-fucking-insane look he gives me tells me I'm too late. I'll never hear the end of it.

"Hi, Jake." Mrs. Carpenter waves at me. "I just stopped by to give you the list I promised."

"You could have emailed me, Mrs. Carpenter." I walk over and take the long-ass list from her while ignoring Lachlan's glower, which is burning a hole through my face.

I glance at the list and notice that she has tasks assigned to each of her pets. Mrs. Carpenter keeps a menagerie in her apartment one floor down from ours.

"You know I hate using that darn computer my grandson gave me."

Lachlan leans closer to peer at my list.

I pull it away. "Do you mind?"

He shakes his blond head before heading over to our open-concept kitchen. Lachlan would never say what's on his mind while Mrs. Carpenter is here. He's a grump, but he's also the best-mannered hockey player I know—outside the rink, that is. During a game, he'll curse like a sailor and get into fights like the rest of us.

"I can't thank you enough, Jake. I know how busy you'll be during hockey season, but knowing you'll be watching my beloved pets is a relief. I had half a mind to cancel my trip."

"It's my pleasure, Mrs. Carpenter. But your grandson will stop by when we're on the road, correct?"

"Yes. I got the little bugger to commit to it. But on the back of the list, I also wrote down the names of pet sitters I've used in the past, in case something happens."

I flip the sheet of paper and see a list of three names. That makes me feel better. When Mrs. Carpenter asked if I could take care of her pets while she was on her three-month trip to Europe, I should have said no, but I couldn't. She's been talking about that trip since we moved into the building five years ago. It's a lifelong dream that she finally gets to fulfill.

"Everything looks good. When do you leave?"

"Tonight. I'm sorry I won't be able to see your first game of the season."

"It's pre-season. You'll be back while we're in the thick of it." I smile.

She pats my arm. "Nevertheless. I expect you to kick ass tonight."

"We will. Have a safe trip, Mrs. Carpenter."

She gives me a mama-bear hug. Even though I have double her body mass, I feel the embrace in my bones.

She steps back and looks at Lachlan. "You make sure Jake stays out of trouble, okay?"

Lachlan cracks a smile—a rare sight. "I'll do my best, Mrs. Carpenter."

As soon as she's gone, Lachlan starts. "Are you mental?"

I roll my eyes. "It'll be fine."

Ryan steps out of his room looking like a million bucks. His brown hair is sleek and carefully styled like the lawyer in his favorite TV show. No wonder he's been named the best-dressed NHL player three years in a row and graced the cover of GQ magazine last month.

"Why is Lachy freaking out?" He veers for our state-of-the-art espresso machine.

"Shut yer face. I'm not freaking out."

"Sure, you aren't." Ryan smirks, his blue eyes twinkling with mischief while he waits for his coffee to brew.

"Jake promised Mrs. Carpenter he'd look after her pets while she's on her trip to Europe."

Ryan laughs. He's too laid back to be concerned about a commitment *I* made. The only time he's ever fazed is when we mess with his cooking. "Better him than me."

"You know he's going to fuck up, and we'll have to help."

"Hey! I'm not going to fuck up anything. Besides, Mrs. Carpenter's grandson is helping too."

Now, both Ryan and Lachlan are giving me droll looks.

"You mean that high-all-the-damn-time, good-for-nothing idiot?" Ryan arches an eyebrow. "You're screwed."

"No, *we* are screwed." Lachlan grabs an apple from the fruit basket and takes a big bite.

Ryan drinks his coffee calmly, then replies. "Speak for yourself. I didn't commit to anything."

"No one is screwed, all right? If Mrs. Carpenter's grandson doesn't step up, I'll call one of the pet sitters from the list."

Ryan stands straighter, mischief shining in his blue eyes. "Can I see that list?"

"Don't even think about it."

"The list didn't come with pictures, Casanova," Lachlan retorts.

Ryan's eyes widen innocently. "Jesus, I just wanted to see if I recognize any of the names."

I put the list in my pocket. "Sure."

He shrugs. "Fine, hide your list. We all know you'll end up calling one of those numbers, and I'll meet the pet sitter anyway."

"Why are you even interested? Don't you have enough women throwing themselves at your feet?" Lachlan asks.

"You know, Lachy, you could have as many admirers as I do if you weren't such a grump."

"Piss off." He flips Ryan off and then strides to his room.

I sigh. "Why do you have to pick on him all the time?"

"Because he makes it so damn easy." He takes another sip of his coffee. "We need to leave for the arena in thirty minutes."

"I know." I open the fridge and grab a salad.

"You're still wearing sweats and a T-shirt."

I dump my salad on a plate, then sit at the counter. "Your point?"

He throws his hands in the air. "I give up. You're hopeless."

A grin spreads across my lips. "Unlike you, I don't need two hours to get dressed."

He runs his hands over his pristine suit jacket.

"Whatever. If you and Lachy aren't ready in half an hour, I'm leaving without you."

"Stop stressing. We'll be ready. When have we ever made you late for anything?"

His brows shoot to the heavens. "Every other day?"

I point my fork at him. "Exactly."

He stares at me without saying a word. Then he shakes his head. "I swear to God, I don't know why I still try to have a normal conversation with you."

"Because you luuv me," I reply with my mouth full to piss him off. He hates it when I do that.

"You're such a child." He stalks out of the kitchen and disappears into his room.

Alone at last. Now I can worry about how I'm going to keep my promise to Mrs. Carpenter. Ryan wasn't wrong. Her grandson is worthless. I hope one of the pet sitters will work out. Otherwise, I'm definitely fucked.

CHAPTER 3
JUNE

By the time I find a parking spot at the arena, my nerves are fried. Thanks to my detour to the dry cleaner, I didn't have time to go home and change. But luckily, I always carry a bag with essentials in my purse. In the parking lot, I do my makeup, spray dry shampoo in my hair, and reapply deodorant and perfume. Then I pop a mint in my mouth and head out. Bill already texted me asking where I am. I have the tickets on my phone.

I find him pacing in front of the entrance with his phone glued to his ear. He's in his work clothes as well, but he ditched his jacket and tie, and his dark hair is messier than usual as if he ran his fingers through it. He still looks better than me, a fact that's obvious when he gives me an overall glance, tightens his lips, and narrows his brown eyes.

"I have to call you back," he tells whoever is on the other end of the line.

What I'm wearing isn't terrible. It's a cute A-line dress with a constellation print, but it has several marker stains on the front. I didn't think they were noticeable, but judging from the way Bill is glowering, maybe they are. He hates messy stuff.

"What the hell do you have on?"

Pulling my best Cher from *Clueless* impression, I reply, "A dress."

"You're wearing the Boston Zodiacs' colors."

I look down, noticing the purple, blue, and black colors. *Ah hell. I actually am.* "It wasn't intentional. I planned to stop by the apartment to change."

His scowl doesn't go away. "Why didn't you, then?"

Is he seriously asking me that? "You asked me to pick up your dry cleaning, remember?"

"So it's my fault now?"

I pinch the bridge of my nose. "Can we not fight over this? So what if I'm wearing the Zodiacs' colors? It isn't like I'm wearing their jersey."

"Might as well be," he retorts. "Let's go in. I'll buy you a Titans shirt to cover that atrocity."

He walks ahead, expecting me to follow. I'm so angry that I could cry. So much for not aggravating Bill tonight. Maybe I should call the whole thing off, but that would mean losing the money I paid for the Jumbotron time. It's nonrefundable.

Maybe Bill will calm down once I cover my offensive dress and he gets food in his belly. He's always cranky when he's hungry.

The place is buzzing with euphoric energy. I don't come to hockey games often, but I always feel invigorated when I do. There's so much positivity around us, I wish it would affect Bill. He doesn't say much on the way to the gift shop, but his mood is much better after he eats two hotdogs and has a beer in hand. He even cracks a smile at a random text.

I narrow my eyes. "Who's that?"

"The office group chat. Someone made a joke." He tosses his arm over my shoulder. "Come on. Let's find our seats. The game is about to start."

My Jumbotron slot is during the break after the first period. Suffice it to say, I haven't paid any attention to the game. There's less than a minute left on the clock, and neither team has scored. Our seats are in the middle of the last row of section one, giving us a perfect view of the ice. Bill has yelled so much that his voice is almost gone.

The buzzer sounds, and the players head to the locker room. My pulse skyrockets, and my hands are clammy. I might throw up.

Bill begins to stand, but I stop him. "Where are you going?"

"I need to pee and get another beer."

Shit. I didn't anticipate that. I'm such an idiot.

"Wait a second. They're doing a giveaway on the Jumbotron, and I don't want to miss it."

His brows furrow. "Stay then."

"It's for couples only."

"June, come on... don't tell me it's a kiss-cam thing."

"It isn't. Just wait a few minutes. Please?"

He sits down again. "Fine."

Another minute ticks by, but it seems like an eternity. I'm on pins and needles when the camera finally points at us.

"Holy shit! It's us!" Bill exclaims, then waves at the camera.

I take a deep breath, then grab his hands, making him look at me. "Bill, we've been together for a long time and survived so many obstacles that I can't even count them anymore. But through all the curveballs life has thrown us, we persevered, and our love has grown stronger. I can't imagine my life without you in it."

He narrows his eyes. "June, what are you doing?"

I take a small box from my purse and open it, revealing the engagement ring I got for him. It's a simple white gold band.

My heart is beating so fast, I can almost hear it. "William Patrick Richardson, will you marry me?"

The entire arena seems to grow quiet as they wait for Bill's answer. I expect him to curl his lips into a slow smile and say a resounding yes right away, but as his silence stretches and his face becomes paler, a horrible feeling makes my heart shrivel in my chest.

"June... I can't marry you."

My pulse is thundering in my ears, and my face is hot as lava. "What?"

"I can't marry you. I'm in love with someone else."

I turn as still as a statue while my brain spirals, trying to process his words.

"Oh shit," the guy sitting next to me blurts out, reminding me that thousands of people are watching my humiliation live.

Then, the background music in the arena returns and the crowd shifts, but it seems it's all happening from a distance.

"Who is she?" I manage to ask, but it comes out weak, almost vapor.

"It doesn't ma—"

"Tell me who she is, Bill. I deserve to know." I force the words out through my choked throat.

"It's Danika."

Tears well up in my eyes, and the growing weight in my chest makes it hard to breathe. Just when I thought the blow couldn't hit any harder, Bill drops this bomb on me. Danika... one of my closest friends.

Nausea hits me, and I jump out of my seat as if electrocuted. I won't add puking in public to the list of my humiliations. I don't know how I manage to exit my row as fast as I do, but once I hit the steps, I don't look back. I wish a black hole would open underneath my feet and swallow me. But since that isn't happening, I skip the line and settle for disappearing into a bathroom stall. People complain, but when they hear me emptying my guts, I don't hear another peep aimed at me.

As I hurl and cry simultaneously, I think back on my life with Bill and my friendship with Danika. Were there signs that he was cheating on me with my friend, or was I that fucking oblivious? She was my roommate in college, and like most of my friends, she didn't like to hang out with me when Bill was around. Maybe she was already screwing him back then. God, I feel so stupid.

With shaking hands, I grab my phone and send her a text.

How could you?

She reads the message, but leaves me on read. *Bitch.*

Katrina calls me, and I just stare at the phone. Oh God. She must have seen my epic fail on TV, and now she's checking on me. But I can't deal with her. I just want to curl into a ball and never leave this bathroom.

CHAPTER 4
LACHLAN

'm sitting in my usual corner in the locker room, replaying the first period of the game in my head, when Melissa Sanders, the VP of Media Relations, strides in my direction.

Shit.

My spine goes rigid. I know that gleam of determination in her eyes. She wants me to give a quick interview.

"Lachlan, I nee—" she starts.

"No, no way."

Glowering, she puts her hands on her hips. "Yes way. It isn't negotiable. Tammy has been begging to interview you since last season, and I owe her a favor. Don't make me look bad."

I open my mouth to retort, but Jake beats me to the punch. "Lachy will be there, Melissa. I'll make sure of it." He squeezes my shoulder, his subtle way of telling me to follow along. He's using his team-captain card. I glare at his profile but know better than to argue.

"Good. Be out in five minutes." She turns on her heels and walks away.

"I hate you," I tell Jake.

He laughs. "No, you don't."

"Why is Lachy giving you his death stare?" Ryan asks.

"Melissa wants him to give a quick interview for Tammy Reynolds."

Ryan's brows arch. "Ah, that explains his sour puss."

"I'm sitting right here, you bloody eejits." I remind them.

"Can you repeat that?" Ryan leans forward. "I can hardly understand you with that thick Scottish accent."

My accent *does* become more noticeable when I'm annoyed.

I stand up and get into Ryan's space. "Shut yer puss."

Our other teammates are used to our antics, and not one bats an eyelid; they just carry on with their conversations. The head coach is distracted by the assistant coaches, not that they'd give me a hard time. No puck got through me tonight.

Jake pulls Ryan back. "Stop goading him. We don't need Lachy biting Tammy's head off during the interview."

"Let's get this over with. She'd better not do my nut in with stupid questions." I'm talking out of my arse. As if Tammy Reynolds would do such a thing. Even though she's only in her twenties, she's already made a name for herself in the pro-sports world. Her exclusive sixty-minute interviews are coveted by rookies and veterans alike. Thank fuck this is a quick one—she can ask four questions max.

I head to the locker room exit, Ryan and Jake following me. I look over my shoulder. "Where do you think you're going?"

"I want to be there for moral support," Jake replies. "I don't know why Ryan is coming."

"Moral support too." He tries to keep a straight face, but the corners of his lips twitch upward.

Moral support, my arse. He's coming to watch me crash and burn. Bawbag.

The best course of action is to ignore them both.

Tammy's informal interview will take place in the wide corridor connecting the rink to the locker room. I see her and her cameraman waiting for me in front of the Titans logo. She notices my approach and smiles. I wish I could reciprocate, but I'm sure my grimace is obvious. I hate giving interviews. I always get flustered, even after almost ten years of playing in the NHL and going through countless media workshops organized by the team.

Across from her, there's a huge TV screen mounted

on the wall. She switches her attention to it and waits for her cue to start the interview.

Jake, Ryan, and I stop in front of the screen as well and watch an attractive strawberry-blonde lass pull a small box from her purse and offer it to her boyfriend. It seems she's proposing to him. We can't hear what she's saying, but the fella's expression isn't what one would expect. He looks horrified.

"Oh shit. I don't think she's getting the answer she's hoping for," Ryan pipes up.

A second later, the boyfriend shakes his head. The pretty blonde's face falls, and even though she's a stranger, my throat closes. I know firsthand what it's like to give your heart to someone only to have it returned mangled beyond repair.

Before the camera cuts to someone else in the crowd, we see the lass get to her feet and exit her row. The camera zooms in on her face, allowing everyone to see the tears rolling down her cheeks.

"Was that necessary?" I grumble.

"No," Jake replies in a cold and tight tone. That's when he's most dangerous. Like myself, he's pissed.

Even I agree that the whole thing was in poor taste. And her boyfriend… what a jackass.

I arch an eyebrow. "Would you have said yes?"

He looks me dead in the eye. "I'd never humiliate someone like that in public. I'd say yes, then break things off later in private."

I shake my head. A typical Ryan answer.

Tammy Reynolds walks over and asks, "Are you ready, Lachlan?"

I'm still upset about what I just saw, but Tammy doesn't need to know that. I force a neutral expression and reply, "Yeah."

I follow her to the spot where the bright lights from the camera are shining against the Titans logo. She stops next to me with a mic in her hand and a kind smile on her face. But my pulse is thundering in my ears, and my face feels hot. Bloody hell. I must be as red as a tomato.

She starts the interview, and I answer her questions to the best of my ability while trying not to sound like an eejit. It goes fast, and then she's thanking me and wishing me luck. I walk away from the spotlight, and it takes a moment for my eyes to adjust to the lack of brightness.

Jake and Ryan are still around, and so is Melissa. I join them and catch the end of their conversation.

"All right. I'll try to get that woman's information. But I can't make any promises."

"What's going on?" I ask.

"We want to invite the chick who got rejected to the Titans' party tonight," Ryan replies, smiling like a fiend.

It makes my blood boil. "For fuck's sake. She just got dumped, and you're hoping to score? How low can you get?"

His eyes widen. "Calm down. It wasn't my idea. It was Jake's."

I turn to him. "Is that true?"

"Yes. I feel bad for her. No one deserves that kind of humiliation. And I promise you, I won't let Ryan get near her."

Ryan throws his hands in the air. "Jesus! I'm not that bad."

"All right, boys. I got her details," Melissa butts in, staring at her phone. "And the security cameras indicate she's still in the arena."

"Wow, that was fast," Ryan replies.

"It's what I do." She smirks. "I'm going to find her. I doubt she'll be answering calls from random numbers."

"Probably not," Jake replies. "Good luck." He turns to us. "Come on, boys. Let's get back to the team."

I follow them to the locker room. I should be thinking about the game against the Boston Zodiacs, but all I can think about is that pretty lass. Melissa had better find her.

CHAPTER 5
JUNE

I have no idea how long I've been hiding in the bathroom when someone calls my name. "June Summers? Are you here?"

My spine goes rigid, and I don't dare breathe. Who's looking for me? Did Bill convince a stranger to enter the women's restroom to find me? I reject the idea immediately. That's not his MO.

"In case you're here, my name is Melissa Sanders. I work for the Titans."

What? Why would the Titans send someone after me? Are they mad that I screwed up their programming with my epic fail?

I press a hand against my forehead, feeling dizzy. I'm glad I'm sitting on the toilet. "I'll be out in a moment."

I'd love to keep hiding in the bathroom stall, but my

curiosity is wins out. I grab a wad of toilet paper to dry off my wet cheeks, then walk out.

Melissa Sanders is a stunning woman—the kind who draws admiration and envy in equal measure. She's standing in front of the bathroom stall I was occupying, wearing a snug pencil skirt that's long enough to be professional and a white button-down blouse. She looks polished, powerful, and sexy—the opposite of me. Her tanned skin is flawless, and her long dark-brown hair shines like silk. If I weren't straight, I might develop a crush on her.

"What can I do for you?" I ask.

"The right question is what can *I* do for *you*."

"I don't understand."

"We're very sorry about what happened at the arena, and we'd like to make it up to you."

My brows furrow. "It wasn't your fault."

"I know, but three of our star players saw the whole thing on TV, and they'd like to invite you to the team party tonight."

My face heats as embarrassment returns to the surface. My fiasco was so terrible that now I have three pro hockey players feeling sorry for me. "That's extremely kind of them, but I'm not sure I want to show my face in public for the next decade."

Melissa tilts her head and arches a brow. "Are you sure? There will be food, and it's an open bar with top-shelf liquor. Besides, I take it your ex is a Titans fan?"

"Yeah… huge fan. He even bought me this T-shirt tonight and made me wear it because my dress had the Zodiacs' colors."

Melissa's lips become a flat line, and her turquoise-blue eyes shine with intensity. "What better way to get even than by hanging out with his idols?"

I nibble on my lower lip, pondering her logic. She has a point. Bill would eat his heart out if he found out I met his favorite players. And the prospect of free booze is enticing. I'm not usually one to turn to alcohol as a coping mechanism, but I'd do anything to forget the pain of his and Danika's betrayal. God, the thought of them together makes me sick.

"What do you say, June? I promise you'll have fun, and I'll be with you the whole time, if that helps."

"Really? You're going to be my wingwoman?"

She laughs. "Sure, if that's what you want."

Melissa sounds sincere, and I used to be a good judge of character. I'm not as confident in my skills anymore—I should have seen Bill and Danika's duplicity. But…

"Okay. What time is the party?"

"Right after the game, at the Four Diamonds Hotel downtown. You're welcome to watch the rest with me from the VIP box."

I glance at my wrinkled and stained dress. "I'm not dressed to attend a fancy party. I should go home and change."

The moment I say those words, my stomach twists savagely. *Home.* The apartment I share with Bill won't be my home for much longer. I can't afford to pay the rent on my own. My heart takes off at breakneck speed, and I stand on the precipice of a panic attack.

"Are you okay?" she asks.

"Not really. I just realized I have to move out." I open the faucet and splash cold water on my face.

"That's tomorrow's problem. I can get you a different dress, if you're open to it."

I turn to her. "What do you mean? Borrow a dress from you?"

"Not exactly. I'll call my personal shopper. She'll bring several options for you to pick from. She can probably be here within the hour."

Wow. Personal shopper. Melissa must be a big deal. I can't believe she's going out of her way, trying to make me feel better. Then again, if the invitation came from the players themselves...

My first instinct is to say no, but I can't shut myself off from opportunities just because I'm scared of making a fool of myself. After being turned down on the Jumbotron, I don't think I can sink any lower. "All right. Let's do it."

Melissa smiles from ear to ear. "Excellent! I'll call my personal shopper right away. She'll have questions for you."

"What kind of questions?"

"Preference in style, colors, size, etc."

"Oh, cool."

A group of loud ladies enter the restroom, and one recognizes me. "Oh, you're the Jumbotron girl! I'm so sorry, dear."

My face gets hot again, and I don't know what to say. I'm frozen, drowning in my shame.

Melissa links her arm with mine. "Let's get back to our seats."

I let her steer me out of the restroom, grateful for her assistance. I wonder if they have alcohol in the VIP box. I could definitely use a shot of tequila right about now.

CHAPTER 6
JUNE

There's a minute left on the clock, and the Titans are winning four to three. The Boston Zodiacs are a tough team to beat, especially with their goalie. Leo Wiseman is a brick wall with ninja-like reflexes. If it weren't for him, the Titans would be winning by a much larger margin.

The Titans are on the offensive, and someone passes the puck to Ryan Bertrand, their hotshot center. He shoots, but Leo, once again, performs a miracle and catches the puck. The guy bends like a pretzel, making me wonder if he has any bones in his body.

"I can't believe it," Melissa blurts out. "How did he manage that? Ryan must be pissed."

My eyes follow the man in question, and he doesn't seem happy. "Maybe the Zodiacs' goalie is a member of the Fantastic Four."

"What?" Melissa looks at me as if I spoke in Klingon.

"Mister Fantastic," I reply, but noticing her blank stare, I add. "He's a Marvel superhero who has the power of elasticity."

Her brows arch. "Oh. I don't know anything about comics. You'll get along wonderfully with Lachy. He's obsessed with them."

"Lachy?"

"Lachlan Stewart. Our goalie."

I feel stupid for asking, and I hope my face isn't showing it. One would think I'd stop getting embarrassed over small things after the Jumbotron incident, but no.

"Ah... sorry. I don't follow hockey."

"Don't feel bad. Many people who come to the games don't. But I should probably tell you more about the players who invited you to the party."

"Yeah, that would be a good idea."

The buzzer sounds, signaling the end of the game. I turn my attention to the ice. The Zodiacs make their way to the locker room, but the Titans remain on the ice to say thank you to the crowd.

"Who invited me, by the way?" I can't believe I didn't ask sooner.

"Jake Phillips had the idea, but Ryan and Lachy were fully on board with it. That's the three of them on camera now."

I look at one of the TV screens in the VIP box just as

it closes in on them. They've removed their helmets, and holy cannoli, I never knew hockey players could be that attractive. My heart flutters in my chest, but I'm blaming my reaction on the two shots of tequila I had.

Right, June. You're not blind, and those men are fiiine. The thought pops into my head in Katrina's voice. Why am I so weird?

"Nayara is here," Melissa tells me. "Let's see what she brought."

Nayara is Melissa's personal shopper. I spent ten minutes answering her questions about my likes and dislikes, and I'm damn curious to see what she brought for me. "Where are we meeting her?"

"In my office."

I follow her out of the VIP box and through a maze of corridors. The farther we go, the less busy it becomes, until we enter a restricted area that only people working for the Titans can access. As I look around in bewilderment, I can't help but think that Bill would give his nut sack for a chance to be here. As heartbroken as I am, the notion does make me feel better.

"Can I take pictures?" I ask.

"Sure. Take pictures, shoot videos. Make sure to tag the team's social media accounts if you decide to post them."

"You won't get in trouble if I do?"

She smirks at me. "I'm the VP of Media Relations. I won't get in trouble."

"Wow. I knew you were a big deal, but I didn't realize you were a VP."

"Most people don't because of my age and appearance. I don't mind. I actually enjoy it when they underestimate me."

"If you don't mind me asking, how old are you?"

Melissa stops in front of a dark wood door with her name and title carved on a brass plaque. "Twenty-seven."

"I'm twenty-five," I say, even though she didn't ask.

She's only two years older than me, and she's already accomplished so much. I can't help but feel gloomy about it. My dream career is a long shot, but if becoming a screenwriter doesn't pan out, I thought I'd be okay as long as I achieved the other items on my bucket list. Marrying Bill was one of them.

No, I won't think about that jackass anymore tonight. Melissa is right. He's tomorrow's problem.

Nayara is already inside Melissa's office, standing in front of a rack of colorful dresses. She turns to us and smiles brightly. She looks like a fairy, with her petite frame and short, bright blue pixie-cut hair that contrasts nicely with her tanned complexion.

"Hello, you must be June." She offers me her hand.

"Hi, nice to meet you."

Melissa has already wandered to the selection on display, and she's browsing the options. She pulls out a purple dress with a flowy skirt and announces, "You need to try this one. It's gorgeous."

I take the dress from her and gasp at the price tag. "It costs fifteen hundred dollars! I can't afford this."

"Don't worry about it. Whatever you pick will be written off as a marketing expense," she replies.

My eyes widen. "Oh, wow. I don't know what to say."

"Try it on, honey. That color with your hair and skin tone will look amazing," Nayara pipes up.

Melissa gives me a pair of silver strappy sandals. "Try it on with these."

I glance at the five-inch stiletto heels and swallow hard. "I'll probably break my neck if I wear those."

"Nonsense. My private bathroom is through that door."

In a daze, I disappear inside the large and luxurious bathroom. I can't believe how this evening is turning out. Maybe I'm passed out in that bathroom stall, and this is just a dream.

I pinch my forearm to test it out. "Ouch!"

"Are you okay in there?" Melissa asks.

"Yeah, I'm fine. Don't mind me." *June, get a grip.*

I take my clothes off and, with care, try on the purple dress. The fabric is delicate—chiffon, I guess—and if I'm not careful, I might tear it. I usually wear sturdy materials that can withstand my clumsiness.

"How is it?" Nayara asks. "Do you need help with the zipper?"

I squish my boobs together and suck in my stomach, then try to zip up the dress. Side zippers and I rarely get along. "Yeah. You can come in."

She sticks in her head and says, "Oh, the color looks amazing on you."

"Yeah, but I'm afraid I'm a size too big for it."

"Let me see."

Nayara moves closer and effortlessly slides the zipper up. The top of the dress has boning like a corset, and it makes my waist look tiny and pushes my boobs up.

"Stunning," she says.

I press a hand over my enhanced cleavage, trying to hide it. "I don't know."

"You look gorgeous, June," Melissa chimes in from the door. "You can try another dress, but I think that's the one."

Staring at my reflection, I smooth the front of the dress. I've never worn anything so luxurious and pretty. It's a tempting indulgence, and any other day, I would resist. But tonight has become all about stepping out of my comfort zone. If I tear a seam or end up showing my ass to a bunch of strangers, it still won't be as bad as finding out Bill was cheating on me with Danika.

"Okay. I'll take it."

"Try the shoes, Cinderella." Melissa smirks.

The bathroom is so large that there's a chair opposite the sink, and the toilet is behind another door.

"If I'm Cinderella, does that mean my clothes turn back to rags at the stroke of midnight?"

"Only if you want them to."

Nayara drops into a crouch in front of me. "Let me help. It's tricky getting these on while you're wearing such a constricting outfit."

"Thanks." I'm glad I got a pedicure last weekend and don't have troll feet. The sandals are surprisingly comfortable, but when I stand up, I'm wobbly. "Shit. How can anyone walk in these?"

"Easy. I do it every day." Melissa points at her stiletto pumps.

I glance at my ballerina flats with longing. I wish I could wear them, but it would be a disservice to this gorgeous dress.

"Do you want to do something with your hair?" Nayara asks. "I'm not a professional hair stylist, but I brought tools."

"What kind of tools?"

"Hair straightener and curler. I can do your makeup too."

I glance at Melissa. I don't want to abuse her generosity. As if sensing my train of thought, she says, "Go ahead, June. Nayara will do my makeup as well. It's all good."

"Okay, sure."

"Melissa is your very own fairy godmother." Nayara laughs.

"The hell I am." She tosses her long hair over her shoulder and stares at her reflection. "I'm too young to be that frumpy old lady."

Nayara and I trade a look, and I don't know why, but we both start to laugh.

"What?" Melissa frowns at us.

"I'm laughing because it feels like I'm stuck in a wonderful dream."

"Wait until you meet the boys." Melissa winks at me.

Butterflies wake in my stomach. I'm getting giddy, and I've only seen them sweaty and with helmet hair.

"I'll probably never want to wake up."

CHAPTER 7
JUNE

We arrive at the Titans' party two hours after the end of the game. Getting ready took an hour, and the drive to the five-star hotel took another thanks to traffic. Melissa changed into a stunning bodycon dress in a deep red that hugs her curves in all the right places but doesn't show any excess skin. She's clearly a master at balancing sexy and classy. My own style is cute and practical, and what I'm wearing tonight is way out there for me.

Once again, Melissa links her arm with mine, and together, we enter the upscale restaurant on the rooftop reserved entirely for the private party. I'm thankful for her support because, one, I'm still getting used to the high heels, and two, I'm shaking like a leaf.

"Relax. Everyone here is a friend," she tells me.

I nod, unable to reply with words. How can I explain

that I get flustered at social events full of strangers? I'm bound to make a fool of myself many times tonight. I hope not in front of my hot benefactors.

"I think I need a drink," I say.

"Sure. Let's head over to the bar."

Halfway there, Melissa stops in her tracks. "Hold on. My purse is vibrating." She unlinks her arm with mine and pulls her phone out. "It's my fiancé. I need to get this. I'll meet you at the bar."

I panic. There are steps leading to the bar, and with my two left feet and wearing shoes I'm not used to, I can foresee the disaster already.

"Fork me gently with a chainsaw," I mutter.

"Did you just say *fork* me?" a man to my right asks.

My eyes widen, and I'm pretty sure my jaw drops all the way to the floor as well. Ryan Bertrand, one of the players who invited me to the party, is next to me, watching me with vibrant and intense blue eyes.

"Yeah. Force of habit."

He raises a brow. "Why? Do you have young kids at home?"

"No, I'm a middle-school teacher."

"I remember cursing a lot in middle school." He smiles broadly, showing a pair of dimples.

My face becomes so hot it could be mistaken for lava. I'm sure my reaction has everything to do with how this gorgeous man is looking at me as if I were something he'd like to eat. Shit. Why did I think that? Now I want him to eat me. My entire body is on fire, and I'm beginning to sweat. This isn't good.

"Oh, I'm sure my students curse, but I can't have a dirty mouth around them."

Fuuuck. Did I just say dirty mouth?

His eyes twinkle with mirth. "I love a girl with a dirty mouth."

My tongue gets stuck to the roof of my wanting-to-be-dirty mouth while my mind spirals. I don't know what to do, so I simply stare at him.

Say something, June. Anything.

"I bet you do," I blurt out.

Not that, you idiot.

He laughs, and the sound is sexy as hell. I don't need a drink. I need a cold shower.

"Ryan, I see that you found our guest of honor already," Melissa chimes in.

I'm glad she's done with her call, because another second chatting with Mr. Sex on a Stick, and I'd have combusted on the spot. Worst of all, I'm sure he wasn't even trying to flirt with me.

"I sure have. I'm Ryan Bertrand." He offers me his hand to shake, and like a dumbass, I wipe my sweaty palm on my skirt first.

Classy, June.

"June Summers."

"Interesting name."

"If by interesting you mean redundant, you're right."

He chuckles. "I like you, June. Where are you from?"

"Baron, Texas. It's a small town."

"It must have been quite a shock to move to LA. How long have you been here?"

"A couple years."

I can't believe I managed to answer all these questions without putting my foot in my mouth. I'm still nervous, but Ryan is charming and nice, and seems truly interested in getting to know me.

"Ah, then you must have already gotten used to the chaos. Can I get you something to drink?"

I open my mouth to reply, but the other two hot-enough-to-melt-popsicles-in-a-freezer players join us.

"You aren't getting her anything," the blond one replies with a Scottish accent. He's glowering at Ryan, but I'm not getting aggressive vibes from him.

Ryan must not be either, because he seems unbothered by his teammate. "June, meet Lachlan Stewart and Jake Phillips."

My mind begins to work in overdrive. I don't want to stare, but it's hard not to. These men are gorgeous. Before I get tongue-tied, I force the words out of my mouth, praying I can still string sentences together. "Hi, nice to meet you."

"Nice to meet *you*," Jake replies, looking into my eyes as if he wants to read my mind. What's with these boys and their stares? "I hope Ryan didn't bother you too much."

"Excuse me?" Ryan butts in. "I was the perfect gentleman, wasn't I, June?"

They're all focused on me now, and their interest is turning me into a fool who forgot how to speak.

"Will you give the poor girl a break?" Melissa intervenes. "Come on, June. Let's get you something to drink."

Before I let Melissa steer me toward the bar, I nod to the guys. "Thanks for inviting me."

"No need to thank us, sugar." Ryan smiles and immediately gets elbowed by Lachlan.

They don't follow us, and I'm a bit disappointed. I want to thank them properly, and maybe ogle the trio some more.

"What would you like to drink?" Melissa asks me when we get to the bar.

I almost go for another shot of tequila but think better of it. I should order a cocktail instead, so my hand is occupied for a while. I never know what to do with my hands in uncomfortable social situations.

"I'll have a dirty martini."

Melissa smirks. "Good choice. I'll have one too."

While she orders the drinks, I look over my shoulder to see if my hockey players are still in the same spot. Sadly, they aren't.

Your *hockey players, June? Get a grip.*

"Here's your drink, hon." The glass is filled to the brim. Jesus.

Melissa sips her drink so the alcohol level isn't dangerously close to spilling everywhere. I follow her example, and damn, this stuff is strong. I have to be careful.

"So, what's the deal with Ryan and Lachlan? Are they not friends?"

Melissa laughs. "They're frenemies. Or maybe they're like brothers who bicker a lot."

"I see."

"The three of them live together in a big-ass loft apartment downtown."

That surprises me. "Really? Don't they make enough money to have their own places?"

"Sure they do, but they've been roommates since their rookie days and... I don't know, they like the arrangement, I guess." She shrugs.

"And their girlfriends don't mind?"

"What girlfriends?" Melissa narrows her eyes. "You just wanted to know if they were off the market, didn't you?"

Cheeks. Flames. Check.

"What? No. I don't care either way. I don't want to go out with any of them." More like they'll never want to go out with me.

"Why not?" She tilts her head. "Any of those boys

are a catch. Well, maybe not Ryan. He's a whore. But Jake and Lachlan are definitely boyfriend material."

I take a large sip of the martini, praying she stops talking about them. I didn't come to this party hoping to hook up with a hockey player. The idea never crossed my mind, even after seeing how attractive the boys were. But Melissa isn't done.

"Or..." she continues. "You could have the three of them for one night."

My eyes bug out. "What?"

She smirks. "They aren't opposed to sharing."

My heart is thundering in my chest now. I've never entertained having a ménage, much less sleeping with three men at the same time. When it comes to sex, I'm as vanilla as a person can be. I've only had sex with Bill, for crying out loud.

"Have you ever..."

Her brows shoot to the heavens. "God no! I'd never cross that line with my players."

"But... how do you know they don't mind sharing?"

Her smile becomes wider. "I just do. Why are you asking? Are you interested?"

Heat spreads across my cheeks. "No," I reply quickly, then take another big sip of my martini, hoping the glass hides my face, which I'm sure is as red as a tomato.

Melissa switches her attention to a point behind me. "Oh, here comes Tammy Reynolds."

I follow Melissa's line of sight and see another stunning woman walking toward us. Her chin-length black hair shines under the light, looking silky smooth and making her blue eyes pop even more.

She looks familiar, so before she's within earshot, I ask, "Who is she?"

"One of the best sports reporters in the business. You really don't know anything about sports, do you?"

"No, but ask me anything about movies or TV series, and I'm your girl." Before Melissa starts to think I'm obsessed with celebrities, I add. "That's why I moved to L.A. I want to be a screenwriter."

Her eyes widen. "Really? I'd love to read something you've written."

My brows arch. "Why?" I blurt out.

Shit. That sounded terrible, but Melissa laughs. "Because I'm curious. Besides, if it's good, I'll show it to my fiancé."

"I have a feeling I'm supposed to know who he is." I take another drink of my martini.

"If you know everything about movies, then you do. His name is Elijah Foreman."

The alcohol goes down in the wrong pipe, making me choke.

"Are you okay?" She watches me with amused concern.

Once the coughing fit stops, I blurt out, "Holy shit!"

"Oh my. What did you say to the poor girl to

warrant that reaction, Melissa?" Tammy Reynolds asks when she finally joins us.

"I just told June about Eli."

"Ah, movie buff?" Tammy looks at me.

"You could say that." I take a large sip of my martini, needing this damn drink to start working faster before I put my foot in my mouth. Not that alcohol will prevent that from happening, but I won't feel as mortified when it does.

I can't believe Melissa is engaged to *the* legendary movie producer. I don't pay much attention to celebrity gossip, but it feels like I failed a test. And Melissa wants to read my stuff and maybe show it to him? I'd have a heart attack if that happened.

"June Summers, meet Tammy Reynolds."

"Nice to meet you, June. Are you a hockey aficionado too?"

I shake my head. "Not at all. My cheating ex is the fan."

God, I can't believe I just said that when I'm trying to avoid the topic.

Tammy's eyes widen. "I hope you're taking all the selfies with the players and posting them on social media then."

"Let's start with you, Tammy," Melissa chimes in. "Give me your phone, June."

I finish the rest of my drink and set it on the bar counter. The tension is finally leaving my body. Tammy and I pose together while Melissa snaps countless pictures of us. Then, she steps next to me and takes another bazillion selfies. My cheeks hurt from smiling so much.

"Do you think you have enough, Melissa?" Tammy asks in a sarcastic tone.

Without looking up from my phone, she replies, "I had to make sure there was one decent picture of you. Would it kill you to keep your eyes open for a second, woman?"

"Shut up. I didn't close my eyes."

Tammy steps closer to Melissa to look at the photos. I stay back and watch the duo. They seem to have the kind of friendship I have with Katrina. Danika and I, on the other hand, weren't like that. Looking back, I think she only enjoyed having a walking disaster as a friend so she would always look like a rockstar.

I should reply to Katrina's texts before posting tonight's pictures on social media.

"Can I have my phone back, please?"

Melissa looks sheepish. "Oops. Sorry, I got carried away."

"Thanks. Now I need to take pictures with all the players on the team." I glance around the room from our vantage point. Even though I don't follow hockey, it's easy to spot them in the crowd. They're taller than most. But I don't see the guys I'm searching for.

"If you're looking for the Unholy Trinity, they're probably hogging the pool table," Melissa chimes in.

I whip my face to her. "There's a pool table here?"

"Yeah. Do you play?"

The corners of my lips twist upward. "I don't play, I slay. Let's find those boys."

CHAPTER 8
JUNE

The pool table is at the far end of the restaurant, and I'm not sure if it belongs or if it was brought in for the party. It doesn't quite fit with the rest of the décor. It's out of place, just like I am. But I'm glad it's here, because playing pool is one of the things I do well. My father had an old pool table in the garage, and he taught my brother and me how to play. Much to August's chagrin, I was a better student than him. My dad said I was a natural.

The Unholy Trinity—as Melissa called Lachlan, Ryan, and Jake—surround the pool table. Ryan and Jake are playing while Lachlan watches with a beer in hand.

He's the first to notice us walking over, and he immediately stands straighter, almost as if he wants to make a good impression. If that's the case, surely he doesn't want to impress *me*.

"It didn't take long, did it?" Melissa asks Ryan and Jake.

"What?" Ryan's eyes widen innocently. "You went through the trouble of getting us a pool table. The least we can do is play."

"You'd better have made your rounds and talked to the sponsors already."

"Don't worry, Melissa. We socialized, and we'll continue to make our rounds after I kick Ryan's ass."

"Who's winning?" I ask.

Ryan twists his face into a grimace. "Jake, but not for long."

I look at the table and notice more striped balls than solid. In fact, there are only two solids left, plus the eight ball.

Jake snorts. "Watch this." He chalks the cue and bends over the table, getting into position to take his shot. He ditched his suit jacket and rolled up his shirt sleeves, showcasing corded muscles and veins. Damn, the look's sexy as hell. He glances at me, catching me staring. Usually, I'd look away, but I hold his stare. He smirks and then winks before focusing on the ball he wants to hit, and then the cue ball. With a powerful strike, he sinks his target. A minute later, the game is over.

"God dammit!" Ryan blurts out.

Smiling, Jake lifts his hand. "Pay up, buddy."

Ryan fishes out a crisp one-hundred-dollar bill from his pocket and shoves it into Jake's hand.

"Do you play, June?" Lachlan asks me.

"Yeah, sometimes."

From the corner of my eye, I catch Melissa's eyebrow raise. I did tell her that I was pretty good. Most guys think girls either have no interest in playing pool or don't know how. I love proving them wrong. And if there's money involved, even better. I never feel bad about taking money from people who underestimate me. Most of the time, I'm unsure of myself, but not when it comes to pool. Or maybe I'm feeling extra confident thanks to the martini. God knows I wouldn't be so bold around these famous hockey players if it weren't for alcohol.

"Why don't you play with June?" Melissa suggests.

"That's a great idea. I'm game," Ryan replies. "You can be my partner, June."

"How about we let her decide?" Jake pipes up. "She might want to pair up with a winner."

Are these guys seriously competing to have me as their partner? This evening keeps getting more surreal. It's obvious that Jake and Ryan are skilled at pool, and they won't hold back—being competitive must be a part of their DNA, or they wouldn't be professional athletes.

There's nothing I like better than wiping the floor with cocky guys.

As I watch the duo, I press my index finger against

my lips and pretend to think about it. Then I switch my attention to Lachlan, who's been quiet. "Do you want to partner with me?"

His blue eyes widen. "Are you sure? Fair warning, I'm not as good as those two."

I shrug. "I don't mind."

Ryan turns to Jake. "I guess it's you and me, buddy."

Jake keeps staring at me in a scrutinizing way. He's trying to figure me out. Good luck with that. *I'm* still trying to figure me out. But if he wants to give it a go, be my guest.

I select my cue stick from the stand and prep it with chalk.

"Since June is the guest of honor, we'll let you two start," Ryan tells us.

In my periphery, I see Melissa sit and get comfortable. I turn to her, and she winks at me. I think she wants me to destroy Jake and Ryan.

I don't want to clue them in on the fact that I know what I'm doing, so I turn to Lachlan. "Can you break?"

"It'll be my pleasure, lass." He finishes his beer and sets the empty glass on a nearby high table. Then he grabs the triangle and racks the balls.

I can't take my eyes off him. He's so handsome, and despite his sheer size—I mean, the guy is probably six-four or five—he moves with incredible grace. But I think what I love the most about how he looks is his shaggy blond hair and boyish face. The long bangs cover part of his right eye in a sexy way. He resembles a surfer more than a Scottish hockey player.

"June," Melissa calls, drawing my attention. A waiter is standing next to her. "Would you like another dirty martini or something else?"

"Martini is good." Even though I want to avoid getting completely trashed tonight, and those drinks are potent, I can handle a second one.

"Boys?" Melissa turns to the trio.

It amuses me that she refers to these three grown men as boys. They don't seem to care. I barely know them, and I'm already thinking about them that way too. It's endearing.

"Another IPA for me," Lachlan replies.

"I'll have a dirty martini too." Ryan smiles at me, making me blush.

When Jake doesn't answer right away, Melissa calls his name. I look and find him staring at me again. His expression is closed off but not unfriendly. It does make me self-conscious though.

He switches his attention to Melissa and finally answers, "An old-fashioned for me."

A whiskey guy. It fits him.

Before Lachlan starts the game, I ask, "What are the stakes?"

"Do you want to play for money?" Ryan raises an eyebrow and curls his lips upward.

He's the cockiest of them all, and wiping that smirk

off his gorgeous face will give me great pleasure. "Of course."

"June... are you sure?" Lachlan asks, frowning slightly.

"Yeah, don't worry. I'm good for the money if we don't win."

Bad, bad, June. Who's being cocky and reckless now? I need to save every penny to rent a new apartment. Never mind that I still have to pay off that stupid Jumbotron slot. I used my emergency credit card for it.

Tomorrow's problems, June.

He shakes his head. "Don't worry, lass. If we don't win, it's on me." He turns to the others. "Same amount?"

"Sure," Ryan replies

I'd fight Lachlan to pay for my half, but I sense it'd be pointless. These boys make a lot of money, and for them, losing one hundred dollars on a bet would be like *me* losing a penny.

Lachlan breaks and sinks a stripe. The table is still open though, meaning he can pocket either a solid or a stripe next and decide which we'll play.

He turns to me. "Wanna give it a go?"

According to the rules, he should keep playing, but I don't think they care, so I shrug. "Sure."

I take my time studying the balls on the table. Even though one stripe is already gone, the solids are better positioned. I can easily pocket two or three, if I play my angles right. I chalk my cue again even though I did it already. It's my ritual; it helps me get into the zone. The restaurant and everyone in it fade away, including my opponents and my partner.

I bend over the table, narrowing my eyes as I line my cue stick at the right angle to take the shot. Then I hit the cue ball with a quick and powerful jab. The loud clack is almost as satisfying as seeing the target ball disappear into the pocket.

"Ah shit. She's good," Ryan mutters.

I don't look at him, keeping my focus on the new spread. I walk around the table, ignoring the pain in my feet thanks to the high-heeled sandals pinching my toes, and repeat the same process three more times. I miscalculate the last shot and end my streak. It's only then that I pay attention to my surroundings. All three men are staring at me with their jaws hanging loose.

"Son of a bitch." Ryan stares at the table as if he can't believe I pocketed three balls in a row.

Lachlan's face splits into a broad grin. "I guess we don't have to worry about losing to these eejits."

I return his smile. "I guess not."

CHAPTER 9
RYAN

don't like to lose. In fact, I hate it. Thus, I make sure it doesn't happen often. But after seeing June destroy Jake and me, I'm grinning from ear to ear. I've never met a girl who could play pool like she did. She didn't just win—she obliterated us. Lachlan barely did a thing in all three games we played. It was so hot.

Right now, she's in the restroom with Melissa. We're supposed to continue mingling, but so far, we haven't moved from our spots near the pool table, and I'm still staring in the direction she went, even though I can't see her anymore.

"What are you smiling about?" Lachlan asks. "You and Jake just lost three hundred bucks."

"I know." I take a sip of my beer. I had to switch to something lighter after the dirty martini. We have practice tomorrow, and I don't want to be hungover.

"You're far too happy though," Jake pipes up, staring at me with his hawk eyes.

"I am." I grin. "And I have two words for you—*triple treat.*"

Jake goes very still, and I can see the interest in his eyes, but then he shakes his head and grumbles. "I didn't invite June to the party for that. What happened to not taking advantage of the situation?"

"I'm not taking advantage of anything." I take another sip of my drink. "I think June wants it as much as we do. And before you try to deny it, let me just say I saw how you and Lachlan were looking at her." Neither rebuffs my statement, so I continue. "Besides, if I'd been dumped on a live broadcast, you bet I'd be looking for a rebound hookup."

"We wouldn't expect anything less from you." Jake finishes his second old-fashioned. He can pound those and be completely fine the next day.

"Don't stand on your morality dais and judge me. I didn't hear you say no to the idea."

He narrows his eyes, then turns to Lachlan. "What do you think?"

Lachlan's brows furrow. "I don't know, mate. I don't think she's that type of lass. She seems so innocent."

"Trust me," I say. "When have I ever been wrong? I can't believe you didn't notice the hungry way she was staring at us."

The first time we shared a girl was when we first

moved into our old apartment almost ten years ago. We threw a housewarming party, and after way too many drinks, it happened. No swords were crossed, but it could have been awkward the following day nonetheless.

It wasn't. We realized we liked sharing. It was a lot of fun, with the right girl. There were many other occasions after that.

I see June returning from the restroom alone. She trips over nothing and collides with Timothy Jensen, a jackass who used to play for the Titans until his contract was up and he wasn't offered a new one by any team. No one was sad to see him go. Now he's a sports commentator, hence why he's here.

"I'm so sorry," she apologizes.

"It's okay, sugar." He grins at her in a sleazy way while his gaze dips to her cleavage, and my entire body tenses. "I don't believe we've met. I'm Timothy Jensen."

He's putting the moves on her? Hell to the fucking no.

"Look at that lavvy heid," Lachlan chimes in.

He and Jake make a motion to head in their direction, but I stop them. "Let me handle that asshat."

In the blink of an eye, I reach Timothy and June, stopping next to her. "Jensen, I didn't know you were on the guest list."

His face twists into a scowl. "What do you want, Bertrand? I was having a pleasant conversation with..." He looks at June, waiting for her to supply her name.

"June Summers," she replies.

"What a lovely name."

I fight the urge to roll my eyes. I don't want June to think I'm a child. Instead of wasting my time with Timothy, I turn to her. "You owe me another game."

Her beautiful hazel eyes widen. "I do?"

"Yes, I'm tired of losing to Lachlan. Please partner with me."

"Are you for real?" Timothy butts in like the annoying fly he is.

I give him my most condescending glance. "Why are you still here? Come on, June." I lace my fingers with hers and steer her away from the dickface.

"What was that?" she asks.

"What was what?"

"That pissing contest." She looks over shoulder, then says, "He's glowering in our direction. You're not his favorite person, are you?"

"You can say that. He used to play for the Titans before he retired from the NHL."

"But why doesn't he like you?"

"I don't think you're going to appreciate the answer."

She stops walking and plants her feet. "I'd like to know anyway."

I glance at Jake and Lachlan, who are watching us with keen interest. I can't believe they haven't joined us yet. But I take advantage of being alone with June to seal the deal. The question is, will she agree to it? She's still expecting an answer, and unfortunately, the truth might be a deal-breaker for her. But I won't lie to her. That's not how I roll.

"All right. I slept with his ex-fiancée." Her mouth makes a perfect *O*, and damn, I wish I could kiss her now. Her plump lips are delectable.

"If they were broken up…"

"An hour after she dumped him."

Her brows furrow. "You could have left that detail out. Are you trying to make me not like you?"

I shake my head. "On the contrary, June. I want you to like me, but I won't lie or omit things. I'm not Prince Charming, and I'll never pretend otherwise."

Blush spreads across her cheeks. "Why do you want me to like you?"

Unable to restrain myself, I caress her face with the back of my fingers. "Because you're a cool chick."

"Oh," she whispers, almost disappointed.

"And really hot. A dynamite combo."

Her entire face is red now. If she blushes like that because of a compliment, I can't imagine what she'll be like in the throes of an orgasm. Shit. Thinking about her like that is giving me a hard-on already.

I clear my throat. "Where's Melissa?"

"She's on a call with her fiancé."

I wonder what Melissa told June about us. She's never mentioned to us that she knows about our bedroom games, but I bet she does. There isn't a thing that happens in this team that she isn't aware of.

"What about another round of pool? Are you in?"

June nibbles her lower lip, drawing my focus to it. Once again, I want to do the dirtiest things to her. She isn't usually the type of woman that I get involved with. Not that I don't find her attractive, but she's a bit timid, and my hookups are usually more aggressive. They know what they want—*me*—and they aren't afraid to show it. It makes it easier to keep things casual. But tonight, I'm willing to break my own rules. Underneath all that sweetness, I saw the firecracker June is. She didn't hold back during the game, and I'd love to see that in the bedroom as well.

"Actually, I was ready to head to my room," she replies. "These sandals are murder, and the events of the day are finally catching up with me."

Disappoint rushes through me, but I try to keep that hidden. "Ah, that's too bad, but I get it."

She tilts her head. "You, Jake, and Lachlan could come up. I barely had a chance to talk to you."

I'd never refuse such an invitation, but I need to be sure she's on the same page we are. I step closer, invading her personal space. She needs to lift her chin to keep her eyes locked with mine. "Do you really want to talk?"

She blinks fast, swallowing hard. "Yes."

I lean down and whisper in her ear, "Nothing else?"

There's a sharp intake of breath, then a pause. "Maybe... maybe something else," she finally replies in a soft and shaky voice.

I pull back to look into her eyes again. "There's no need to be nervous. We'll come up, and if you decide you just want to get to know us and nothing more, that's cool."

"Okay."

Jake and Lachlan finally decide to join us. It took them long enough.

"Did you survive meeting Timothy, June?" Jake asks, looking at her in his intense way.

She touches a strand of her hair, running her fingers up and down the length of it. "Oh, Ryan rescued me just in time."

"That guy's a total gommy," Lachlan pipes up. "Where did Melissa go?"

"She's on a phone call," I reply. "June is tired, and I volunteered us to escort her to her room."

She invited us, but judging by how nervous she is, the white lie won't hurt. I honestly think she'd combust on the spot if I told the guys it was her idea. First timers need to be handled with care.

"Yeah, I'm beat," she chimes in. "But I told Ryan we can totally hang out for a bit longer, that is, if you aren't needed at the party anymore."

My eyes widen. I guess she isn't as timid as I thought.

"We can hang out," Jake replies. "I'll text Melissa so she won't worry about you."

"Thank you."

We make our way to the restaurant's exit. I walk next to June, and to test the waters—and because I can't resist—I place my hand on the small of her back. She doesn't tense, nor does she increase the distance between us.

I smile. I wasn't expecting tonight to end in a foursome with a hot middle-school teacher, but I love to be surprised.

CHAPTER 10
JUNE

Holy shit. Ryan has his hand on me. It's an innocent gesture, but also protective, and it's giving me all sorts of feelings. I can't remember the last time jerkface Bill did that. My heart doesn't know if it should do somersaults or jump out of my chest. And I can still feel the gentle touch of Ryan's fingers against my cheek. I didn't realize I was so deprived of affection until I got it from a guy I just met.

I have no illusions though. Even before he confessed that he isn't Prince Charming, I had already figured that out. Ryan, Jake, and Lachlan are famous hockey players. What could they possibly want with me besides a night of fun?

A night of fun you totally deserve, June.

In the elevator, Ryan stays on my left side, and Lachlan on my right. Jake leans against the right wall and proceeds to stare at me. I still have a buzz going thanks to the dirty martinis, so my tongue is looser than normal.

"Why do you keep looking at me like that?" I ask him.

His brows arch. Maybe he's not used to people calling him on it. "I'm trying to figure you out."

"If you succeed, please share. I haven't accomplished that yet."

He cocks his head. "Are you saying you're an enigma even to yourself?"

"Yep."

"I love a good mystery." Ryan takes my hand, lacing his fingers with mine.

It feels like an electric charge goes up my arm and spreads everywhere, igniting a fire in the pit of my stomach. The elevator finally arrives on my floor, and since Jake is ahead of us, he walks out first. Ryan and I follow.

Lachlan is the last out. "What's your room number, lass?" he asks.

I glance at the card Melissa gave me earlier, and hell and damn, I don't want to say it out loud.

Since Ryan is standing next to me, he peeks, and chuckles. "Room eleven sixty-nine."

Face. Flames. Check.

I make the mistake of looking at Jake. His expression is serious, but the corners of his lips are curling upward.

I don't know if he's trying not to laugh at me, but he *is* amused.

If saying a stupid number gets me all flustered, do I really have what it takes to get down and dirty with three men at the same time? My pulse skyrockets and my palms are starting to get clammy. Shit. And Ryan is still holding my hand. I'm beginning to unravel, and not in a good way.

No, June. Stop letting your head get in the way. Screwing three sinfully sexy hockey players is exactly *what you need tonight.*

Now that we know the room number, Jake and Lachlan walk ahead, and I trail them with Ryan. I'm too busy freaking out to pay attention to my surroundings. Besides, there are two hot guys walking in front of me. They're tall and muscular and exude male dominance. Fuckity fuck. I'm way out of my depth. Not only do I have no idea what to expect, but also my skills in the bedroom are lacking. Bill wasn't the most adventurous lover.

Why am I thinking about that asshole when I'm surrounded by these gorgeous men? I won't let him ruin this for me.

Jake and Lachlan stop, and Jake announces, "Room eleven sixty-nine."

"That's me," I say like a dumbass.

They move away from the door, allowing me access to it. I let go of Ryan's hand and scan the card, praying it works on the first try. It does and, before I lose my nerve, I open the door, expecting to find a regular-size room on the other side, not a huge suite with panoramic windows and a blue L-shaped couch with a massive TV screen against the wall opposite it.

"Wow." I walk in, looking at everything in bewilderment. There's even a mini-kitchen with top-of-the-line stainless steel appliances, and a counter with high stools.

From the corner of my eye, I spy Ryan making a beeline for the fridge. He opens the door and says, "Nice."

I turn. "What is it?"

Grinning broadly, he takes out an ice bucket with a bottle of champagne inside and a medium-sized black box with a big red bow on top.

"Melissa gave you the VIP treatment, lass." Lachlan pats my shoulder the way a friend would. Funnily enough, that makes me feel less nervous to be alone with them.

Ryan sets the ice bucket and the box on the coffee table in front of the couch.

I follow him, eyeing the box. "What's inside?" I ask.

"It's a gift for you, June. You open it."

I sit on the couch and get rid of my sandals. Immediate relief follows and I sigh loudly.

"I don't know how women do it," Jake chimes in.

"Do what?"

"Walk in those high heels. It looks painful."

"Not as painful as getting checked against the boards, I imagine." I smirk.

He grins as well. "We wear protective gear."

"Even so, but you're right. High heels are torture. I don't usually wear them. I'd be in the emergency room too often if I did. It's a miracle I only tripped once tonight."

"Too bad you landed on the worst person in the room," Ryan pipes up. "Shall I open the champagne?"

Tomorrow is a work day, but hell, it'd be a waste not to drink it. Besides, my nerves have killed my martini buzz. "Yes, please."

While Ryan takes care of the champagne bottle, I open the box with the red bow. Jake and Lachlan sit on either side of me but leave a respectful amount of space between our bodies. It doesn't matter; their proximity makes me shake from head to toe. I'm nervous, but I'm also turned on.

I focus on the box, not how they're making me feel. Inside, I find an assortment of chocolate-covered straw-berries, from dark chocolate to white. "Oh, I *love* choco-late-covered strawberries," I say.

"What's your favorite type of chocolate?" Jakes asks.

"Hmm, I like them all, but white is my favorite."

He takes a strawberry covered in white chocolate and brings it to my lips. *Oh my God.* He wants to feed me, and I'm going to let him. Locking eyes with him, I take a bite, and the juice from the strawberry drips down my chin. Before I can wipe it off, Jake rubs his thumb over the mess, holding my stare. The space between us crackles with electricity. With the way my heart is beating so damn fast, it seems as if there's a hummingbird trapped in my chest. Never mind the butterflies in my stomach, which are now wide awake.

The loud *pop* of the champagne bottle opening breaks the spell. I look away, knowing very well my face is bright red. I jump to my feet. "We need glasses."

I try to walk past Lachlan, but his legs are too long.

"Let me get out of the way, lass." He stands as well, and now we're in each other's space. He should move, but he doesn't. I look into his light-blue eyes and easily get lost there. His gaze drops to my lips, and I freeze, waiting for him to lean down and kiss me.

"Here's your glass, June." Ryan appears with a flute in hand.

Lachlan finally steps back, and I can breathe again. "Thanks."

"We should toas—" Ryan starts, but I'm already halfway done with my drink. "Or maybe not." He chuckles.

"Sorry. I was thirsty."

"Let me refill your glass, and then we can do a proper toast." Ryan winks at me.

The champagne isn't as strong as the dirty martini,

and I'll need more than one glass to relax. When everyone has a drink, I ask. "What should we toast to?"

"Serendipity," Jake replies.

I smile, lifting my glass. "To serendipity."

Glasses clink, and then I'm inhaling my second flute of champagne.

"Whoa, you *are* thirsty." Lachlan laughs.

The alcohol is finally taking effect, so without blushing like a virgin, I manage to say, "You have no idea."

Ryan takes my empty glass and sets it down on the table, then raises his hand, palm up. "Can I have your phone?"

"What for?"

"We didn't take any selfies."

I smile. "Oh, yeah. I got distracted kicking your ass at pool."

"Ouch." Jake chimes in, shaking his head. "Go ahead, rub it in."

"I just did. Ha!"

"Man, what happened to the sweet middle-school teacher from earlier?" He gives me a proper smile, and I realize it's the first time he's done so tonight.

My heart does several backflips. "You thought I was sweet? Aw, that's so… *sweet.*" *Jesus, did I really say that?* I start to giggle like an idiot.

"I think the bubbles went to her head already," Lachlan pipes up.

"Maybe," I say. "All right. Come closer. Let's take all the selfies, but with the window as the background."

Ryan, who's closest to me, stands on my left side. Jake joins on my right, and Lachlan, being the tallest, stands in the back and rests his chin on my shoulder. I jump a little, not expecting that, then turn my face to look at him.

"Relax, lass. I don't bite."

"It'd be okay if you did."

His face splits into a lazy smile. "Careful what you wish for."

"All right, everyone look at the camera and say *hockey*!" Ryan says.

I snort. "What?"

Ryan doesn't wait for us to strike a pose or smile. He starts to take pictures, and I already know several will end up in the delete pile. I try my best to smile like I'm a cool chick, innocently taking pictures with three hotties, but when one—Jake—has his arm wrapped around my waist and all of them are flush against my body, it's a hard task. I'm getting hot and bothered, and I hope it doesn't show in the pictures.

"I think you took plenty," I say after a while, stepping forward. "Let me see them."

Some are ridiculous, and in others my eyes are closed.

"Oh, that's a good one, lass." Lachlan, who's still standing behind me, points at the phone.

He's not wrong. It's a good picture to post on social media. Well, the boys look better than I do, but they don't have to try. I bet they look like rock stars as soon as they wake up.

"Yeah. I'm posting this one. What should I write in the caption?"

"Hmm… how about hanging out with my new friends?" Jake suggests.

I nod. "Yeah, that's good." After I finish typing and posting, I look up. "What should we do next?"

"Whatever you want, June." Ryan takes a strand of my hair and tucks it behind my ear, sending rivulets of desire down my spine.

I close my eyes, gathering the courage to answer him honestly. "I want to spend the night with you—all of you."

When I open my eyes again, I'm taken aback by how Jake and Ryan are looking at me. Lachlan is still behind me, so near that I can feel the heat emanating from his body. I've never felt more desired by anyone than I do now. The insecure part of me still thinks this is a sick joke and the punchline will come soon.

"We want that too, June, but only if you're sure," Jake replies.

"I'm sure but…" I bite my lower lip. "I've never done this before."

"It's okay, lass." Lachlan whispers in my ear, placing his hand on my hip. "We'll be gentle." He kisses my neck, and I close my eyes again, leaning into him.

Someone kisses me between my breasts, and curiosity makes me peek. It's Ryan. He draws his tongue across my cleavage and cups my right breast with his large hand. I gasp. Lachlan continues to shower my neck with open kisses, digging his fingers into my hips while pressing his erection against my butt.

Jake pinches my chin between his forefinger and thumb and turns my face to his. His green eyes are pure fire as he moves closer and brushes my lips with his. Then he uses his tongue to tease my lips open, and when his tongue connects with mine, I almost melt on the spot. The kiss is slow and gentle, but it's fanning the fire that started in the pit of my stomach, turning it into a blaze. All the attention my body is receiving is making me lightheaded.

He leans back, ending the kiss too soon, and swipes his thumb over my lower lip. "You taste as good as I thought you would, sweetheart."

Ryan stands straighter and captures my face between his hands. "I want a taste too."

His kiss is not as gentle as Jake's was. Ryan slants his mouth over mine, possessive and hungry, almost as if he wants to erase Jake's taste from my tongue. Lachlan shifts behind me, creating a bit of space between our bodies. I miss the contact immediately, but I have no complaints when he runs his fingers down my ass, and then lifts my skirt, bunching the delicate fabric around my waist.

"I love yer curves, lass," he says in a husky whisper, before grabbing my ass and squeezing it.

And I love your accent, I would have said, if Ryan wasn't currently devouring my mouth. He ends the kiss with a swipe of his tongue over my lips and steps back.

His blue eyes are electric and filled with hunger as he stares. "You were right, Jake. She's delicious."

They both stand in front of me, watching me like two powerful Greek gods who want to do wicked things to me. I'm distracted by their attention, so when Lachlan curls his arm around my waist and cups my pussy with his free hand, it startles me.

"It's okay, lass. I'll make you feel good," he murmurs in his thick Scottish brogue.

He delivers on his promise by swiping two fingers left and right over my clit. The sensation is so good, it makes my knees buckle. I can't remember the last time I had an orgasm ignited by a living person and not a sex toy. If he keeps this up, I'll climax soon. I arch my back, lifting my arm to grab a fistful of his hair.

"Do you like that, lass?" he asks.

"Yes," I hiss.

"Do you want my fingers inside you?" He alternates between flicking my clit and running his fingers in a circular motion.

"Please," I moan like a kitten.

I have no idea what Jake and Ryan are doing, so I open my eyes. And swallow hard. They've gotten rid of their shirts, and holy shit, they're more breathtaking than I expected. Both have broad shoulders and abs that are so defined, I could wash clothes on them. I want to run my tongue over those hard ridges.

"Do you like what you see, darling?" Ryan asks, his lips curling up.

"Yes." The word barely leaves my mouth at all, thanks to Lachlan's fingers. He's toying with my entrance now, driving me insane.

"I want to see that pussy." Jake drops to his knees and peels my underwear down my legs.

Lachlan pulls his hand away, leaving me bare for his teammate. He turns his attention to my breasts, pulling the strapless top down so my boobs are exposed too.

"Beautiful," Jake says.

"Yes, she is." Ryan steps closer again and brings his mouth to my left nipple.

My breathing is already ragged, but it becomes much worse with the triple attack on my nerves—Lachlan kneading my breast and kissing my neck, Ryan sucking my nipple until it becomes as hard as a pebble, and then Jake, parting my legs and licking my clit.

"Oh my *God*," I blurt out.

They keep going, not stopping their torture to say a word. As for me, I'm unraveling quickly and becoming boneless. If it weren't for Lachlan holding me up, I'd have collapsed to the floor already. For a while, the only noise in the room is of our lovemaking. When the orgasm hits me, it's like fireworks, an explosion of senses that makes my body shake from head to toe. I'm turning into stardust, and all my thoughts scatter into space. Jake keeps licking and sucking, working his tongue like a magician.

"Yes, yes, yes!" I yell, and it's a surprise. I've never been this vocal in bed, probably because I've never come this hard until now.

Even after the tsunami of pleasure recedes, my body is trembling. Soon I regain feeling in my limbs. Ryan lets go of my nipple and kisses me hard and fast, making my toes curl. When he retreats, I would follow if it weren't for Lachlan keeping me in place.

Jake unfurls from his lower position, wiping the corner of his mouth with his thumb. "Fucking delicious."

Before I get the chance to reply, Lachlan turns me around, grabs a fistful of my hair, and captures my lips with his. Greedily, I curl my arms around his neck and jump into his arms, bringing my wet pussy and throbbing clit to his rock-hard erection. I gyrate my hips to increase the friction between our bodies. These boys have turned me into an insatiable woman.

"Lass, do you want me to explode in my pants?" he asks against my lips.

"It's not my fault you're still wearing them."

His eyes widen before he narrows them. "You're a sassy girl, aren't ya?"

"I am now." I kiss him again, and then bite his lower lip.

The deep groan that comes from him gives me goosebumps and sends tingles of pleasure all over my body.

"Don't be selfish, Lachy. You have to share," Ryan chimes in.

Lachlan doesn't make a move to let me go, though. Instead, he whispers in my ear, "You're ours tonight, all of you. All your holes are ours, aren't they, lass?"

My pussy clenches in anticipation, even though his words make me nervous. I've never been fucked in the ass before. Despite that, I say breathlessly, "Yes, I'm yours, all of me."

"Good girl."

He sets me on the couch and steps back, unbuttoning his shirt. I look at Jake and Ryan and see that they're completely naked and playing with themselves. I swallow hard, taking note of their sizes. They *are* proportional to their heights. And Jake's dick is pierced vertically through the glans. *Holy shit.*

"What's the matter, sweetheart? Never seen an Apadravya piercing before?" Jake strokes his shaft up and down.

"I've never seen *any* piercing of that sort."

He chuckles. "If you want, you can not only see it, but feel it inside you."

I swallow hard, wondering what it'd be like. Instead of answering him, I ask, "Can I help you two with what you're doing?"

They step closer, two giants that could bend me like a pretzel—I hope they do. I look up while wrapping my fingers around their cocks. Holding their stares, I run my hands up and down their shafts, in awe at how smooth their skins feel against my palms. I've never imagined that being ambidextrous would be so advantageous, but I also never dreamed of being in a situation like this. They grunt in unison, and I marvel that my touch can elicit those sounds from them.

I press my thumb over Ryan's slit, then spread precum over the sensitive skin. His eyes become hooded and burn with desire. I switch my attention to Jake's pierced cock, taking my time to run my fingers over the jewelry.

"You like playing with that, sweetheart?" he asks in a rough voice.

"I do."

"Go ahead, wrap your luscious mouth around it."

Holding the base, I lick his length from bottom to top then flick my tongue back and forth over the piercing.

"Open your pretty mouth wide, honey," he commands.

I do as he says and swallow his length until it reaches the back of my throat.

"That's it, babe. Take it all." He grabs a fistful of my hair, twisting it over his hand and pulling just enough to cause a little pain. "Now suck Ryan."

I turn to his friend, repeating the same thing while Jake keeps a hold of my hair. Then Lachlan comes from behind, leaning over the back of the couch to put his hands on my shoulders, and to whisper in my ear, "You're doing such a good job, lass, but I want in on the fun."

Jake promptly releases me. Free from the restraint, I let go of Ryan's cock with a loud wet *pop* and look over my shoulder. "Tell me what to do."

"Get on your hands and knees on the couch, lass."

My pulse is drumming in my ears. This is it. I'm going to get railed by three hockey players. I begin to get in position but stop halfway there, realizing some-thing. "I look ridiculous with my tits hanging out like this."

"*Ridiculous* isn't a word I'd use to describe you, darling," Ryan replies.

Heat spreads through my cheeks. I don't know why compliments from them are still doing this to me. "I need help getting out of my dress. The side zipper is tricky."

"I'll help you," Ryan volunteers.

He claims my mouth while he does it, but unlike his

other kisses, this one is slow and delicious, and it turns me into a puddle. The corseted top slackens, making me feel much better. I had somehow blocked that the dress, even though gorgeous, wasn't comfortable. I lift my arms so he can pull the dress off me… and now I'm in my birthday suit in front of them. I should feel vulnerable—I'm naked in front of three men I just met—but I've never been more comfortable. I wonder if it's the champagne that's giving me confidence.

"You're a vision, June," Jake says in a voice that's tight with need.

"You have to stop giving me praise. I might start to believe you."

He furrows his brows. "It's the truth, sweetheart. Don't let any asshole tell you otherwise."

And by *asshole*, I'm pretty sure he means Bill.

Immediately, I force him out of my mind. He doesn't belong here, not even in my thoughts.

I get on my hands and knees alongside the length of the couch, positioning myself so I'm at the edge of it and giving Lachlan a view of the goods from the other end.

He caresses my butt cheeks with a feather light touch, then parts them. "Look at this pretty little cunt, all pink and juicy." He teases my entrance, making lazy circles, then inserts two fingers, drawing a ragged moan from me. "You're nice and ready for us, aren't you, lass?"

"*Yes.*"

He inserts two more fingers and begins to fuck me in earnest. I'm already delirious with pleasure when I look at Ryan and Jake, who are jerking off as they watch us. I beckon them. "Come here, you two. I barely had a taste."

They trade a glance, and judging by their arched eyebrows, they weren't expecting my bossy side.

Lachlan chuckles. "You tell them, lass."

Feeling sassy, I look over my shoulder. "I want your cock inside me now."

He rewards me with a crooked smile and pulls his fingers from my pussy. "As you wish."

It occurs to me I don't have any condoms in my purse, and having unprotected sex tonight is a deal-breaker. Mercifully, I don't have to say anything, because Lachlan produces a condom wrapper.

Ryan pinches my chin with his fingers and turns my face toward him and Jake. "Eyes on us, beautiful."

My body is quaking in anticipation, but I refuse to show them I'm nervous. I focus on giving them the best blowjobs I can, but when Lachlan penetrates me, it's a little hard to concentrate on my task. He's stretching me in the best possible way, going slow until he's completely sheathed inside me.

"You're so tight, lass. Fuck." He digs his fingers into my hips and pulls out almost all the way only to slam back in.

I let out a gasp, which is quickly silenced by Jake's

cock deep in my throat. Grabbing me by the hair, he starts to fuck my mouth at almost the same pace as Lachlan is pounding my pussy. Jake pulls back, and then I'm sucking Ryan. At this point, I'm glad they've taken over, because all I can think about is how quickly Lachlan is sending me toward the edge.

I begin to shake even more, and then the orgasm hits me and my internal walls squeeze Lachlan's dick.

"Och, lass. You take me so well."

His accent sounds thicker, or maybe I can't understand English anymore, because I'm climaxing and my brain has stopped functioning properly. His thrusts become faster and harder, and he's pounding into me so fast, I begin to slide forward on the couch. Then in the next second, he grunts, coming as well.

After one final, hard thrust, Lachlan stops moving and squeezes my hips before pulling out, leaving me obliterated. Maybe guessing I need a minute to recover, Ryan and Jake step away. I collapse on the couch, completely boneless, and shut my eyes.

"Are you all right, lass?" Lachlan brushes my hair off my face.

"More than all right." I look at him, then at Ryan and Jake, who are hovering nearby. "I want more."

Lachlan kisses my cheek. "And you'll get more, lass. Don't worry."

CHAPTER 11
JUNE

I sit up on the couch after a moment, even though my body is still jelly and my breathing hasn't returned to normal. Lachlan walks to the kitchen to get rid of the condom, but Ryan and Jake are standing in front of me, still as hard as rocks. I couldn't finish them off while Lachlan was fucking me in earnest.

Lachlan's words come back to me. I promised them all my holes, and it's time to deliver. A shiver runs down my spine. I should be more nervous. I've never been fucked in the ass before, and I can't imagine it'll be easy, taking into account their sizes. Yet, imagining getting railed by all three of them at the same time, I get even wetter.

"What's on your mind, sugar?" Jake asks me.

"I'm ready for round two."

Ryan smiles lazily. "Oh yeah? And what would you like to do in round two?"

My eyes focus on Jake's piercing, and immediately I know I want to feel what a pierced cock can do to my G-spot.

I turn my attention to Ryan, holding his stare. "I want you to take my other virginity while Jake obliterates my pussy."

Ryan steps closer and rubs his thumb over my lower lip. "I'm loving your dirty mouth, June."

Lachlan walks over and, from behind the couch, leans forward to whisper in my ear, "I want that filthy mouth wrapped around my cock, lass."

His hot breath against my skin gives me goose bumps. I turn my face, and he wastes no time capturing my lips, prying them open with his expert tongue. His hand cups my cheek tenderly, making me feel protected and cherished. Something else mixes with the desire coursing through my veins, and it goes straight to my heart—yearning.

He pulls back too quick but holds my stare for a couple beats. I'm a little shocked by the new emotion swirling in my chest. Catching feelings isn't on the menu tonight.

You're only feeling this way because Lachlan is sweet, and your heart is mangled. It's not real, June.

"Stand up for a second, gorgeous." Ryan takes my hand and pulls me up.

I'm a little confused, but when he captures my face between his hands and kisses me deeply, the daze comes. Oh my God. I'm dazed and confused. I'd laugh if my mouth wasn't being devoured by Ryan. I wrap my arms around his waist and lean into him. His erection presses against my stomach, all hard and sleek, making my belly flutter. I'm more nervous about this first time than when I lost my virginity to Bill.

Hot lips press against the base of my spine, sending chills of pleasure straight to my throbbing clit.

I lean back, breaking the kiss with Ryan to look over my shoulder. Jake is sitting on the couch now, eyes dark with desire.

"You're going to ride me, cowgirl." Holding my forearm, he detangles me from Ryan and pulls me to him.

The condom is already in place, and all I have to do is sit astride him and let his cock impale me slowly. My pussy is drenched from before, and he goes in nice and easy. His eyes are smoldering when he cups the back of my head and pulls me down to kiss me. I don't move my hips, I just stay in that position, getting used to his piercing.

I tense when someone touches my asshole, teasing the entrance. I pull back from Jake's kiss and find Ryan there, bent over a little with one knee propped on the edge of the couch. He has a cat-who-got-the-cream grin on his sexy face.

"We're going to need lube, gorgeous. You're as tight as can be."

"I don't have any."

His grin turns into a toothy smile. "Lucky for you, I'm always prepared."

My eyes widen when I notice the small packet already torn open in the corner, and lube pouring out of it. "Is it going to hurt?"

"I'll be gentle, and this will help." He smears lube around my hole, and the coolness of it gives me goosebumps.

I forget for a second that Jake's inside of me, but he's quick to get my attention by sucking one of my nipples into his mouth. I gasp, letting my head roll back.

Lachlan is still behind the couch, and he's watching me as if he wants to eat me. "You look so beautiful, lass." He grabs my chin and slants his mouth over mine possessively.

I jerk a little when Ryan inserts a finger inside of me, but Lachlan keeps my head in place so he can keep kissing me.

"Relax, June. This will feel good, I promise," Ryan says, pumping his finger in and out.

He keeps doing that while Jake grabs my hips, digging his fingers into my skin. He releases my nipple at the same time that Lachlan leans back, ending the kiss.

"Ready to have some fun, beautiful?" Jake asks, already guiding my movements.

It's hard to focus on riding him while Ryan is fingering my asshole. Why did I think I could do this?

As if reading my mind, Ryan pulls his finger out, allowing me to get the full impact of riding Jake's pierced cock. Whoever looked at a dick and thought *Hmm, I think I'll run a piece of metal through it*, I thank them. The Apadravya piercing is hitting me in a spot that's turning my body into mush. I'm moaning out loud, and I don't even care what I sound like.

"Are you enjoying yourself, kitten?" Jake asks in a voice that's tight, almost as if he's trying to control himself.

"Yes," I hiss.

"Lean toward Jake, sugar. Show me your pretty hole."

I swallow the ball of nerves that's making my stomach tighten. This is it. I know if I said I changed my mind, they'd stop, but I want this... I *need* this.

Following Ryan's command, I lean forward and lift my ass a bit, careful to keep Jake inside of me. He caresses my cheek and smiles. "You're doing so well, June."

"Don't jinx me!"

Jake and Lachlan chuckle, making me laugh too. My amusement is cut short when Jake presses his thumb over my clit, then swipes left and right.

I close my eyes for a second. "Oh, this feels good."

Ryan teases my hole with the head of his cock, and involuntarily, my legs tense.

"It's okay, June. Try to relax," he says.

Lachlan pinches my chin with his thumb and index finger and turns my face to him. He kisses me again, slow and delicious. Jake keeps teasing my clit, and the pressure continues building between my legs. My muscles start to relax, and Ryan slides in a bit more. It burns a little but nothing unbearable. He keeps moving, going deeper inch by inch until his pelvis is flush with my butt. He's all the way in.

"Fuck, June. You're squeezing me so good. How does it feel for you?"

Lachlan breaks the kiss, allowing me to answer, "Really good."

"Are you ready to kick this up a notch?" Jake asks.

I first lock eyes with him, then I look at Lachlan. "I still have one hole to fill."

The right corner of his lips twists upward. "That you have, lass." He curls his fingers around the base of his cock, then, with his free hand, he cups the back of my head, guiding me toward his erection. "Open that filthy mouth wide, beautiful."

I swallow his entire length until the tip hits the back of my throat, drawing a groan from him. Jake is still gripping my hips, and he takes control. He moves his pelvis upward, impaling me with each thrust. His piercing is wreaking havoc inside me already. My body tingles as the pressure builds, front and back. Ryan is moving faster now, stretching me in a way I didn't know was possible. It burns a little, but the pain is mixed with a different kind of pleasure. Different sensations assault me, and I'm suddenly caught in a vortex, not knowing which way is up or down. Lachlan pistons in and out of my mouth, fucking me in earnest now. He grabs a fistful of my hair, twisting it around his hand tightly. His grunts become louder and mix with Jake's and Ryan's groans of pleasure. I'd be making sounds too, if my mouth wasn't occupied.

This is the ultimate test on multitasking. I have no clue if I'm doing things right, but I'm on the verge of ecstasy, and I can't be bothered to worry. My body is fragmenting into a million pieces, and when the climax hits me, it's like everything in my life finally makes sense. I'm nothing but stardust, but I've never felt more whole.

CHAPTER 12
JUNE

I wake up on my back in the middle of a king-size bed with a strong arm wrapped around my stomach. Lachlan's. On my other side, Jake is snuggled against me, and his leg is covering mine. I'm the meat in a delicious hockey-player sandwich. The bed wasn't big enough for four people, so Ryan ended up sleeping on the couch. He said he sleeps better alone anyway.

I crane my neck, trying to see the clock on the nightstand. It's ten to six. Shit. Time to go. The dream is over, and now I must face reality, and deal with the fact I'm not Cinderella and this isn't a fairy tale. I can't believe I actually slept with three men last night. I'm still not sure how I feel about it. Do I regret it? No. It was the best experience of my life, but guilt sneaks in. If my mother ever found out, she'd say I belong to Sodom or Gomorrah.

Carefully, I slide Lachlan's arm off me and dislodge Jake's leg from the top of mine. The last thing I want is to suffer an awkward morning-after. I don't know the protocol, because I've never had one before. Slowly, since the sides are blocked, I slink toward the end of the bed. I manage to escape without waking the boys, and it's a miracle. Now I need to find my clothes, get dressed, and skedaddle.

My bladder is about to burst, but using the bathroom is not an option. The toilet flushing will surely wake them. I'll use the restroom in the hotel lobby.

Ryan is sleeping on his stomach, completely naked. I stop for a second to admire the view and commit it to memory. The defined muscles of his wide back are visible even in that relaxed position. And don't get me started on his tush. I touched and scratched his butt a few times last night, and I can see the red marks I left behind.

His face is turned toward the back of the couch, resting over his left arm. My chest feels heavy as the realization hits me that this is the last time I'll see him, Lachlan, and Jake.

No, I can't get sad now. Catching feelings for them after one night would be too damn stupid.

I spot my dress and underwear neatly folded on top of the coffee table, and my purse right next to the pile. That's not where I left them. Ryan must have put them there. Since he's not facing me and seems to be in a deep sleep, I get dressed in the living room as quickly as I can. I can zip up my dress only halfway, but it'll have to do. My sandals are still under the table.

I drop to my knees to retrieve them, but I need to stretch my arm to grab them. When I straighten and look up, my gaze collides with Ryan's. Shit. He's awake.

His lips curl into a lazy smile. "Leaving so soon?"

My pulse goes from zero to a hundred in a couple seconds. I jump to my feet, clutching my sandals against my chest. "Yeah. I have to be at work before eight."

He sits up and stretches his arms. "What time is it?"

I try to take my phone out of my purse fast to check the time, but it catches on something, so I yank on the damn thing to dislodge it.

"It's six on the dot," Ryan answers his own question. He's looking at his wristwatch on the side table. He must have taken it off last night before falling asleep. "Would you like some coffee?"

He asks as if this is his hotel room, not mine.

"No, I have to run."

He stands, unfazed by his nakedness. My cheeks are burning, and I try my best to keep my eyes focused on his face. He walks over, and when he stops in front of me, I turn into stone.

Tucking a loose strand of my hair behind my ear, he says, "I had fun last night. Did you?"

"Yeah, sure." *Jesus, could I be more lame?*

He arches an eyebrow, but besides the upturn of his

lips, he doesn't comment on my uninspired reply. "Can I walk you to your car?"

Do I want to spend more time with Ryan? You betcha, but that isn't the smart thing to do. It's bad enough I couldn't escape without talking to him.

I swallow hard. "It's better if you're not seen with me."

His brows arch a little, and something passes through his eyes. I'd guess disappointment, but I'm probably reading him wrong.

"Yeah, you're right." He leans closer and kisses me on my cheek. "It was nice to meet you, June."

Now my heart is galloping at breakneck speed. I wasn't prepared for that sweet gesture. "It was nice to meet you too," I croak. "And Lachlan and Jake. Tell them I said that."

"Will do. Take care, Peaches."

"Peaches?"

He smiles in a cheeky way that makes my body temperature rise. Why does he have to be so adorable and sexy?

"Yeah, you taste like them."

Omygod, omygod. I'm hyperventilating now. Damnit, Ryan.

I nod, unable to find my voice. Clutching my purse and sandals to my chest, I walk out of the hotel suite in a hurry. My mind is spiraling. I'm so confused. After an evening of multiple orgasms, I should be on cloud nine.

Instead, I'm depressed, and it has nothing to do with Bill and Danika's betrayal.

Shake it off, June. There's no time for morose feelings. It's time to deal with yesterday's tomorrow's problem. Hell, that's a mouthful.

That's what she said.

Oh my God. I'm a dumbass in my thoughts too.

RYAN

I watch June walk out of the door. It's been a minute since she left, and I'm still rooted to the floor. I usually don't kiss hookups on the cheek when they leave, and it was a fucking mistake to break that rule today. I'm a second away from going after her and... I don't know what for. To fuck her again? Probably, even though I'd be breaking another rule. I don't go for seconds.

I'm saved from the crazy impulse when Lachlan walks out of the bedroom in his birthday suit, yawning.

I shake my head. What the fuck is wrong with me? I'm usually relieved when a hookup leaves without wanting more. The heaviness in my chest isn't normal.

"Where's June?" Lachlan asks.

"She left a minute ago." I head to the kitchen lest he sees the turmoil in my expression.

"What? Without saying goodbye?"

I open the cupboard, searching for the coffee mugs. The hotel suite has a decent coffee maker and I'm in dire need of an espresso.

"Yes, Lachy. She was in a hurry." I set three mugs on the counter, knowing he and Jake will ask for coffee too, and then I look for the coffee pods.

"Do you think she regrets last night?"

The wistfulness in Lachlan's tone makes me turn around. He's sitting on one of the high chairs, resting his forearms on the counter, looking dejected.

"I don't know. I'm not like your comic characters that can read minds."

"But you can read body language."

I cross my arms, narrowing my eyes. "Why do you want to know?"

"No reason." He sits up straighter, his expression now shut off.

Yeah, Lachy. You're looking hella suspicious.

I keep looking at him without saying a word, but he can't hold my stare for more than a second. That's unlike him. He never backs down from a staring contest. "Please don't tell me you caught feelings for the middle-school teacher."

His face twists into a grimace. "I didn't catch feelings, ye eejit."

"Who didn't catch feelings?" Jake joins us, the only one already dressed.

"Lachy, or so he says." My tone is cheerfully forced. I

love to antagonize Lachlan, but I'm not behaving like myself either in relation to June.

"Piss off and make me some coffee. I'm only half awake."

"You can make it yourself," I say, knowing very well I'll give the first mug to him.

"Yer such a nyaff," he grumbles.

"Is June gone?" Jake asks while staring at something on the living room floor.

"Yes," Lachy and I reply in unison.

"How long ago?"

I look over my shoulder. He can't possibly be upset that she left without saying goodbye. I understand Lachy getting all mushy. Underneath that grumpiness, he's a softie. "I don't know. Five minutes or so. Why?"

He bends over and picks up a pink wallet from the floor. "She left something behind. I'll try to catch up with her."

Lachy jumps from his chair. "I'll come too."

Jake frowns and gives him an overall glance. "You're naked."

"I can get dressed in under a minute."

"I'm not waiting." Jake veers for the door.

"She'll probably realize she doesn't have her wallet and come back," I say.

"She might not look in her purse until she needs to pay for something," he replies, and then he's gone.

"We could call her," Lachy suggests.

Excitement and jealousy pinch my chest. "When did you exchange digits?"

He grimaces. "I didn't. Did you?"

Fuck. I didn't, and I'm regretting it now. Can't let any of the guys know, though. "Why would I do that?"

He rubs his face. "I bet Melissa has her phone number."

I give him a meaningful look. "You aren't seriously considering calling Melissa this early, are you? She'll set up a bunch of interviews for you in retaliation."

"Bloody hell. You do it, then."

I shake my head. "Not a chance. You'd get interviews, I'd get my nut sack ripped off. Don't worry. I'm sure Jake will find June."

I'm not one to say things I don't mean, but I'm actually rooting for Jake to fail on his mission, so we have an excuse to deliver June's wallet in person.

CHAPTER 13
JUNE

The closer I get to my apartment, the worse the pain in my stomach becomes. My palms are sweaty and the lump in my throat is the size of Texas. I have a few unread messages from Katrina, but I'm too nervous to read them. I don't know if she saw the selfie with the boys I posted last night. I'm trying not to think too much about what happened after. Not a difficult task when my imminent confrontation with Bill is taking up most of my head space.

It's early enough that I avoid the heavy morning traffic. It takes me half an hour to get home. Ugh. I really need to stop thinking of the apartment I share with Bill as home. It won't be home for much longer. I should move out immediately, but I'm broke, and finding an affordable place to live in LA will be a difficult task. I'm sure I could stay with Katrina for a while, but she lives in a small house, and with her four kids and husband, her place is already at max capacity.

I have to park my beat-up car on the street because the apartment has only one designated garage spot and, naturally, Bill claimed that. With so many apartment buildings and all the commerce on my street, it's always stressful to find parking. I can't believe I let him get away with so much over the years. No wonder he thought it was okay to cheat on me with Danika.

I'm still wearing my party dress, because I didn't think to change before I was on the road, and I left my work clothes in my car. I did manage to zip it up, but I'm wearing my flats. When I see someone drive away from a parking spot, I take it, even though it isn't near my apartment's entrance. As I back into it, I notice the dry cleaning bag with Bill's lucky suit in the back seat. Hell. I forgot the jackass asked me to pick it up for him. I'm tempted to toss it in the trash, but I'm not that petty. With a sigh, I grab the bag.

My heart is beating loud and fast as I take the stairs to the second-floor apartment. It's early, and Bill must be home. Or maybe he spent the night at Danika's.

What if she spent the night here?

Shit. I'm starting to panic. As much as I want to tell them both to go to hell, I want to do it from a position of strength.

When I reach the landing, I pause and stare. I thought the worst possible scenario would be finding my snake of a former friend in my apartment. But I couldn't have foreseen how low Bill would go. All my stuff is sitting in the hallway in trash bags and boxes. I know those are my things, because among them, I spot my pink carryon bag, and one-eyed Toby—my first teddy bear and most valued possession—sticking out of one of the boxes.

"What the hell!"

Fury erupts from the pit of my stomach and spreads through my veins like wildfire. My hands are shaking when I fish my key out of my purse and insert it in the keyhole. It doesn't work. Oh my God. Did he change the lock?

I curl my hand into a fist and bang hard. "Bill! Open the door."

I keep slamming my fists until I hear the click of a lock releasing. But the asshole keeps the chain on, and I can see him only partially.

"What do you want, June?"

My jaw drops. *The nerve!* "I want to get into my fucking apartment."

"This isn't your apartment anymore."

"Bullshit it isn't. I pay half the rent every month, and we used *my* savings for the deposit."

"You should have thought about that before you decided to party with *my* hockey team. Do you know how humiliating that was for me? My entire office saw your selfies and they were giving me shit all night."

My eyes bug out. "Are you seriously going to talk about humiliation after I proposed to you on the damn Jumbotron and you turned me down because you're sleeping with my friend?"

He scowls. "Don't blame me for that. You know I hate public declarations of love. And after seeing the pictures you posted online, I'm convinced you only did it for attention."

I close my eyes and pinch the bridge of my nose. "Let me get this straight. You're saying I made that romantic gesture to gain media exposure?"

"Didn't you? You want to break into Hollywood, and you're going nowhere in your career. Now you're the jilted woman who got consoled by a bunch of hockey players and I'm the bad guy." His eyes focus on the garment bag in my hand. "Is that my lucky suit?"

My mind is spiraling. I can hardly believe all that nonsense that came out of Bill's mouth. Does he really believe he's the victim in all this?

"Yes. If you want it, you'd better open the door," I grit out.

He narrows his eyes, but instead of acting like an adult, he glares harder. "You know what? Keep it. Danika says I should get rid of old stuff anyway."

My chest constricts painfully. I didn't expect that hearing her name come out of his mouth again would hurt this much. Never mind the meaning of his reply. "That includes me, huh?"

He sighs. "Just take your things and leave, June."

My eyes are tearing up, but I don't want to give Bill the satisfaction of seeing me cry. "You can't do that. My name is on the lease."

He arches a brow. "Are you sure about that?"

My stomach bottoms out. I swear I signed a lease—I know I signed a bunch of stuff when we got the apartment. Could I be wrong? "My name is not on the lease?"

"You catch on fast."

"Are you kidding me?" I shriek.

"Calm down. I don't need a circus on my doorstep. Just go, before I call the cops." He slams the door in my face.

I don't move a muscle, stunned that the man I thought was *the one* could do such a vile thing. Hot tears run down my cheeks. I hastily wipe them away and glance at all my things, disposed of like trash.

A door down the hallway opens, making me turn. Who's coming to witness my humiliation? At least it won't be a crowd this time.

A teenager with dark long hair carrying a backpack hoisted over one shoulder walks down the corridor toward me. I've never seen him before, but I don't know all the neighbors. He glances at my stuff lined up against the wall, then at me. "Got kicked out?"

His tone is nonchalant as if this is a common occurrence. There's no pity in his gaze, but shame makes my face burn nonetheless. "Yes."

"Need help getting your stuff downstairs?"

His kind offer almost makes me cry again. I bite the inside of my cheek, hoping the pain will help me keep my shit together.

"Aren't you going to be late for school?"

"My ride won't be here for another ten minutes."

"Okay. Then yes, and thank you."

He shrugs. "No problem."

He adjusts his backpack so it's carried on both shoulders and then stacks a few boxes and lifts them up. I stuff Bill's suit into another box—I'm not sure what to do with it yet—then grab a couple of the trash bags and follow my helper to the elevator.

"We should fit as much as we can in the elevator and take the stairs," he says.

"Yeah, that's a good idea. I'm June, by the way."

"Paul," he mumbles.

"Nice to meet you, Paul."

He doesn't reply, but he's helping me, so I don't care that he's a little grumpy. I'm not in the mood to chat anyway. With Paul's help, I clear the front of Bill's apartment in record time. I'm not a packrat, thus I don't own a lot of things.

I press the elevator button to send it to the ground floor, and when I turn, Paul has already disappeared down the stairs.

"Thank you, Paul," I say, loud enough so he can hear me.

I wish he could have stayed longer to assist me in getting everything out of the elevator and into my car, but oh well. I race down the stairs and arrive before the elevator. Then I place one box in front of its door to prevent it from closing, and begin to take everything out.

I'm halfway done when someone yells from a few floors up. "Who's holding the elevator?"

"I'm sorry. I'll be done in a minute," I reply.

A moment later, an angry man stomps down the stairs and points a judgmental finger at me. "You're not allowed to move during peak hours."

"I didn't plan to move at all," I grit out. "I'm almost finished."

"I'm still going to write an email to the building's administration."

"What for? I'm moving out. What are they going to do about it?"

"They can send you a fine."

I'm about to tell him to go to hell but think better of it. They can send the fine to Bill. "Go ahead. I'm apartment 202."

He scowls as he types on his phone, then strides out of the building. The altercation has left me shaking and on the verge of tears again. I resume unloading the elevator, making sure I put all my things in a corner of the lobby and out of the way, but I take Toby out of the box. I have to get my car and park in front of the building, and I'm not going to risk him being stolen.

Outside, I finally decide to call Katrina. I need to stay at her place for a few days to sort out my living situation. But of course, my phone is dead. "Son of a *bitch*."

I stride toward my car. I can charge my phone using the car charger. The most important thing now is to load my things in it and get to work. Then it dawns on me. I'm still wearing a cocktail dress and probably smell like a sex dungeon. I can't teach like this.

As if things weren't already going swimmingly well for me, when I try to start the car, nothing happens.

"No, no. Come on, Betty. Don't do this to me."

I try again… and nada. I rest my forehead against the steering wheel, fighting more tears. This cannot be happening. Is it punishment for sleeping with three men last night? My very religious parents would say so.

I can't even call roadside assistance, because the charger won't work if the car won't start. Hell. I have to return to the apartment and beg Bill to let me charge my phone. The thought of further humiliating myself in front of that jerk makes me sick. But sitting in my car while all my belongings are in the foyer won't do.

I return to the building, but just as I'm about to enter, I see Bill's car exit the garage. I wave at him with both arms, but if he sees me, he chooses to ignore me. Dejected, I sit on the curb, and rest my forearms on my knees, dropping my head between them. Tired of keeping my sadness bottled inside, I finally allow myself to cry. I know not all is lost. I can bother a neighbor, but right now, I want to feel sorry for myself.

The sound of car doors opening and shutting nearby makes me look up. My eyes widen, and I stare at Lachlan, Jake, and Ryan in disbelief. Am I hallucinating now?

They walk over, and thanks to my utter shock, I forget to wipe off my wet cheeks.

They all furrow their brows, but it's Lachlan who drops into a crouch in front of me and asks, "What happened to you, lass?"

Concern shines in his eyes as he searches mine. Even though it's bruised, my heart does a backflip. But instead of answering him, I ask, "What are you doing here?"

CHAPTER 14
JAKE

When I couldn't find June to return her wallet, there was no question about what we should do. Unanimously, we decided to drive by her place and return the wallet in person. I didn't expect to find her sitting on the curb, crying her eyes out.

I tense, guessing her asshole ex put her in this state. The instincts to protect and avenge her mix in my veins, a powerful and dangerous combo. I'm on thin ice already with the organization, thanks to my bad temper. If I pick a fight with June's ex, there'll be hell to pay. Melissa will kill me.

I hang back while Lachy drops into a crouch and asks what happened. June's beautiful hazel eyes are brighter thanks to the tears swimming in them.

"What are you doing here?" she asks instead of

answering him.

"You forgot your wallet, lass."

"Oh?" Her brows arch. "I didn't even notice."

"Come on. Back on your feet." He takes her hands and pulls her up.

Ryan moves closer, staring at June with a serious expression. I only see that look on his face when he's utterly pissed. "Are you going to tell us what happened, Peaches?"

I frown. *Peaches?* That's new. I've never heard Ryan give any girl a special nickname. It's always the generic stuff with him.

"Bill kicked me out of the apartment. I got here and found all my stuff in trash bags and boxes out in the hallway. He even changed the lock."

"Son of a *bitch*," I blurt out. "What's your apartment number, June? I'd like to have a word with Bill."

My voice is low and tight, and she probably noticed the menacing tone, because her eyes widen. "He already left for work."

"He's lucky then," Ryan pipes up, glowering at the tall red brick building.

"Where's your stuff?" Lachy asks.

"I brought it all down to the foyer. But when I went to get my car, it wouldn't start. I'm beginning to think I'm being punished for..."

She trails off, but it's not hard to guess where she was going with her train of thought. She must believe having a foursome with us was bad. I might be jumping to conclusions, but knowing she's from a small town in Texas—Ryan told us—it isn't a giant leap to imagine she was brought up in a religious household.

"Do you have a place to go?" Ryan asks.

"Not really. I mean, I'm sure I can stay with my friend from work for a few days, but I don't want to impose longer than that."

Ryan and Lachlan both look at me, and I can almost read their minds. In any case, the idea also occurred to me. "I may have a solution for that."

"What? Do you know a place I can rent for cheap in L.A.?"

"Is free cheap enough for you?"

She blinks fast, and then she surprises me by shaking her head. "If you're suggesting I move in with you, then the answer is no. I'm not a mooch."

Her indignant answer makes me chuckle. "That's not my solution."

"All right. What is it then?"

Ryan throws an arm around my shoulder. "Jakey here looks tough, but he's a softy at heart. He volunteered to watch our neighbors' pets while she's on a three-month trip to Europe."

June looks at me. "You did?"

"It was her lifelong dream. I couldn't say no."

"But aren't you guys on the road all the time? Who's going to watch the pets then?"

"There's where you come in. You can stay in Mrs. Carpenter's apartment while she's away. I'm sure she won't mind."

June bites her lower lip, drawing my attention to it and bringing memories of last night to the forefront of my mind. I legit want to help her and get out of a bind at the same time. But that's not the only reason I'd love to live next door to her for a while. She intrigues me with her sweet nature that changes into fierceness when she's in competing mode, and I wouldn't mind getting to know her better. Besides, I don't have the same rule as Ryan of not hooking up with the same girl more than once. Judging by the way Lachy is looking at her, I'd say he's on the same page as me.

"You said pets. How many and what kind?"

"Two cats, a semi-blind dog, a few fish, and a parrot," Lachlan replies.

June laughs. "That's all?"

"You forgot Humberto, the turtle," Ryan pipes up.

"Oh yeah."

"Are you sure your neighbor won't mind? She doesn't know me, and to be fair, neither do you."

"If the city of L.A. trusts you to teach middle-graders, then I'm sure we can trust you too." Ryan smiles brightly.

Her eyes widen. "Oh crap. I need to call the school. There's no way I can make it to work on time now."

"We'll load your stuff in my car while you call them," I say.

"Could I borrow one of your phones? My battery is dead."

Lachlan offers his. "You can use mine. It's unlocked."

"Thank you." She glances at the screen and smiles. "You have a Highland calf as your screensaver?"

His cheeks turn red. "They're adorable."

Watching their interaction, I'm now certain I'm not the only one who wouldn't mind getting to know June better. Lachlan is usually a grump, but in front of her, he melts like butter. That doesn't bother me. I can share her with him and Ryan for one night or many. But only them, no one else.

I head into the building to see what we're dealing with and get angry all over again when I see the trash bags filled with June's belongings. Her ex should count his blessings that he isn't around. The motherfucker deserves an ass whipping. I'd risk Melissa's wrath for the chance to teach him a lesson.

Ryan follows me in, and before I can say a word, he starts, "We have a problem."

I narrow my eyes. "What now?"

"I want to break my number-one rule, and you need to stop me."

"I can't be your chastity belt, Ryan." I grab a few boxes.

He follows my lead and takes some of the trash bags. "You know I don't do seconds."

"Then don't." I head for the exit.

"How am I supposed to resist when she'll be living right next door?"

I laugh. "You're assuming she wants a repeat."

"Are you saying she doesn't?" He sounds almost unsure, and it's fucking hilarious.

I refrain from answering him as we walk outside the building. That's not a conversation I want June to over-hear. She's standing close to my car, talking on the phone under the watchful gaze of Lachlan.

He switches his attention to us and asks, "Is that all?"

"No, there are a few more bags inside," I reply.

"Okay. I'll get them." He hurries into the building, and then June ends the call.

"Everything okay at work?" I ask.

"Yes. The principal is a nice lady, and she saw my fiasco of a proposal on TV. She was already expecting me not to show up at work today and called in a sub."

"Good. You need to rest," Ryan chimes in.

"I need to call roadside assistance to see about my car, but you guys probably need to get going."

We do have practice in an hour, but I don't want her to worry. "Let's get you settled, and then we'll see about your car." I open the trunk and start to arrange the boxes inside.

"I don't think it'll all fit," she says.

"It will, but I'm afraid the guys will need to call an Uber."

"Oh no. I feel terrible now," she says.

Her reaction is too adorable for her own good and it gives me fuzzy feelings. I grew up surrounded by phony people who only pretended to be nice to get something from me. I can tell when someone is being genuine.

Ryan and Lachlan give me the stink eye, and I know it isn't because they have to call a ride. They want to spend more time with June, but she obviously wouldn't guess that.

Ryan rubs June's arm. "Don't worry, Peaches. I feel sorry for you though. Jake's a terrible driver. Maybe you should come with us."

I narrow my eyes, and I'm about to call him on his bullshit, but June beats me to the punch. "If he's a bad driver, why did you ride with him in the first place?"

I'm trying not to laugh, which is usually easy for me because I'm not easily amused, but June giving Ryan shit is not only funny, it's also hot as hell. I pegged her to be shy at first, but maybe she's only like that with strangers. I saw a glimpse of her fiery nature during that game of pool, and then she went from timid to a wildcat during sex. Today, we're getting more of her sassy personality.

When Ryan can't reply soon enough, Lachlan says,

"Lass, I've never seen Ryan not have a fast retort. You're a keeper."

Her cheeks turn bright pink, and then she looks at me. "I'll ride with you, Jake."

Feeling like I won the lottery, I nod. "Sounds good."

"I need to get something from my car. Be right back." She runs down the sidewalk and stops next to a faded blue sedan near the street corner. I wonder why she didn't park in the garage. She returns holding an old teddy that's missing an eye.

"What's that?" Ryan asks.

"Toby. I've had him since I was a baby."

Ryan and I turn to Lachlan. He shakes his head, his round eyes begging us to keep our mouths shut, but obviously, Ryan can't resist teasing him. "Just like you and your old baby blanket, Lachy."

His eyes narrow, and I can almost hear the insults popping into his head. But he doesn't say a word, probably restraining himself on June's account.

June tilts her head. "Do they tease you a lot because of your blankie?"

"Nah," he lies.

Ryan opens his big mouth, and I know he's going to contradict Lachlan, so I chime in before he can say anything. "If you have everything, June, we should go and try to beat traffic."

"Right." She looks at Lachlan and Ryan. "I guess I'll see you later."

I open the passenger door for June but can't help glancing at Ryan and Lachlan with a smug grin on my face. They're both glowering. I can see already spending quality time with June will turn into a competition. Bring it on.

CHAPTER 15
JUNE

don't speak for the first couple minutes of the ride. My head keeps replaying everything that happened in the last hour, and my emotions bounce from anger to disbelief to heartbreak, never settling on one.

Jake lets me be, but I soon realize I'm being extremely rude by not saying anything.

"Thanks for helping me," I murmur.

He turns to me and smiles. "Happy to do it."

"And for returning my wallet in person. You must think I'm a walking disaster."

"I don't think that. I happen to have met you while you're going for a rough patch, that's all."

I cross my arms. "That's a rough patch, all right."

"Don't take this the wrong way but… it isn't all bad."

I turn to him. "No, it isn't. If it weren't for my asshole ex-boyfriend, I wouldn't have met you and the boys."

Jake glances at me again, one of his brows raised. "Boys?"

My face becomes hot in zero-point-two seconds. Crap. "I'm sorry. I obviously don't think you're boys... ugh. Melissa said it, and I thought it was a cute endearment. I don't have the history she has with you to call you that, and—"

He places his hand on my leg, giving me instant radioactive butterflies. "Relax. I'm not mad. You can call them boys."

"And you?"

His hand slides off my leg as he looks at the road. I miss the contact immediately. "If you want to. Although I've never considered myself cute."

"Hot guys can be cute too."

He laughs. "You think I'm hot?"

Shit. I can't believe I said that out loud. I sink further into the supple leather seat, hoping it will swallow me. Here it is, the awkward morning-after moment I was dreading.

"Forget I said anything."

"You're blushing. It's adorable," he replies, amusement lacing his tone.

"It doesn't take much when I'm around you guys."

He chuckles. "I noticed."

Oh God. Is he thinking about last night? He must be, because I am too. I'm still tender in certain parts.

I clear my throat. "Tell me about your neighbor."

"Oh, she's a hoot, the grandmother I wish I had."

His comment makes me curious about his family, but we're on the neighbor topic now, and I'm not about to change it to pry into his personal life. "Is she a hockey fan?"

"Not when we met her, but she is now. She comes to every home game and even converted some of her friends to fans as well."

"How did you officially meet?"

He laughs. "That's a funny story, but not mine to tell. You need to ask Ryan."

"Curiouser and curiouser," I mumble. "Do you think Mrs. Carpenter will be okay with me staying at her place?"

"I'm sure, but if it makes you feel better, I can call her and make the introductions."

"Yeah, I'd like that. Thank you."

I begin to relax, until some jackass cuts in front of Jake's car, forcing him to step on the brakes hard to avoid a collision. The seat belt digs into my chest painfully, but it's better than my face smashing against the windshield. One of the boxes in the backseat slides forward, and judging by the noise, something fell out.

"Motherfucker!" Jake yells as he slams the heel of his

hand against the car's horn. Then he turns to me. "Are you okay?"

"Yeah. I'm fine." I check what fell out of the box and see my ukulele case on the floor. I try to pick it up, but the strap catches on something.

"What fell?" he asks but doesn't look away from the traffic ahead. "I heard something."

"Just my ukulele. It should be fine."

"You play?"

"Yeah, or at least, I used to. Bill hates it, so I stopped practicing when he was around."

Jake's jaw tenses. "I'm glad he's out of the picture."

My heart constricts. I'm glad too, but I'm also super depressed that I wasted years of my life with him. Speaking about all the things I stopped doing because of him, and the stuff I let him get away with… it makes me so mad at myself. I was an idiot.

When I don't say anything, Jake continues. "You're happy too, right?"

"Yeah. I am. It's just… the coin hasn't dropped yet."

"It will once you're settled in your new place."

I almost say *temporary new place* but that might sound ungrateful.

"I hope so."

"Well, here we are." He points at a historic commercial building. We're on Broadway in the heart of the Historic Core district of Downtown Los Angeles.

"You live in a commercial building?"

"The top two floors have been converted to apartments, and our penthouse is on the top floor. Mrs. Carpenter lives in an apartment below us."

"That's so cool. I didn't realize you lived so close to me. We might even have bumped into each other at a market."

"I think I'd remember if our paths had crossed before." We enter the garage, and it becomes darker for a moment, which helps cover the blush I must be sporting right now.

I want to say *I'd remember you too*, but the words stay lodged in my throat. I don't want to give him the impression I'm hoping there'll be a repeat of last night. He probably has a mile-long list of gorgeous women he can pick from. Why would he want me when not even my lame-ass ex-boyfriend did? Last night, I was a novelty. Today, I'm a solution to his problem.

He parks the car. "I'll get the dolly. Be right back."

"Okay."

I get out of the car too, and open the trunk. Before Jake returns, Ryan and Lachlan find me.

"Did you just arrive?" Ryan asks.

"Yeah. How did you get here so fast?"

"Our ride didn't take long, and Ryan told him there would be an extra tip if he got here fast," Lachlan replies.

"I'm sorry this is taking so much of your time. I can probably get everything upstairs by myself."

Both make faces, but it's Lachlan who replies, "Don't be silly, lass. We're glad to help."

Jake returns with the dolly. "Damn, did you fly here?"

"We were very motivated." Ryan gives me a look that it's meant to make my panties shimmy down my legs on their own. Talk about a smoldering glance.

Heat spreads across my cheeks, and I quickly avoid his gaze, taking some bags out of the trunk. The boys load the dolly with most of the boxes, and what doesn't fit, Lachlan and Ryan carry while Jake pushes the dolly. I follow them toward the elevator, but Jake splits from the group.

"Where is he going?" I ask.

"The service elevator is on the other side," Ryan replies.

"Shouldn't we all take that?" I eye the box in his hands.

"We won't all fit. It's okay, lass."

My pulse accelerates when I find myself alone in the metal box sandwiched between Ryan and Lachlan. This is deja vu. Are they thinking about last night too? My face must be redder than a tomato, because it feels so hot.

I should say something because the silence is beginning to smother me. But I don't know what to say. I'm as nervous now as I was last night when we were making our way to my hotel room. My heart is beating so loudly, it's hard to believe they can't hear it.

"How was the ride with Jake?" Ryan breaks the silence.

"We almost crashed," I blurt out.

Shit. Why did I say that? Oh yeah. Nerves. I just threw Jake under the bus. Where's my sense of loyalty? He's been nothing but super nice to me.

"For real?" Lachlan brows arch.

"What did I tell you?" Ryan pipes up.

"It wasn't his fault. A jackass cut in front of us." I turn to him and catch the upturn of his lips. Crap. "Please don't say anything."

He stares into my eyes, mischief written all over them. "What would I get in return?"

My jaw hangs loose, but my tongue remains tied. I don't know how to answer that. Is he flirting with me, or is he just yanking my chain?

"Stop teasing June. Don't worry, lass. He won't say a word." Lachlan glowers at Ryan, and the intensity of his stare tells me there'll be hell to pay if Ryan opens his big mouth.

"You guys are no fun." Now Ryan's pouting.

The elevator's door slides open, and that's when I notice we've reached their floor. I step out first and see that the door to their apartment is wide open.

I don't move, and Ryan and Lachlan stop on either side of me.

"Go on, June. Ladies first," Ryan tells me.

I swallow hard. I'm not sure why the jitters are getting the better of me now. I've already done many naughty things with these men, and if they want a repeat, I won't say no. Maybe that's why I'm nervous. If we're going to be neighbors for the next three months, I shouldn't let that happen again. I can't afford to fall for men who are way out of my league.

CHAPTER 16
JUNE

I can't help but gawk at everything. The boys' apartment is the most beautiful place I've ever seen. There's a sense of grandeur and sophistication that's evoked by the many unique art pieces displayed on the walls of the expansive loft-style open space. A skylight with retractable shades floods the area with natural light.

As I walk past the dining area, which holds a twelve-seater table in solid wood and colorful chairs, and into the great room, the gourmet kitchen equipped with state-of-the-art appliances, double sinks, and a large island comes into view.

"Wow," I say.

"Not too shabby, huh?" Ryan chuckles.

"Not at all. This place is amazing."

"And you haven't seen the rest yet," Lachlan chimes in.

Jake joins us in the living room. He's changed into jeans and a sweater, making me even more aware that we're all wearing last night's clothes. My wrinkled party dress feels like a neon sign flashing to the word that I did bad things.

"Hey, I called Mrs. Carpenter, but she didn't answer. We'll try again later. In the meantime, you can stay here," Jake tells me.

"You have to be somewhere, don't you?"

He rubs the back of his neck. "Yeah, we have practice. But we should be back in a few hours." He looks at Lachlan and Ryan. "Aren't you changing?"

"Right," Ryan says, but keeps staring at me.

Lachlan smiles and then veers toward a hallway to my left. Ryan follows him. Shit. I'm totally imposing and don't know what to do with myself. I could still ask Katrina for help, but then I'd be imposing on her too. What a fucking mess.

"I need to walk Winston. Feel like joining me?" Jake asks.

"Uh…" I glance at my dress.

"Here. You can wear my sweatshirt." He offers me a big and warm navy sweatshirt that I know will look like a dress on me. Perfect. It'll cover my cocktail dress and make this outing feel less like a walk of shame.

"Thanks."

I put it on, and not only do I get swallowed up by the fabric, but also Jake's heady scent envelops me. It's fresh, all-male, and giving me serious goose bumps. My stomach flutters as I recall his mouth on my body, doing the dirtiest and most delicious things to me.

Control yourself, June.

I return to the here and now and find Jake staring as if he read my thoughts. Shit. I hope my expression wasn't obvious.

"I'm ready," I say.

We head out together, and once again, I'm trapped in an elevator with one of the boys. Mercifully, it's a short ride down to Mrs. Carpenter's floor. There are four doors in this hallway. Jake turns to the left and stops in front of the first with the key in hand.

No sooner does he open the door than I smell his neighbor's menagerie. It's not unpleasant per se, but you can definitely tell many pets live inside. Winston, the half-blind dog, is a grey mutt that comes running toward Jake and jumps on his legs in excitement. He reminds me of Benji.

"Hey buddy, are you ready to go out?" Jake rubs the dog's head affectionately.

He barks in response, then turns his attention to me. I drop into a crouch to properly greet the cutie pie. "Hello, Winston. I'm June."

Jake hands me the leash. "We'd better get going, or he might do his business here in the hallway."

I wrinkle my nose. "We don't want that, do we, Winston?"

The dog is super excited, but I manage to attach the leash to his collar without getting my face licked. When I unfurl from my crouch and turn, I catch Jake watching me so intensely that it makes my heart skip a beat. I was going to ask about the other pets, but I rush down the corridor with Winston. I need fresh air, stat.

JAKE

The more time I spend with June, the more I want to get her back in bed, with or without the guys. I'm not quite sure yet why I'm so drawn to her. She's hot, cute, and sweet, a combination proving to be irresistible to me. But there's more to it, and I haven't figured out what yet.

I let her handle Winston, since she'll walk him when I'm not around. When I'm in town, I plan to join her. I could say Mrs. Carpenter's pets are still my responsibility, but deep down, I know I just want to spend more time with June.

"Too bad there isn't a park in this area," she says.

"True. The loft is convenient since it's only ten minutes from the arena, but the neighborhood lacks green spaces. I never stay here off-season."

"Where do you go?"

"I have a house in Birchen Beach, North Carolina."

"Oh, I bet it's beautiful. Are you originally from there?"

I snort. "I wish."

I keep my eyes straight ahead. The sidewalk is busy with people hurrying to their offices, and I don't want to bump into anyone. But I sense June's gaze burning a hole through my face, so I glance at her. "What is it?"

"Where are you from then?"

"I think you're the first person I've talked to in a long time who doesn't know that."

She averts her gaze, and her cheeks turn pink. "I don't follow sports."

"It's okay. It wasn't a critique, just an observation. I'm not a narcissist asshole who expects everyone to know who I am."

"But you mostly deal with people in the business or who follow hockey, so they all know everything about you."

"They *think* they know everything about me."

She tilts her head. "I'd love to get to know the real you, not the image you project to the world."

Warmth spreads through my chest. I didn't expect June to say that, or my reaction to her words.

Before I can reply, my phone rings. I fish it out, betting it's either Ryan or Lachlan. My mood sours when I see my brother's name flash on the screen.

There's no chance in hell I'm going to answer that. I decline the call quickly. Those conversations are never pleasant. Gregory only calls me to criticize me, just like my father does. He's learned from the master.

"What's wrong?" June asks, looking at me with her big, bright, curious eyes while Winston does his business on a corner.

"Nothing." I start to put my phone away, but then Ryan calls me. Perfect timing. "Hello?"

"Where are you?"

I glance at the traffic. It's already going at a snail's pace. We might arrive late for practice. "Walking Winston. We'll be back in a minute."

"All right. See you soon."

When I turn to June, she's unfurling from a crouch, holding a small bag. "All done. We can go back."

"Good. Winston was quick today. It can sometimes take ten minutes before he's done. You need to keep that in mind."

"Noted. I'm usually an early riser. I'll walk him first thing in the morning." Her expression grows serious, and she bites her lower lip, drawing my attention to her mouth.

I lose focus. It hasn't been a day since I feasted on those luscious lips, and I'm already craving another taste.

"What about during the day? I don't get off work until four," she continues, dispelling my lust haze.

I shake my head. "Don't worry about it. *I'm* the one who agreed to watch Mrs. Carpenter's pets. I'll make arrangements for during the day."

"But it doesn't seem fair that I'll stay in her apartment, and you'll still have to pay for a dog walker."

Her eyes are troubled, and usually, I'd use only words to lessen her worry, but I feel compelled to do more. I touch her shoulder and squeeze. "It's okay. You have a job, and you'll be helping plenty."

She glances at my hand and then back into my eyes. As much as I'd like to keep the connection, I pull my hand away. June doesn't seem convinced, but as long as she doesn't make other living arrangements, it's okay with me. I don't want her going anywhere.

CHAPTER 17
RYAN

"Do you think June will be all right?" Lachy asks as soon as we hit the road.

"Oh my god. Don't worry about her. She's a big girl," I reply, irritated.

"What crawled up your arse?" he barks back.

I'd level him with a glower if I weren't driving. Sitting in the back seat, Jake chuckles.

"What's so funny?" I glance at the rearview mirror.

"You two are acting like June is a shiny new toy you're fighting over."

I narrow my eyes, regretting having told Jake that I wanted seconds. "I'm not fighting over anyone. I'm annoyed that Lachy is acting like she's a breakable doll."

"Piss off," he grumbles. "We're breaking all our rules when it comes to June. We left her alone in our apartment. We've never let any lass stay there when we aren't around."

And for good reason. There are way too many nutjobs in this city. Then why didn't I even blink before letting June stay? I rub my face. I'm overthinking this. June isn't some crazy chick interested in hooking up with a hockey player. She's a nice woman who got dealt a horrible blow. Being cheated on by someone you trust is one of the hardest things a person can go through. I saw the devastation firsthand with my dad.

"We can trust, June," Jake grits out.

I try to catch Jake's eyes through the rearview mirror again, but he's looking out the window with his jaw locked tight.

"What's up, Jakey?" I ask.

"Nothing."

"Bullshit. You might not be worried about June, but something is bothering you."

He sighs. "My douche brother called earlier."

Lachy groans. "What did that bawbag want?"

"Don't know. I didn't answer."

Jake's family is just as messed up as mine. His father is a certified asshole, constantly comparing Jake to his brother, always bitching about his life choices. Never mind that Jake is one of the best hockey players in the league, has played in two All-Star games, and has a Stanley Cup under his belt. It's never good enough for the scumbag.

He's the reason Jake will never play for any team in New York, his home state. He's made that clear since the beginning of his career. Sometimes, we don't have a choice where we wind up, but we can put teams on our absolutely-fucking-no list.

"He won't stop calling until you answer," Lachy points out.

"I don't care."

His tone is final, and both Lachy and I know to drop the subject. The ride is silent until we're a minute from the training facility. It's not in the arena but a block away from it.

Melissa calls my phone, which is connected to the car's audio system. She doesn't usually call me unless I've done something stupid. Maybe she's unhappy about last night's activities with her guest of honor.

Too fucking bad. "Good morning, Mel. What can I do for you?"

"Just checking to make sure you guys took good care of June."

I should bite my tongue, but she totally teed that up for me. "Don't worry. We took *excellent* care of Peaches."

Lachy turns to me, sporting a what-the-fuck look.

"Peaches?" Melissa's voice rises a pitch. "You gave her a nickname?"

"Sure did."

"Oh boy… So it *did* go well. I called her, but it went to voicemail."

"Her phone is dead. I'll pass on the message that you want to talk to her."

Lachy shakes his head and mutters, "Bloody eejit."

"Wait… what? You're planning on seeing her again?" Melissa asks.

I laugh. "Sure, why not?"

A moment of silence follows, and I can't help grinning. Stunning Melissa is always fun. She's on top of things ninety-nine percent of the time and takes pride in always knowing shit before anyone else does. Catching her by surprise is rare.

"I don't believe it. You're yanking my chain, aren't you?"

"It's not what you think," Jake butts in from the backseat. "I'll explain later."

"You'd better. And it goes without saying, don't mess with June. She's been through enough, and she doesn't need more complications in her life."

Lachy sinks in his seat, crossing his arms. Jake decides to shut his piehole as well. They don't want to assure Melissa we'll stay out of June's life because no one wants to keep that promise. I have no problem answering though. "No worries, Mel. June is safe."

"All right. I have to run. See you at the meeting this afternoon."

"Byeee." I press the end-call button, and Lachy starts immediately.

"Why did you have to tell Melissa about June?"

"Technically, I didn't say anything." I stop the car and lower the window to scan my card and gain entrance to the garage.

"Let's drop the subject," Jake chimes in. "We can talk about June later. It's in our best interests to not let anyone know what happened last night, or that she's staying in our building."

I grow serious. We definitely shouldn't broadcast what we did. Too many snakes would try to exploit our private lives for their own gain. We could take the hit, but June couldn't. The last thing I want is for her to get hurt.

CHAPTER 18
JUNE

When Jake and I returned to the apartment, there wasn't time for a tour. He showed me where the bathroom was and told me I could eat anything. After they left, I felt pretty glum. It's been fifteen minutes, and the sensation of abandonment hasn't gone away. I've been sitting on their comfortable L-shaped leather couch without moving, staring into nothing.

My stomach grumbles, reminding me I haven't eaten anything today. And I've been operating without coffee. I need to fix that pronto, before I develop a headache. I get up and head to the kitchen, but my hope for coffee plummets when I stare at the fancy espresso machine.

"Shit. How does this thing work?"

I look at all the buttons and knobs but can't figure it

out. It looks super expensive. *You'll end up breaking it, June.* I might have to head out to grab a coffee.

I open the fridge in search of something to eat. It's fully stocked with all kinds of promising things, but my eyes immediately zero in on the bottle of cold brew. Katrina hates iced coffee, but I could mainline it.

"Thank God."

Besides the coffee, I grab cheese, ham, butter, and bread. It takes me a few minutes to whip up a sandwich and less than that to inhale the whole thing. I guess last night's sex marathon worked up my appetite.

Energized and with caffeine running through my veins, I'm motivated to get organized. The first order of business is to charge my phone and then call roadside assistance to tow my car to a garage. I hope it's nothing major. I can't afford an expensive car repair.

While my phone charges, I take my laptop out of its bag and search for places to live. Even if I can stay at Mrs. Carpenter's apartment for now, it's temporary. I need to know what my prospects are. But after ten minutes of checking listings, I'm sick to my stomach. As I already suspected, I won't be able to afford my own place.

My phone pings as it comes back to life. Several different people are waiting for replies to texts, including Mom and my brother, August. Ugh. They know about my epic fiasco. I didn't tell them I planned to propose to Bill last night, and they don't watch hockey, so I didn't worry about them. Someone must have told them, and I bet my humiliation is juicy gossip in good old Baron, Texas.

The messages from my mother start with *Honey, what were you thinking?* and the last one is all-caps: *CALL ME!*

"Yeah, fat chance of that happening this second."

August's text is better.

> Never liked that guy. Do you want me to come over and beat the shit out of the douche?

I laugh despite the growing sadness in my chest. I don't think I want Bill back. I'm mourning the death of the relationship I thought I had.

Katrina left several messages too, and the last one is about the selfie with the boys I posted on social media. I want to call her and tell her everything, but first period has already started, so I reply with a text instead.

> Girl, those hockey players are hot. I want all the deets.

> Call me as soon as you can.

I don't expect a reply right away, so when my phone rings a minute later, it startles me. It's Katrina.

"Hey."

"June, how are you, baby girl?"

"I'm okay. Aren't you supposed to be in class?"

"I couldn't wait until the end of the first period. I'm in the bathroom. Tell me everything."

"I can't tell you everything over the phone. There's a lot to tell."

"Ugh... don't do this to me. At least tell me you hooked up with one of those boys," she whispers.

My face becomes hot in an instant. "The answer is yes."

"Yes! Who?"

"I'll tell you later."

"You're impossible. What did you do about Bill?"

"I've moved out."

"Good. He doesn't deserve to share the air you breathe. He'd better not cross my path, or he'll get punched in the throat."

I totally believe Katrina would do such a thing, but then Bill would press charges and ruin her life. "I appreciate the sentiment, but I don't want you getting in trouble because of that scumbag."

"Where are you staying now? You know you can totally stay at my place."

Shit. I can't be evasive about my whereabouts too. She'd worry. "Right now, I'm at the boys' apartment."

"The boys? Oh my God, the hockey players?"

"Yep. They share a loft downtown. It's amazing."

"Damn, girl. Talk about an upgrade. I have to get back to class, but text me the address. I'm coming over after work."

Oh crap. What if they don't want anyone to know where they live? Also, do I want Katrina to come here and meet the boys before I tell her I was railed by them? She has the uncanny ability to figure that shit out. She always knows who's banging who at work before anyone else. But I don't have a choice. She's my best friend, and she needs to know I'm in a safe place. I'd do the same thing for her.

"Will do," I reply. "Talk later."

"Bye!"

Although I'm nervous about Katrina's visit—and the spilling the beans part—I do want to see her. Maybe I can meet her in a public place. There must be a coffee shop nearby. The past twelve hours have been a whirl-wind—sleeping with three men and then moving into their building. I'm so confused about my feelings, and I need guidance.

I glance at the apartment listings again and, with a sigh, close my laptop. Looking at them will only depress me. What I need is a shower and comfy clothes. Grimac-ing, I look at the boxes and bags with all my stuff. Nothing is labeled, so I have no idea where fuckface Bill put my clothes. I bet he didn't pack everything, and I have no illusions about what he's done with the rest.

They're just things, June. At least my teddy bear and the ukulele made it.

I start with the bags. My underwear is in one bag, and my loungewear is in another. I keep things simple, since I don't have to go to work. Leggings and a vintage T-shirt it is. I laugh when I see which top I pulled from the bag. It's a *Youngblood* movie T-shirt with Rob Lowe and Patrick Swayze on it. Appropriate.

With my bundle of clothes in hand, I head to Lachlan's room. He told me I could use his bathroom to shower. I'm sure Jake and Ryan would have offered as well, but they were already out the door when Lachlan said it. My guess is they were late, and it slipped their minds.

My jaw drops when I step foot in his room. Melissa mentioned he was into comics, but now I see he's obsessed. He has an entire wall dedicated to his comic and figurine collections. I set my clothes on his king-size bed and walk over to inspect the shelves. I don't dare to touch anything. With my luck, I'd probably knock a figurine down and break it.

He has hardcover graphic novels on display, but most of his comics collection is stored alphabetically in glass paneled filing cabinets. That's how I store my comics collection back at my parents' house. I didn't want to bring it to LA, knowing there would be limited space. I'm glad I didn't, because I bet Bill would have thrown it in the trash.

The room is light and airy, thanks to the tall windows. A desk is in front of them, and I notice a closed sketchbook and drawing pencils. I'm tempted to look, but art is personal. I'm intruding on his privacy as it is.

I head to the en suite bathroom, and I'm not even surprised that it's three times the size of my old one. Considering Lachlan's size, he needs the space. There isn't a tub, but the shower stall is enormous; he could throw a small party inside. There are two regular showerheads—one on each side—and a rainfall showerhead in the middle. I can't help but wonder who Lachlan had shared this stall with. It'd be a waste not to use all this room for some hanky panky. Immediately, I picture myself pinned against the wall with my legs wrapped around Lachlan's hips while he pounds into me. My clit throbs with arousal.

No, bad, June. You can't start having sexy dreams about any of the boys—that's a danger zone.

Great, now that song is playing in my head.

Despite my inner monologue, I can't control my body. I'm aching for Lachlan, Ryan, and Jake. It's not only because they're sinfully hot guys, and they gave me so many orgasms last night. It's also their attention and care toward me. Hell, who could resist three knights in shining armor? I want a repeat, even if it's a bad idea.

"Fuck. A cold shower it is."

CHAPTER 19
JAKE

The meeting with Melissa lasts so long that by the time it's over, I have a headache. I try to pay attention, especially since she's going over events that require our presence, and I have a bad reputation to salvage. Shoving a drunk patron into the swimming pool during a charity event last year put me on Melissa's shit list. In my defense, he was being extremely obnoxious toward the waitressing staff.

Ryan pays zero attention and keeps checking his phone while Lachy remains unmovable, arms crossed and glowering at anyone who looks at him.

When the meeting finally ends, I jump from my chair, but Melissa's gaze finds mine. "Jake, may I have a word?"

I glance at Ryan and Lachy, but since Melissa didn't

ask to speak with them, they leave the room with everyone else.

"What's up, Mel?" I ask once we're alone.

"You know what's up. You said you'd explain Ryan's enigmatic answer later. This is later."

Her expression is serious, which means there's no room for jokes. "You don't want all the details."

She narrows her eyes. "No, I don't need that. I just want to know if any of you plan to keep seeing June."

"As in date her?"

She waves her hand. "Date her, hook up with her, whatever. What happened at the arena with June is still newsworthy. Several online sites have written about her fiasco, and they've also shared the picture she posted online with you."

My brows arch. "Are you mad about that?"

She shakes her head. "No. I encouraged her to do just that. I'm not judging, but I need to know if she's going to be around. If that's the case, she needs media training."

I cross my arms. "I don't recall any other WAG receiving media training."

Melissa smirks. "June's circumstance is special. She isn't like the others."

You got that right. She isn't.

"All right. Then you should definitely speak with June about that training."

Melissa's eyes widen a bit. "Really? You're interested in dating her?"

Am I? I want to spend time with her, but dating is another story. "You know I don't date."

She rolls her eyes. "Oh yeah. I forgot. You and Ryan suffer from the same commitment phobia. Lachy then."

"I can't speak for him. All I'm saying is, I think June should get media training, because she'll be our neighbor for the next three months, and it's very likely she'll be seen with us."

Melissa's mouth makes a perfect O. "I didn't think there were apartments available for rent in your building."

"She's staying in Mrs. Carpenter's apartment while she's on her trip."

"Ah, that's the lady with all the pets." Understanding shines in her eyes. "Oh my God. You've asked June to pet sit for you. Jake..."

"What?" I shrug. "She needed a place to stay after her douche ex kicked her out of their apartment, and I offered her a solution. It's a good trade."

Melissa's spine goes straight. "He kicked her out?"

"Yeah, all her things were in the hallway when she got home."

Melissa loses some of the sharpness in her gaze. She's in business mode most of the time, but it seems June made an impression on her as well. Melissa likes her. "I can't believe he did that. How is she holding up?"

"When we dropped by her place to return her wallet, she was a mess. Her ex is lucky he was already gone when we got there."

She levels me with a glare. "No. *You* were lucky. You can't get into another fight, Jake. You're the captain, for fuck's sake. You need to set the example."

Rubbing my face, I look away. "I know. I promise I'll try to be on my best behavior."

"You'd better. You know there's a reception after the game with the New York Bobcats tomorrow."

I frown. "So? I have no issues with anyone in the organization."

She gives me a loaded stare that I can feel in my bones. "Your father and your brother will be in attendance."

My stomach coils tightly and painfully. Hell, now I know why my brother was calling me. "Why?"

"One of your father's clients is a major sponsor of the Bobcats."

Fuck me.

Melissa tilts her head. "Will that be a problem, Jake?"

I stand straighter. "No. Is that all?"

She nods.

I'm in a piss-poor mood when I walk out of the meeting room. Ryan and Lachy are waiting for me in the hallway.

Lachy pushes off the wall and turns to me. "What did Melissa want?"

"To ask if June needs media training."

Ryan jerks back. "Why would she need that?"

"Because she has a spotlight on her right now, thanks to what happened at the game last night."

"That wouldn't warrant training unless... Does she think one of us is with June?" Lachy asks.

"She thought maybe you."

His brows arch. "Me?"

Ryan snorts. "And you're surprised? Out of the three of us, you're the only one who's been in a serious relationship before and wants to jump into another one."

"I doona want to jump into anything," he grits out.

"It doesn't matter. If June wants it, she'll get media training. End of story."

Both Lachy and Ryan check their phones quickly, then look at each other.

"Anything?" Ryan asks.

Lachy shakes his head. "Bloody nothing."

"What's going on now?"

Fuck. It'd better not be another complication. I'm stressed enough as it is, knowing my father and brother will be at the game tomorrow. My father's presence in the arena is triggering because the jackass always insists on coming to see me afterward, and it doesn't matter the game's outcome. Win or lose, he always has a list of things I could improve.

He played hockey in college, but he wasn't good enough to make it to the pros. Not that he would have pursued that anyway. We come from a long line of powerful attorneys, and that's the only accepted path for any man in our family. If I had any sisters, they'd be expected to marry well and be good housewives.

"Nothing is going on. We texted June, and she hasn't replied yet," Ryan answers, scowling at his phone.

I check my own phone. I sent a text to June before the meeting to let her know I arranged for a dog walker to start today. I got no response either. "I'm sure she's fine."

I want to believe my own words, but I'm beginning to worry too. She'd better be okay.

I do everything I can think of to keep busy, but noon rolls around, and I'm bored out of my mind, which presents a problem. I have too much time to think about Bill, Danika, and the mess that is my life right now. Speaking with my mother didn't help either. She didn't flat-out say it, but I know she thinks I'm to blame for what Bill did. Maybe I am.

When Katrina video calls me, I answer on the first ring. "Thank God."

"What's the matter, hon?"

"Everything." I laugh in derision. "Maybe I should have gone to work. Being alone has given me too much time to beat myself down."

"No, we can't have that. I have twenty minutes of my lunch break remaining. Tell me about your hockey boy. Who did you bang? And don't you dare say you can't spill the tea over the phone. I'm going crazy here with curiosity."

"Oh, all right. They're all wonderful," I reply dreamily.

"Oh my. Too bad you had to pick only one."

My face is burning something fierce. I'm nervous about sharing the truth with Katrina, but I take a deep breath and say, "Who said I did?"

She doesn't speak for a couple beats, and her eyes blink fast. "Wait. What?"

Before I lose my nerve, I blurt out, "I slept with all three of them last night."

Katrina's jaw drops. "Oh. My. God. You're not joking, are you?"

"Nope. I wasn't even drunk when I made the decision, although I needed some liquid courage to go through with it."

A sly smile unfurls on Katrina's face. "It's always the innocent-looking ones. I knew there was a sex goddess hidden behind those freckles. Tell me more. I want *all* the details."

"I still can't believe I did it. Me, boring old June, who had slept with only one man until last night."

"You were never boring. You were with the wrong man. Having a hot evening with three hockey gods was exactly what you needed, baby girl."

"It was amazing. Also, I never knew I was so... *bendy*."

Katrina throws her head back and laughs. "Nothing like trying to handle three penises to discover that. I had a threesome once in college with my boyfriend at the time and his roommate. It was hard work. I can't imagine adding another sausage to the party."

I frown. "You never told me about that."

Her brows arch. "It's hardly a topic you can spring on someone out of the blue. Besides, after you told me you had only slept with Bill, I didn't want to scare you off by oversharing."

"I guess that's fair. Was it awkward for you the day after your threesome?"

She twists her face into a grimace. "Yeah. My boyfriend started to act super jealous whenever his roomie was around. We broke up a month later. Some people can't handle sharing."

My chest tightens. My situation with the boys isn't the same, but they *are* roommates, and I *am* their new neighbor.

"What's the matter, June?"

"I don't know how to behave around them. Last night, I thought I'd never see them again, and now I'm living in their building, hanging out in their apartment."

"Were they acting differently this morning?"

"Not at all."

"Then I wouldn't worry about it. Just be yourself."

"What if they want a repeat?"

She tilts her head. "Do *you* want a repeat?"

I nibble on my lower lip. "Maybe?"

Shaking her head, she chuckles. "You'd be crazy not to. I googled them, and damn, girl. They are fiiine."

I laugh. "They are. And they're used to sharing. This wasn't their first time."

"Then I don't see why you shouldn't entertain the possibility. You need to explore, gain experience, and find out what you like in bed. You've been living in a cage for too long. It's time to spread those legs and ride some hot men."

I start to laugh and end up choking on my saliva, which results in a coughing fit.

"Are you okay, June?"

"I'm fine," I croak.

"Good. I have some time left. Let's go for a tour of their apartment. I wanna see their bedrooms."

"Uh... I don't know. Doing that doesn't feel right when they aren't home."

She gives me a droll stare. "And how are they going to find out?"

"I don't know. They might have hidden cameras."

"If they do and didn't tell you, that's on them. They'd be invading *your* privacy."

"I guess...."

"Come on, June. Let's explore. You need to make sure they aren't psychos."

I snort, already in motion toward Lachlan's room. "They aren't."

"You don't know that. That's how they get you—by earning your trust."

"You've been watching too much *True Detective*."

"Shut up."

I enter Lachlan's room and flip the camera so Katrina can see his impressive collection. "This is Lachlan's room."

"Wow, he's a nerd like you. Remind me again, which one is Lachlan?"

"He's the goalie."

"That doesn't help me."

"The blond one."

"Oooh, he's so cute and *tall*. Does that translate to... you know?"

I feel the blush creep onto my cheeks again. I'm glad the camera is pointed away from my face. "Yes, very much so."

"Nice."

I leave Lachlan's room and continue down the hallway. "I've only been in Lachy's room."

"Lachy, is it?" Katrina laughs.

"His name is a mouthful."

"That's what she said."

"Oh my God. You're as bad as your students."

"I'm an eighth-grade teacher. I have to be."

I open the first door to my right, and without stepping inside, I know it's Jake's room. The scent that hits me in the face is undeniable. Even though this room gets as much natural light as Lachlan's, everything is much darker. The walls are blue-gray, and all the furniture is dark wood.

"Oh, whoever sleeps in this bedroom is a total alpha," Katrina chimes in.

"I'm pretty sure this is Jake's room. He's the team captain."

"Are there any pictures anywhere?"

I look at the dresser, then the desk near the window, and see no photo frames. "No. But it smells like him."

"What does he smell like?"

I close my eyes and take a deep breath. "Like a dark room and wicked promises."

"Hmm... that sounds lovely."

I shake my head, trying to dispel the sudden lust haze that wrapped around me. I'm glad I'm on a call with Katrina, or I might do a little self-care on Jake's bed. Needing to clear my head, I quickly walk out and continue to the last door in the hallway.

"This must be Ryan's bedroom." I try the knob, but the door is locked.

"Did he lock it?" Katrina asks.

"Yeah."

I'm unsure why, but I'm disappointed Ryan locked his bedroom door. Did he think I'd steal from him?

"That's a little sus, isn't it?"

"He must have trust issues. It's no big deal. I *am* a

stranger." I pivot and return to the living room. "What time are you coming?"

"About that, I completely forgot Beau has a work thing tonight, and I need to head straight home from work."

Relief washes through me, making me feel guilty. Is it selfish that I want to keep the boys to myself for a bit longer?

"Oh, don't worry. As you can see, I'm not a prisoner. I'm perfectly safe."

"Come over tomorrow. I need to see you in person."

"Okay, sounds like a plan."

"Gotta go. Make sure you go for seconds."

"Sure thing."

I can't tell Katrina that getting more entangled with the boys could be dangerous. They could be a trap for my heart. If I weren't so broke, I'd find my own place as soon as possible. But the prospect of not paying rent for the next three months is too good to pass up. I need to save for a deposit.

I stare at the open space before me, hands on my hips. "What should I do now?"

The corner with all my stuff piled up catches my attention first. It's an eyesore in this beautiful space. But I can't do anything, because I'll have to move everything to Mrs. Carpenter's apartment. I turn my attention to the kitchen. Maybe I can cook dinner as a thank you. Everyone loves a home-cooked meal, right?

I open the fridge to do a more thorough inspection. The ratio of meat to vegetables indicates that no one here is a vegetarian. Plus, there aren't any vegan substitutes for anything either. I could cook my famous lasagna. I see there's enough cheese and ham, plus the milk jug is full. All I need is tomato sauce and pasta.

I check all the cabinets, but don't see any jars with tomato sauce; there are only whole tomatoes in a can. They're from Italy. Making sauce with those will probably taste better. I also don't see lasagna noodles. I can make them from scratch. I have plenty of time.

Soon, I get in the zone, working like a determined bee. Cooking always makes me hyper-focused, and during the first hour of prep time, I don't think about my problems. But once I finish part one of the process and take a step back, I see the chaos I left behind. The kitchen is a disaster. I have to clean up before I continue.

I fill one of the sinks with water and soap, and I'm about to start when my phone vibrates on the counter. It's a text from Jake checking on me. I smile, but in my hurry to text him back, I grab the phone with my soapy hand and watch in disbelief as it slips through my fingers and dives into the sink filled with water.

"No!!!!"

I fish the phone out as fast as I can. My heart is stuck in my throat as I pat it dry with a towel and press the home button to unlock the screen. It works, but only for a second before the screen goes black.

"Don't die on me, phone."

Panicking, I grab the rice I spotted earlier. Maybe I can resuscitate my phone if I stick it in a bag filled with rice and let the grain soak up the moisture from the device. It will be a while until I can try turning on the phone again, which means I can't reply to Jake's message. What if he takes my radio silence as a sign I raided their apartment and took off?

Son of a bitch. Why does shit like this keep happening to me?

CHAPTER 21
LACHLAN

Jake is a pro at making people relax. It's why he's a bloody good captain. But his words of reassurance sound hollow to my ears, probably because I can read in his eyes that he's also concerned about June's lack of response.

It doesn't escape my notice that we know nothing about her. Maybe there's another reason her ex-boyfriend said no to her proposal and kicked her out of their apartment. June reeled me in with her sweetness and sassiness, but I've been fooled before. I'd hate to think I let a pretty lass wrap me around her finger so fast that I lost my sense of reason.

We're quiet on the ride home until Ryan opens his mouth as we enter our garage. "Wouldn't it be a kick in the nuts if we came home to find the place swept clean of anything valuable and June long gone?"

"Shut yer hole. June isn't a thief," I retort.

"How do you know? Maybe she's a con artist, and that entire circus last night was part of her act."

Jake turns to him. "That's the stupidest thing that ever came out of your mouth. There's no way she could have known we would see the failed proposal and ask Melissa to intervene."

"Fine. Maybe that part was true, but then she conveniently forgets her wallet, and gets kicked out of her apartment? That could be a con."

Jake shakes his head. "You watch way too many television shows."

Ryan parks the car, and I'm the first one out. My pulse is accelerated, and I don't know what's causing it —the possibility that Ryan could be right or that something happened to June. Both scenarios are horrible, but I'd pick the first. I'd rather she be a con artist than hurt.

Stop being so bloody pessimistic.

In the elevator, Ryan pipes up again. "In case I'm wrong about my theory, have you heard from Mrs. Carpenter yet?"

"No," Jake grumbles.

Ryan's eyes sparkle. "June might have to spend the night with us."

I watch him through narrowed eyes. "You don't do repeats."

He shrugs. "I'll make an exception this time. It's all

about opportunity, my friend. Besides, I can't let you two have all the fun."

"Do you even listen to yourself when you talk? You were just saying June was a con artist," Jake retorts.

"I said she *could* be. Don't twist my words."

"Just shut up," Jake retorts as the elevator door opens.

Ryan whistles. "What's with him? He's as grumpy as you are, Lachy."

"And the common denominator is you." I follow Jake out of the elevator.

"I'm not the cause," he mumbles, following me.

True, Jake has been in a bad mood since speaking with Melissa alone. It can't be because she wants June to go through media training. Something else was discussed. Bloody hell. I wonder if it's related to Jake's bad behavior last year. He was dubbed by the press as the most problematic player off the ice, and almost lost his position as captain.

The most mouth-watering smell hits my nose as soon as Jake opens the front door. June turns toward the entry foyer, where we all huddle together and stare at her standing in the middle of our kitchen. Her hair is up in a messy bun, and she's wearing leggings and a T-shirt. She has zero makeup on, and the only thing on her cheek is a smear of flour. I've never seen a more breath-taking view.

She smiles from ear to ear, and my heart takes off. Bloody hell. I'm so fucked.

"Hey, guys. I cooked dinner. I hope you don't mind."

Jake and I look at Ryan and wait for him to blow a fuse. The kitchen is off-limits. We aren't allowed to do any serious cooking in it, because he claims we'd ruin all his pans and the food would be inedible. We only have access to the microwave.

Ryan's jaw clenches tight, and a vein on his forehead throbs. "What did you cook?" he asks through gritted teeth.

June doesn't seem to notice Ryan's reaction to her taking over his sanctuary. Still sporting a smile, she replies, "Lasagna. It's a family recipe. It should be done in about five minutes."

Ryan walks over, glances at the sink, and then turns to the stove. We all know he's inspecting everything, but June is oblivious.

I step closer to Jake and whisper, "If Ryan says anything to June about his bloody pans, I'll turn him into haggis."

"We didn't have lasagna noodles," Ryan points out.

"I know. I made them from scratch."

"Really?" He pauses, then his attention drops to her T-shirt. "What are you wearing?"

His expression is a mix now of aggravation and amusement. I can't see what's on her T-shirt that's making him react that way, because Ryan is blocking the view. Jake and I move closer.

Looking down, June stretches the fabric of her top. "Rob Lowe and Patrick Swayze." When she looks up, she's smirking. "What? They were babes."

I grin. "Did you wear that in our honor, lass?"

Her cheeks turn bright pink. There's a fluttering in my stomach that I've felt only once before. All because of June's blushing. I've never met anyone who did that so often, but I'm beginning to realize that might be my weakness when it comes to her.

"No. It was the first T-shirt I grabbed from the bag."

"Maybe it's a sign that you should stick around," I say.

"I thought I was, or has that changed?" She turns to Jake. "Did you speak to Mrs. Carpenter?"

"Not yet. But don't worry. She'll say yes."

She frowns. "I can't stay at her place tonight, then."

"You can stay here," Jake replies.

From my peripheral, I catch Ryan checking the oven. "I think your lasagna is burning."

June whips her face toward him. "What? No, for real?"

He opens the oven, and the smell of delicious melted cheese makes my stomach grumble.

Ryan says, "It's done," while June says, "Another minute."

They stare at each other briefly before June closes the oven door.

"Ohhh, someone is challenging your skills, Ryan." Jake laughs.

June tilts her head, still looking at Ryan. "You cook?"

"You could say that."

"He thinks he's a chef," I tell her.

"I don't think. I *am*."

"Wow, cool. My dish is nothing fancy. Just good old home cooking."

"If you ask me, that's the best type," Jake butts in, earning a glower from Ryan.

"Says the man who licks his plate every time I cook."

"Only because there's never enough food." I pile on, then high-five Jake.

The cooking timer starts beeping, prompting June to turn the oven off. "Where do you keep your oven mitts?"

Ryan opens the drawer next to the oven and hands her a set.

"Are we eating now? I'd better set the table..." I start before realizing June has already set the table.

"We're eating now, unless you're not hungry." She brings the steaming lasagna to the table.

"Wait." Ryan rushes after her with a trivet and places it on the table with a look of sheer horror. It's fucking hilarious.

June looks at him and sets down the dish. "Oh, thanks. Now go wash your hands."

I'm not sure what's more comical—June's unawareness that Ryan is losing his mind, or his reaction to her. He looks dazed as he walks to the kitchen sink to do what she asked.

"We all texted you," Jake chimes in. "Didn't you receive them?"

June grimaces. "I had a small accident." She shows us her phone inside a ziplock bag filled with rice. "My phone decided to have a bubble bath."

"Is it dead?" Jake asks.

"I don't know. I'm afraid to check."

"Can I see it?" Ryan reaches for it.

June hands him the bag and stares at the device while Ryan tries to turn it on. "Yeah, I'd say you need a new phone."

Her shoulders sag. "Great. Another broken thing to add to the list."

Ryan returns the phone to her without saying a word and then leaves the dining room. June watches him go, furrowing her brows. What's that eejit doing now? He'd better not be rude and skip dinner.

"Aren't you gonna eat?" I ask him.

"Be right back."

I relax a bit, then Jake and I veer for the table, but June hangs back. "Sit down, lass."

"I'm not sure where."

I pull out the chair next to mine. "You can sit here."

"Thanks."

We're all seated when Ryan returns and places a white box next to June's plate. She looks up. "What's this?"

"Your new phone." He walks to his side of the table without looking at her.

"What?" She flips the box over, revealing a picture of the latest iPhone. "It's brand new."

Smirking, Ryan sits next to Jake and across from June. "Of course it is."

"I can't accept this." She pushes the box away from her.

"He didn't pay for it," Jake butts in.

"But still..."

"I forgot I had it lying around. I did a marketing campaign for the mobile phone provider, and they gave me that as a bonus. I don't need it, you do. Take it, Peaches."

"He really doesn't need it, June," Jake points out.

"My phone is customized." Ryan shows her the sleek design of the case.

I'm a little annoyed at myself for not offering her my freebie. I also have a new phone somewhere in my room. It completely slipped my mind.

"What if my chip is also ruined?" she asks.

"Then you get a new one," Ryan shrugs. "Chips are cheap."

"Thank you, then. I truly appreciate everything you're all doing for me. If there's anything I can do for you in return, please tell me."

I cover her hand with mine. "You're already returning the favor, lass. The lasagna smells divine."

She turns to me, her cheeks pink again. If we were alone, I'd lean in for a kiss. But I don't want to risk getting shot down in front of Jake and Ryan. It could also give her the idea we expect sex in return for helping her out. That'd be horrible and so wrong.

"I hope you like it," she replies.

"Let's dig in. I'm starving." Jake grabs a knife and cuts the lasagna in equal squares. "June, hand over your plate, please."

"Oh, I can serve myself. You go first."

I grab her plate and stick it out so Jake can give her the first piece. "Ladies always come first here."

She shakes her head, but the corners of her lips twist upward.

Jake serves everyone else before putting a piece of lasagna on his plate. I take a bite and moan. "Fuck. This is good."

"Really?" June asks.

Jake nods as he chews his own bite and swallows. "It's amazing. Best lasagna I've ever had. Sorry, Ryan."

He scowls. "I've never cooked lasagna before, jerkface."

"But even if you had, June's would be better."

Ryan snorts. "Let's see about that."

We all watch him take his first bite. He chews slowly, and his expression remains stone-cold. I notice that June hasn't eaten yet, and she's leaning forward just a little, her body tense.

"So?" I ask once he swallows.

Ryan holds my stare for a second, then switches his attention to June but replies only once his gaze is down on his plate again, and he's forking up another piece of lasagna. "June would win a lasagna bake-off."

"Do you mean that?" she asks.

His mouth is full now, so he nods. I nudge her arm with my elbow. "You got Ryan's seal of approval, lass. That's huge."

"But you're still not allowed in the kitchen unsupervised," he tells her.

Jake shakes his head. "So close."

"You couldn't let it go, could you?" I add.

June's gaze darts around. "What's going on?"

"Ryan has a rule. No one is allowed to cook in the kitchen beside him," Jake replies.

June seems to shrink in her chair. "I'm so sorry. I didn't know. I didn't break anything. I swear."

Ryan has the decency to look remorseful, but he's still an arsehole in my book.

"It's okay. I should have told you," he replies.

"It's a ridiculous rule. I vote to lift the ban and allow June to cook here whenever she likes," I grumble.

Ryan opens his mouth, but June cuts him off. "Oh no. I wouldn't want that. If the kitchen is Ryan's domain, I will avoid it. Besides, I can cook at Mrs. Carpenter's apartment. Today, I was bored and wanted to do something nice for you."

Ryan's expression falls. "No. *I'm* sorry. I appreciate you cooking dinner for us. I didn't mean to come across as ungrateful. I'm a little... *particular* about certain things."

"I totally understand. Now, let's eat before the food gets cold."

I watch June for a couple beats just to be sure she's not pretending she's okay. She catches me looking and holds my stare before smiling and squeezing my leg under the table. I jolt a little, not expecting the contact. It happens fast, then her hand is gone, but it makes me smile. I know now she'd have reciprocated my kiss. But it's best if we're alone. The next time I'm with her, I don't want to share.

CHAPTER 22
RYAN

'm an asshole. The disapproving stares I keep receiving from Jake and Lachy during dinner are deserved. The kitchen survived, and June's lasagna is out of this world. I didn't need to ban her from my space.

I'm a control freak and never hide that from anyone, especially women. I'm never interested in keeping them around anyway. But now, I regret showing June my dark side. My feelings are a fucking mystery to me. Why do I want her to like me? It isn't as if I want to date her. Maybe it's because Lachy and Jake are into her, and my competitive nature wants her too. That must be it.

Smiling, I lean back in my chair with my hand pressed over my full stomach. "This was truly delicious, June. I'll need an extra hour at the gym to burn off the calories."

"Thanks. I'm glad you liked it." She pushes her chair back and stands with her empty plate in hand.

"What do you think you're doing?" Jake asks.

"Cleaning up."

I stand up too. "Absolutely not. You cooked—leave the cleaning part to me."

She tilts her head. "Are you offering because you're afraid I won't do a proper job?"

Jake and Lachy promptly say "Yes" while I say "No." I glower at them.

"That's not the reason," I grit out. "Get up and help me if you don't believe me."

Jake and Lachy trade a look before Lachy replies, "Nah, pass. You offered."

I shake my head. "It figures."

"What's for dessert?" Lachy asks, immediately getting June flustered.

"Oh, I didn't have time to make dessert."

His face turns beet red. "No, no, lass. That question wasn't for you."

"We have Jake's butter pecan ice cream in the freezer." I smirk.

Jake glares at me. That's his favorite dessert, and he hates to share it with us. It's payback for telling June I don't allow anyone in the kitchen.

"Oh, I love ice cream," June pipes up.

"Yeah, me too." He smiles at her, annoying me. He didn't fall for my trap.

I collect all the dirty plates in a huff and stride to the kitchen, trying to ignore everyone. I'm not angry or jealous that he's being nice to June. I'm pissed that I acted like a jerk to her earlier, and I was hoping to even the playing field. We all have negative traits, but I'm the only one who didn't try harder to curb mine. It's been a long time since I cared what other people think of me.

While I load the dishes into the dishwasher, Lachy and June head to the living room while Jake veers for the freezer. Whistling, he sets the gallon of ice cream on the counter and grabs three bowls.

"Let me guess. I'm not getting any ice cream," I say.

"You don't like store-bought ice cream."

"I never said that."

"'Store-bought ice cream is a sin against desserts.' Did I hallucinate you telling a waiter that?"

"I expect house-made ice cream from a fancy restaurant," I grumble.

He's yanking my chain, and I'm letting him. God, now I know how Lachy feels when I tease him. I'm not myself, and I know that's June's influence. I look at her. She's laughing about something Lachy said, and the sound is addictive. I've never met a woman as naturally stunning as she is. I shake my head, trying to wake from the daze. Somehow, the plate in my hand slips through my fingers and breaks into pieces when it hits the floor.

"Son of a bitch!"

"Is everything all right?" June asks.

"Yeah." My ears are burning as I drop into a crouch to clean up the mess. I can't remember the last time I broke anything in the kitchen. I'll never hear the end of this.

"What do you want to do tonight, June?" Lachy asks.

"How about a movie? But I need to take Winston out for a walk first."

"Don't worry about it, June. The dog walker came an hour ago. She also fed all the pets. We can walk Winton after the movie.

"Oh, you hired one already?"

Jake joins them in the living room, carrying the ice cream bowls. "Yeah. She was number one on Mrs. Carpenter's list. I'll introduce you to her when we have a chance."

I finish cleaning up, then grimace when I see the ice cream still on the counter, melting.

"Yo, Jake. Do you want to turn your favorite dessert into soup?"

"Oops. Forgot. Do you mind putting it back in the freezer?"

If we were alone, I'd tell him to fuck off and do it himself. But I bite my tongue and just stick the ice cream back into the freezer.

"Do you have any preferences, lass?" Lachy asks.

"Not really. I'm good with whatever you guys want to watch."

I walk into the living room and, no surprise, June is

in the middle of the couch with Lachy and Jake on either side.

"How about *Braveheart*?" I suggest just to be a pest.

"Fuck no," Lachy blurts out. "That movie is a disgrace."

June looks at him. "Why?"

"Too many inaccuracies."

"*Braveheart* is Lachy's pet peeve." Jake laughs.

"But you like *Highlander*, right?" she asks.

He snorts. "Of course. That's a classic."

"I know what we should watch," Jake pipes up, looking straight at me. I already know what he'll suggest, and my skin crawls. "*Ratatouille*."

Lachy perks up. "Oh, I like that idea."

"I've never seen it. It's supposed to be good, right?"

If by good, you mean disgusting? Sure. A bunch of rats cooking. Unpleasant chills run down my spine.

Mercifully, I keep my thoughts to myself.

"It's Ryan's favorite," Lachy adds.

I hope he can read in my eyes how much I hate him right now.

"Awesome. Let's watch it then," June replies.

I should tell her the guys are messing with me, but she's too eager to watch that damn cartoon movie. Besides, if I say anything, they win.

Forcing a smile, I say, "Great. Let's do it."

"I can't believe it. He bloody did it," Lachy says as the end credits roll.

I'm as stiff as a board, and I've never wanted to take a shower as badly as I do now, but pretending to be unbothered, I reply, "Sorry to disappoint." I turn and see that June fell asleep with her head propped against Jake's shoulder. "When did that happen?"

"Halfway through the movie I think," he replies.

I narrow my eyes. "And instead of stopping the movie you made me suffer through the worst part?"

Lachy laughs. "Are you surprised?"

"You suck. Where's June going to sleep?"

"My room," Jake and Lachlan reply in unison.

"She's already been in my room. She'll be more comfortable there. I'll take the couch," Lachy adds.

I laugh. "Shall we decide this in a rock, paper, scissors game?"

"You don't like anyone in your room," Jake points out.

"I'm not entering. I'm talking about you two."

Jake and Lachy lock into a staring contest until Jake sighs heavily. "June can sleep in your room. I don't care."

Don't care, my ass.

I'm not bothered by the arrangement. When she's in my bed, I'd rather be with her.

CHAPTER 23
JUNE

I wake with a start, don't recognize my surroundings, and have a minor panic attack. My heart speeds up as I wait for my eyes to adjust to the darkness. Before it happens, a yummy scent reaches my nose, and it takes me only a couple beats to recognize Lachlan's aftershave.

Shit. Did I sleep with him and don't remember?

I spread my arms little by little and find nothing. I'm alone in bed. My body relaxes against the comfortable mattress. I bet it's late. I must have fallen asleep during the movie, and he brought me here. But if I'm alone, where is he sleeping?

I get out of bed and slowly open the door. The hallway is dark, and Ryan's and Jake's doors are closed. However, there's a soft light coming from the living room. Lachlan must have fallen asleep watching TV.

I'm thirsty, so I walk to the kitchen to grab a glass of water.

Lachlan is lying on the couch, and I believe for a second he's indeed sleeping, but then he turns to me and whispers, "June? Why are you awake?"

I walk closer to him. "I'm thirsty. What are you doing up? What time is it?"

He sits up and looks at his watch. "It's ten past one."

"You shouldn't have given up your bed. I could have slept on the couch."

"Nonsense, lass. We'd never let you sleep on the couch."

A fuzzy feeling spreads through my chest, making me giddy. This shouldn't be happening. I don't want to fall for any of these boys just because they're being nice to me. I don't belong to their world. Besides, at the rate things are going, I wouldn't be able to choose.

"I'd insist, but I already know you won't budge."

Thanks to the TV, I can see his smile. "You learn fast."

"Would you like some water too?"

"I can get it." He springs to his feet, and there's nothing I can do but shake my head.

He grabs two glasses from the cupboard in the kitchen and hands me one. He's super close to me now, and as much as I'd like to pretend that I'm not affected by his nearness, my heart is beating furiously fast, and my stomach flutters.

Suddenly, the simple task of filling a glass with water requires as much concentration as trying to solve a math equation.

"Do you ever let anyone do something nice for you?" I step aside so he can get to the fridge.

He chuckles. "Yes."

He turns to me, and even in the gloom, I can feel the weight of his heated stare. Heaven help me. I drink the whole glass in one go, and it's a miracle I don't choke on the water. Lachlan takes only a sip before setting the glass on the counter. He takes my empty glass and sets it next to his.

I'm frozen in place save for my heart, which is beating at breakneck speed. Lachlan steps into my space, and I have to crane my neck to look into his eyes. He's so damn tall. When he cups my cheek, I shiver.

"Lass, you were on my mind all day yesterday."

"I was?" I croak.

"Aye. I was dying for another taste."

He slants his lips over mine softly, teasing them open with his tongue. I sigh into him, surrendering to his sweet invasion. He cradles my face with both hands and deepens the kiss. The amber in the pit of my stomach flares into wild flames, burning me from within. I curl my fingers into his shirt, pulling him closer to me while I drown in the taste of him. I can feel the inferno building around us, and the need to get rid of our clothes and feel his bare skin against mine intensifies.

He pulls back but keeps cupping my cheeks. "We'd better stop."

My stomach falls. "Why?"

"Because I want you, lass. One evening wasn't enough for me, but I don't want to take advantage of you."

"You aren't. I want you too, Lachy."

"Thank fuck." He picks me, fusing his lips with mine.

My legs wrap around his hips, and I sense then how much he wants me. I keep my arms looped around his neck as he exits the kitchen. Within seconds, we're in his bedroom. He leans forward to set me on the mattress, but I don't let go and pull him to me. I part my legs to accommodate him better, and even though I want our clothes gone, I love the friction of his erection over my throbbing clit.

He releases my lips to leave a trail of hot kisses down my neck.

I sigh loudly, arching my back and running my fingers through his hair. "Lachy... you're driving me crazy."

"This is just the beginning." He pulls my T-shirt up until my breasts are exposed. "Your tits are lovely, lass."

He runs lazy circles around one nipple, turning it as hard as a pebble. I never knew I was that sensitive there. Lachlan's ministrations are making my toes curl already. I grab a fistful of his hair, twisting it around my hand while he destroys my self-control with each stroke of his tongue. He switches his attention to my left breast while kneading the other.

The ache between my legs intensifies. I need more friction, more of him down there. I reach for his jeans, cursing that he isn't wearing something more accessible, like sweats. I manage to lower the zipper, but I can't free the button.

"Lachy, I need your clothes gone."

He releases my nipple and kisses me again, deep and hard, before pulling back. "Aye."

I watch him jump out of bed and remove his clothes. The man is beautiful, with his taut abs and broad shoulders. And don't get me started on that messy hair. I love it all, but what pulls me into his orbit isn't his looks. It's the way he looks at me as if I were the most precious thing in the world. It makes my heart skip a beat.

"It's your turn, lass." His voice is throaty and so damn sexy.

I take my T-shirt off first, then pull my leggings and panties down my legs. Lachlan doesn't move, but his chest expands and contracts faster. Feeling bold, I part my legs, lifting my knees. "See how wet I am for you already, Lachy."

"You're a temptation I can't resist." He drops to his knees and brings his face to my pussy.

A moan escapes my throat when he sucks my clit into his mouth, sending electric sparks of pleasure throughout my body. His scruff rubbing against my sensitive skin adds a layer of sensations that quickly unravels me. But as much as I'm enjoying myself, I want to reciprocate.

"I want your cock in my mouth again."

Lachlan lifts his head and smiles. "Are you suggesting a sixty-nine, lass?"

I lean on my elbows. "Yes."

He jumps to his feet and spins me so my head rests at the edge of the mattress. "How is that?"

I reach for his cock, curling my fingers around it. "You're too far away."

"Not for long." He rests one knee next to my head and leans forward.

Now I can properly do my job. Lachlan doesn't waste a second before he resumes his work. My climax is looming on the horizon, but I don't want to come before I bring him to the edge too. I open my mouth wide, sucking him in until his cock hits the back of my throat, then use my hand to jerk him off a bit. His fingers dig into my skin, and his tongue becomes more ferocious. I can't stop the orgasm from shattering me, but I don't stop working him. If anything, I suck him harder as I ride the wave of pleasure.

Lachlan's dick grows harder, and then he takes control, fucking my mouth with enthusiasm. I've never done anything like this, but I love every second of it. I'm making him lose control, and it makes me feel powerful.

He jerks one more time before his cum fills my mouth. A muffled groan comes from deep in his throat, but I keep milking him until I swallow the last drop.

He stops thrusting and turns his face to kiss my inner thigh. "Och, lass. That was... wow."

I pull his cock from my mouth so I can reply, "Ditto."

He gets off the bed and crouches by the edge, bringing his face close to mine. He runs his fingers over my hairline with a featherlight touch. "Thank you."

I roll onto my stomach and lean on my forearms. "You're welcome, and also, thank you."

He smiles. "Would I be greedy if I said I want more?"

Lachy, stop being so adorable.

I touch his face. "If the answer is yes, then I'm greedy too."

CHAPTER 24
JUNE

wake up alone, but Lachlan's side of the bed is still warm. His bathroom door isn't shut all the way, and I can hear him singing "You're All I Have" by Snow Patrol in the shower. It's a little off-key, but a smile tugs the corners of my lips. I can't believe I spent the night with him. It was as memorable as the first time. The butterflies in my stomach are alive and busy, fluttering their wings like crazy.

The shades are closed, making it hard to discern the time. Lachlan doesn't have a clock, and my phone is still in the living room. I wish I could stay in bed and wait for him to come out of the shower, but I don't want to risk an awkward situation.

I slide out of bed quickly and get dressed. I need a shower, but that can wait. Hopefully, I'll be able to move into Mrs. Carpenter's apartment today. Of one thing I'm sure—I can't spend another night here. I've already abused their hospitality too much. If Jake doesn't have an answer from his neighbor, I'll stay with Katrina.

My hand is on the doorknob when Lachlan walks out of the bathroom with a towel wrapped around his waist and another draped over his shoulders. My stomach does a backflip. He's even sexier like that, and my body is humming with desire. I want to tug that towel off him and ride him until I can't remember my name.

"Don't tell me you were planning to slip out without a word."

I blink fast, hoping my face doesn't show the nature of my thoughts. "I was just going to grab my phone," I say.

He smirks. "Right."

"I was!"

He walks over and steps into my space, his arms going around my waist. He smells fresh and divine, and it's hard not to melt. My heart thumps faster.

"Even if you were trying to escape, you wouldn't get far." He leans in for a kiss, but I remember I just woke up and have morning breath.

I push him away before I can add another embarrassing moment to my long list. "I haven't brushed my teeth yet. No kissing."

Lachlan laughs. "I don't care."

"I do."

"Okay. Go freshen up. You're more than welcome to use my shower again."

My face is in flames now. So much for not showing him my mortification. "Thank you."

LACHLAN

I'm still smiling even after June closes the bathroom door. I don't think she realizes how irresistible she is like that, all flustered. I get dressed and leave the room. She'll probably be more comfortable if I'm not around when she gets out. As much as I love seeing her blush, I'm not an arsehole. Everyone needs privacy, and she hasn't had much of that since coming to our place.

Ryan and Jake are up, eating breakfast at the table. It's the usual spread on game day; lots of carbs, which means pancakes and French toast with a side of eggs, sausage, and bacon.

They stop eating and stare at me. Ryan smiles smugly when he says, "I thought you were going to sleep on the couch, Lachy."

"Well… change of plans."

Ryan turns to Jake, extending his hand. "Pay up."

Jake grimaces but fishes out a fifty-dollar bill from his pocket.

"You bloody eejits. You bet that I'd sleep with June?" My voice rises.

Calmy, Ryan replies, "No. We bet that you wouldn't last on the couch."

I narrow my eyes and point a finger at the duo. "You'd better not say anything to June about that."

"Of course we won't tell her," Jake grumbles, then resumes eating.

I grab orange juice from the fridge and join them at the table. "You aren't mad that I hooked up with her again, are you?"

"I'm not mad," Ryan replies, then looks at Jake. "Are you?"

Jake takes his time chewing, keeping his expression neutral. Is he stalling because he doesn't want to answer? Finally, he replies, "Why would I be mad? I'm not interested in dating her."

"Yeah. Me neither." Ryan drops his gaze to his plate.

Their answer should satisfy me, but I've known them for too long not to notice when they aren't being completely honest. Maybe they don't realize the truth yet. June has a hold on them, just like she has a hold on me.

"What if you *were* interested in a serious relationship? What if we all were?" I ask.

Ryan and Jake stare at me, but neither answers my question immediately.

"It would be up to June to decide. I'd never fight with either of you over a girl," Jake replies.

"Same with me," Ryan adds.

I'm not sure of my feelings toward June yet, but I know I want more than just casual sex. But she might not feel the same. We were her rebound adventure, after all.

"But what if she does want to date all of us?" Ryan asks a moment later.

Now it's my turn to ponder. There have been quite a few instances where we shared a woman, but those were only one-night stands. There were no feelings involved, only lust. Could I share a girlfriend with my mates? I picture June with Ryan or Jake, and wait for jealousy to present itself, but it doesn't come. I know my answer.

"That wouldn't be a problem for me," I say.

"Me neither," Jake replies.

Ryan doesn't comment, and I'm having trouble reading his mood. "What about you, mate?"

"Hypothetically, I wouldn't care. But if we're being honest, I only want to have fun with her. Nothing more."

I have no reason to believe otherwise. That's Ryan's MO.

"Make sure she knows that," Jake chimes in.

"Make sure I know what?" June walks in, and both Ryan and Jake share a panicked glance.

"That you're welcome to his extensive arsenal of hair products," I pipe up.

Ryan's death glare gives me undiluted satisfaction. Finally, I found a way to get under his skin. *Payback, mate.*

"Good morning, June. Did you sleep well?" Jake changes the subject.

She quickly glances at me, then drops her gaze. Blush creeps up her cheeks. *June, darling, yer such an open book.*

"I did. Thanks for asking."

The seating arrangement is different this morning. Jake is across from me, and Ryan is at the head of the table. June pulls out the chair next to Jake, which is the closest to her. I don't mind. I can stare at her better when she's sitting across from me.

"What do you want to eat, Peaches?" Ryan asks.

"Oh my. There's so much food."

"Game day," we all say in unison.

Her eyes widen. "I didn't know you were playing today, and here I am intruding."

"You're not intruding, lass."

Jake wipes his mouth on a napkin, then angles his body to her. "I spoke with Mrs. Carpenter earlier. She's more than okay with you staying at her place."

June's shoulders relax. "She is? Oh good. I was already planning on staying at my friend's place if we hadn't heard from her."

"Why?" Ryan asks. "Tired of us already?"

She shakes her head. "No, of course not. I don't want to impose more than necessary."

Jake covers her hand with his. "You're not imposing. We're happy to have you here. By the way, I have a favor to ask."

Ryan and I trade a look. What's Jake up to now?

"Name it. Anything."

"I have to attend an event after tonight's game, and it'd be a huge favor if you were my plus one."

That smart son of a bitch. Why didn't I have the forethought to invite June?

"Uh... are you sure?" she asks.

"I'm sure. But I'll understand if you say no. The press will be there."

She bites her lower lip and stares at the stack of pancakes for a beat. "What if I do something stupid? I don't want to embarrass you."

"You're not going to embarrass Jake. Nothing you do could ever top Lachy's most embarrassing moments." Ryan laughs.

"Shut yer mouth." I try to sound harsh, but he isn't wrong, and I don't bloody care about my awkward moments in front of the press.

"You're not going to embarrass me." Jake smiles reassuringly.

"Okay, then. Count me in. What's the dress code?"

"Cocktail attire."

"Will Melissa be there?"

Ryan nods. "We'll all be there. It'll be fun."

Jake grimaces but keeps his mouth shut. It's never fun for him when his father is around.

"You're coming to the game too, right, lass?" I ask.

She frowns. "I don't know. I have to find out if I still have a car or if I need to start shopping for one."

"When will you hear from the shop?" Jake asks.

"I'll call them after breakfast."

"I can order a car to take you to the arena if your car isn't ready," Ryan offers.

Her widens. "Oh no. That won't be necessary. I could always walk. The arena isn't that far from here."

"No." Once again, we reply at the same time.

June blinks fast, and her stare bounces around. "Uh, why not?"

"It's not safe to walk alone at night in the city," I reply.

"Oh, you're probably right."

"Maybe you want to bring some friends? I can get as many tickets as you want." Jake chimes in, making her eyes sparkle.

"I bet Katrina and her husband would love to come, if they can find a babysitter."

Jake grabs his phone and sends a text. "It's settled then. The game starts at seven, but you all can come early and hang out in the family lounge."

"Wow, that'd be cool. What time you need to leave for the arena?"

"We have a few hours. After breakfast, we'll take your things down to Mrs. Carpenter's apartment," Jake replies.

"Thank you. I'm happy to be out of your hair finally. I don't want to overstay my welcome."

"That'll never happen, lass." I wink, and on cue, her cheeks turn pink.

I can't wait to spend more quality time with her, alone or with the lads. She's turning into my sweet obsession, and she has no idea.

CHAPTER 25
JUNE

"Thanks for breakfast. It was delicious," I tell Ryan.

His face breaks into a warm smile. "My pleasure."

I get up and start to collect the dirty dishes, but Jake holds my wrist. "What are you doing? You don't need to clean up."

I frown. "Of course I do."

"You're our guest." Jake insists, still holding my wrist, not that I mind. I like his warm and callused hand on me.

I immediately berate myself for the thought. I just spent the night with Lachlan, for crying out loud.

"And guests help," I reply. "That's how I was raised. Sorry, but I won't budge on this."

We keep our gazes locked in a staring contest, until

finally, Jake releases my wrist, sighing in resignation. "Okay, you win. But I'll help."

Lachlan stands as well. "Me too."

"I've never seen my roomies so eager to clean up. Eat here more often, Peaches." Ryan winks at me.

"Don't tempt me."

He curls his lips into a devious smile, making my body temperature kick up a notch. "Oh, I plan to do just that."

"Stop flirting with her," Lachlan grumbles.

My face is on fire. Does he think I was encouraging Ryan? Oh God. Am I messing things up already? I put on the serious face I wear when I want my students to behave, and head to the kitchen sink. Lachlan and Jake bring the rest of the dishes, and we work together in silence. There's not much to do but load the dishwasher. Ryan is probably the type of person that cleans as he goes.

"All right. All done here," I say. "I'll start moving my things to Mrs. Carpenter's apartment now."

"We'll help you, lass."

"I'll get the dolly. It'll be faster," Jake says, then heads for the door.

Lachlan turns to Ryan, who's sitting at the table, scrolling through his phone. "Are you going to help?"

He looks up. "I will, but Jake's not back yet with the dolly. Chill."

I feel uncomfortable with the exchange, and the idea that I'm a burden returns with a vengeance.

"I'm sure I don't need everyone's help. I don't have a lot of boxes."

Ryan's brows furrow together. "I want to help, Peaches."

"All right. I'll start bringing the bags to the hallway." I grab a couple of garbage bags and try to not wince. I'm still not over the fact that Bill did this. I can't help but see his action as a metaphor for what he thinks about our relationship.

Before I can get to the door, Jake returns with the dolly and takes something from his pocket. "Here's your copy of the apartment key."

Our fingers touch in the exchange, and I swear I feel electric sparks. "Thanks."

Lachlan follows me to the hallway, carrying a few bags himself. He presses the button for the elevator before I can get to it.

"Shouldn't we use the service one?"

"It's just us on this floor. Who's going to complain?"

We get inside, and just as the door is about to shut, Ryan calls out, "Wait for me."

"Take the stairs." Lachlan laughs, and the door closes completely.

"That was mean."

He looks at me, his eyes widely innocent. "What?

Our hands are full. We couldn't stop the door from closing."

I shake my head. "Right."

He bumps his arm with mine. "You can't blame me for wanting more time alone with you, lass."

I don't make eye contact, but I can't hide the smile that blossoms on my face. I'm in so much trouble already.

When we arrive on the floor below, Ryan is already there, waiting for us with a scowl aimed at Lachlan. "You suck."

Lachlan laughs. "I'm not sorry."

"Boys... play nice."

I don't think anything about my reply until I see the look in their eyes. It's like a fire lit up in them. Oh God. What I said wasn't meant to be an innuendo to sexy times. I pretend I don't notice how they're staring at me and focus on opening the door to the apartment. The moment I step foot inside, Winston comes running and barking. I've only met him once, but he seems happy to greet me.

"Hi, boy. It's nice to see you too." He jumps on my legs. "I'd pet you if my hands were free."

Lachlan and Ryan follow me, which draws Winston's attention. Now that I don't have him distracting me, I can soak in my surroundings. Mrs. Carpenter's apartment is exactly as I expected it to be. Her furniture is a mix of odd pieces, some vintage, some just plain old, that shouldn't go together but somehow do. The walls are painted a light neutral color, eggshell if I were to guess, and there are several colorful paintings and photographs hanging on them.

It's an open-space layout with the kitchen being the first thing you see as you walk in. Just like the boys' apartment, there's a lot of light coming from the tall windows. All sorts of plants are spread throughout the living room, something Jake forgot to mention. They'll need tending too. In fact, I'm sure they should be watered asap.

"You can put your bags in the bedroom, June," Lachlan tells me.

"Right."

"I've never been in Mrs. Carpenter's bedroom," Ryan pipes up. "Have you?"

"Once, when she needed help with her light fixture."

It's strange to sleep in someone else's room, but if there was a guest room, Jake would have told me. I hope she doesn't have personal pictures on display. I'd feel like they were watching me.

On the way to the bedroom, we walk past the big aquarium in the living room. There are three exotic fish in there, but I can't tell what they are. "Do the fish have names?"

"Yes. Frodo, Bilbo, and Sam," Jake replies.

I turn and see him by the front door with the dolly and most of my boxes stacked up.

"Oh, she's a Lord of Rings fan. Cool."

"Her cats are called Eros and Apollo," Ryan chimes in. "Where are they by the way?"

"They must be hiding. They're a little shy."

"Oh. Do you think they'll come to me?" I ask, worried that they'll be afraid of me.

"Open a can of tuna, and they'll come running." Jake smiles. "Where do you want the boxes?"

I bite my lower lip and glance at the space available. "I think we can set them in the living room for now. I'll unpack whatever I need then put the rest in storage."

"Jaaake!" a parrot in a cage in the corner of the living room calls.

"Hey, hi Admiral."

I chuckle. "The parrot is called Admiral?"

Jake smirks. "Mrs. Carpenter was very creative when she named her pets."

"I'll say. Where do you think Humberto is?" I have no clue how big the turtle is, but I know they can be difficult to find sometimes.

"He should be in this little habitat on the balcony," Jake says.

Lachlan returns to the living room—I didn't even notice him leaving—and he's holding a melon-size turtle in his hands. "He was in Mrs. Carpenter's bathroom."

"Uh? How did he get there?" Ryan asks.

Lachlan walks toward the balcony. "Through the pet

door. Mrs. Carpenter had it installed because Eros and Apollo like to chill outside."

"No, Winston. That's not a toy!"

I look and find Jake trying to yank something free from Winston's clenched teeth. It's a dark piece of fabric I don't recognize at first. He must have snagged it from the box Jake set down. The lid is open.

"What did he get?" I walk over.

"A pair of slacks from your box. He thinks it's a toy. I'm sorry, June."

Up close, I recognize the material. Instead of being upset, I laugh. "Let him play with it. I don't care."

Jake looks at me, brows scrunched together. "Are you sure?"

"Those are Bill's pants. I had his dry cleaning with me on the day he kicked me out of the apartment. He decided he'd rather give up his favorite suit than let me inside."

Jake releases the fabric and stands straight. "In that case, go to town, Winston."

"Where's the jacket?" Ryan peers inside the box and pulls it out. "Oh, this isn't a cheap suit."

I was amused before, but Ryan's comment about the suit's price tag makes me feel guilty. "I know. I planned to donate it to charity."

Ryan grimaces. "Nah. You don't want anyone getting exposed to your ex's douche energy."

Now that Jake is no longer trying to snag the pants

from Winston, he loses interest in them and jumps to catch a sleeve of the jacket Ryan's holding. Ryan pulls it back, hard, and the sleeve rips at the seam. "Oops. I guess Bill's suit is Winston's bitch now."

I shrug. "Oh well."

Ryan steps closer and throws an arm over my shoulder. "I'll donate one of my suits to charity, Peaches."

My entire body tingles from his proximity, and my ability to form sentences is hindered for a moment. "You don't have to."

"That's a great idea. I'll donate too," Jake butts in.

Ryan drops his arm from my shoulder and steps back. "Sure, Jakey, steal my thunder, why don't you?"

"And me." Lachlan smirks. "I'm donating too."

Ryan shakes his head then looks at me. "Watch out for those two."

I'm not sure how I'm supposed to take his statement. It sounds like he's joking, but I do have to be careful… with *all* of them. They're way too dreamy for my bruised heart.

CHAPTER 26
JUNE

After the boys helped me bring all my things to Mrs. Carpenter's apartment and I got organized, I called Katrina to ask if she and Beau would be free to come to the game with me. I was relieved when Jake said I could bring friends. The prospect of attending their game and hanging out in the family lounge solo was terrifying. I didn't expect Melissa to play babysitter again. Besides, I'm a grown-ass woman; I shouldn't need one.

Unfortunately, Katrina couldn't find a sitter at the last minute, so Beau had to stay behind with the kids. I guess it was unfortunate only for him. Having a girl's night out is an even better outcome. There's so much to talk about.

Instead of going to the family lounge, Katrina and I decide to watch the players warm up. We find a place by the glass close to Lachlan's goal. My skin is humming with excitement. I can't believe it's only been a couple days since the most humiliating day of my life. It feels like it's been years.

I look at the Jumbotron screen, which is currently showing players' highlights. It's hard to believe I was on that screen, learning that the man I thought was the one had been cheating on me. Now I can't even remember why I thought he was husband material.

Lights flash, and loud music explodes from the speakers when the Titans enter the ice. My pulse accelerates as I search for my guys. *My guys? When did they become mine?* I'm getting ahead of myself and doing exactly what I shouldn't—becoming attached. Ugh. I'm a dumbass.

Katrina touches my arm and squeezes. "I can't believe you were railed by those men!"

"Shhh! Do you think I want to broadcast that to the entire arena?"

"Relax. No one can hear us over all the noise." She takes a sip of her beer.

I'm not drinking at the game, since I'm going to the charity event with Jake and the last thing I want is to show up buzzed. The goal is to avoid a disaster and not embarrass Jake in front of his peers.

Naturally, Lachlan is the first I spot on the ice. He looks like a giant in all that goalie gear. He doesn't see me though. I think he's in the zone already. Unfortunately, the helmet hides his beautiful face—a face that was between my legs last night. My body temperature rises.

"Do you feel hot? Why is it hot here?" I fan myself.

Katrina laughs, then thrusts her beer cup at me. "Here. Take a sip."

I accept her offer only because I do need to cool down. "Thanks."

I'm between gulps when a player knocks on the glass before me, and obviously, I spill the beer all over my chin. Ryan grins on the other side of the glass while I wipe my face with my sleeve. He winks and then waves before skating away to join his teammates.

"Oh my God. Was that one of your boys?" Katrina asks.

"He's not mine," I grit out.

"You know what I mean. He's more handsome in person. You're a lucky girl, June."

The butterflies in my stomach seem to agree with Katrina, and my stupid heart as well, despite my brain telling me this is a fairytale that won't last. It's already on an unexpected extension.

Jake skates by us but doesn't make eye contact with me. The quick glimpse I catch of his face reveals an entirely different man. There's no warmth, just a cold and hard expression.

"Wow, Jake Phillips is one scary dude. I wouldn't want to pick a fight with him."

"He's not like that outside of the ice though."

"He'd better be a cinnamon roll with you, girl. I mean, a *sin*namon roll." She bumps her hip with mine. "He's scary, but he's hot as hell."

Other people join us, and it becomes too crowded to keep talking about the guys in such an intimate way. I'm more than okay to continue exploring this new world of pleasure with them, even if my heart receives another blow. But what I can't allow to happen is for this secret to come out. I could lose my job, and my family would never speak to me again. It would ruin me.

Once the warm-up is over, Katrina and I head to our excellent seats. They aren't by the glass, but a few rows up and in the middle.

"Wow, I've never sat so close to the action before. Let's take a selfie with the ice in the background." Katrina turns around and throws her arm around my shoulder. "Say, sausage party!"

"Oh my God. You're terrible."

"Seriously, June. Smile. You have more than one reason." She pushes our heads together and points the camera at us.

We take a few photos before she's satisfied. "I'll send this to Beau. He'll be so jealous."

I laugh. "That's cruel, Kat."

"Cruel my ass. I pushed four of his giant babies through my veejay. This is nothing."

"We still have time until the puck drop. Should we get snacks?"

"I'm not hungry but I could use another beer." She chugs what's left in her cup, and then we head to the food court.

"I'm surprised you want to eat. Don't you have a party after the game?" she asks.

"Yes. So?"

She shakes her head. "Ugh. I forget that you're still in your twenties. If I eat any of the crap they sell here, I blow up like a balloon."

"I'll just grab some gummy bears and a water bottle."

"June, if you're hungry, eat."

"I'm not hungry, just nervous."

"About the party?"

I nod. "I have no idea what to expect, and if I do something stupid, Jake will suffer."

"He's a big boy. I'm sure he'll be fine. Besides, you won't do anything stupid. What are you going to wear?"

"It's cocktail attire, so I thought about that emerald-green dress I wore to the Christmas party last year."

"You look so good in that dress. That poor boy won't know what hit him."

"I'm pretty sure he's had his fair share of gorgeous women by his side."

"And none of them were June motherfucking Summers."

I smirk. "Did you just use the *Pretty Woman* line on me?"

"You know it." She laces her arm with mine. "Come on. Let's get you the gummies so we can watch some eye candy."

CHAPTER 27
JAKE

saw June during warm-ups, but I couldn't bring myself to acknowledge her. I had to remain focused. I've never had a problem getting in the zone before. I've had hookups come to see me play, but they were never on my radar while I was on the ice. It was different with June. I was too aware of her presence.

Winning tonight was a must. Not only did I want to impress June, but I couldn't lose to the New York Bobcats while my father was in attendance. All the checks, hits, fights, and one swollen-shut eye were worth it. We won.

On the way home, I keep an ice bag over my eye. My right shoulder is sore, but the team physician cleared me. Everything is intact and in the right place.

"How's yer eye, mate?" Lachy asks from the shotgun seat. I'm riding in the back.

"All right. I've had worse."

"That Bobcat punk did get his worst tonight." Ryan laughs. "I've never seen a guy turtle up so fast."

"What did you expect from that bawbag? He's been running his mouth and picking fights since the start of the season. It was about time someone taught him a lesson."

I flex my right hand. My knuckles are a little rough after the fight. That douchebag caught me by surprise while the ref was between us. I didn't let him touch me after. My gloves came off, and the game turned into a massive brawl, with players from both teams joining the fight. In the heat of the moment, I didn't think. Now I worry I might have scared June.

"The charity event tonight will be interesting," Ryan pipes up.

My stomach sours. The last thing I want to do tonight is play nice with a bunch of phonies and deal with my father. I'd much rather take June to a nice restaurant and enjoy her company.

Whoa. Where did that thought come from? I told Melissa the other day I wasn't interested in dating June.

"No. It'll be a nightmare," I grumble.

"You're in a bad mood. Maybe you shouldn't take June," Lachy replies.

"Right, so you can take her." Ryan laughs. "You're so transparent, Lachy."

"I'm not. Yer aff yer heid."

"I'm not canceling on June," I retort.

"Yeah, Jake needs June there, or he might go berserk on his father."

Ryan isn't wrong.

Lachy and Ryan head to the party in separate cars. We usually ride together to practice and games, but we don't to social events. It would be an inconvenience.

June didn't cancel being my date tonight, but I'm a little tense as I stand in front of Mrs. Carpenter's door. I'm not confident taking her to the party is a good call. I'll be forced to introduce her to my father and brother, and if they're rude to her, I can't promise I'll behave.

I knock on the door and wait. Immediately, Winston barks, and a moment later, I hear June telling the dog to settle down. She opens the door next and stuns me with her beauty. I shouldn't be surprised. She caught my eye the moment I saw her at the Titans party. But tonight, she's even more beautiful to me. Maybe because I already know her a little, and she isn't just a pretty face in the crowd.

"You look stunning," I say.

She beams. "Thank you. Would you like to come in? I just need to find my purse."

"Sure."

She opens the door wider but sticks her leg in the

gap to prevent the dog from escaping. I slide through the opening and shut the door fast.

"Are you all settled in?" I ask.

"Almost. I still have to finish unpacking, and I don't know where Mrs. Carpenter keeps everything, but I'll figure it out."

"What about the pets? Do you need any help with them?"

"Oh, I'm good on that front. The trick with the tuna can worked. I'm now besties with Eros and Apollo." She smirks.

I chuckle. "That's good to know. But if you have questions, write them down, and I'll pass them along."

"That'd be great. But would it be possible to speak to her directly? I'm sure she'll feel more at ease meeting me, even if it's through a video call."

"Yeah, I can make that happen."

She focuses on my swollen eye and grimaces. "Does that hurt a lot?"

"Nah. I barely feel a thing."

"I can't believe he punched you like that."

"It happens. The fight didn't put you off, did it?"

"No. But I was pissed. I'm happy that you kicked his ass and that you guys won. I never liked the Bobcats."

Her comment makes my chest feel less tight. I'm on edge, dreading seeing my father, but being in June's presence is already helping me. I have no clue what magic she possesses that makes me feel this way, but I won't ignore it.

I take her hand and pull her to me. Her beautiful eyes widen a fraction, and her lips part. Such a temptation. Looking into her eyes, I say, "I'm glad you're here, June."

"Jake..."

I rub my thumb over her lower lip, waiting for her to push me away. She slept with Lachy last night, and there's a chance she wants to be with only him.

"Tell me to stop, and I will."

Guilt shines in her eyes. "I don't, but..."

"You think kissing me after you spent the night with Lachy is wrong."

"Yes."

"What if you didn't have to choose?" I kiss the corner of her mouth, and she shivers.

"I... I'd let you kiss me."

"Good answer." I slant my lips over hers, coaxing her mouth open with my tongue while I wrap my arms around her waist.

Sighing softly, June melts into me, causing a stir in my pants. I'm getting a hard-on already. Jesus. I pull back with regret.

"What's wrong?" she asks, her brows furrowing.

"Nothing. Go find your purse, sweetheart," I reply in a restrained voice and step back.

"Right. Okay. Yeah, we don't want to be late."

She disappears down the hallway, and I veer for the kitchen to grab a glass of water. I can't remember the last time a woman set me on fire this fast from only a kiss. I have to watch out for June. She's dangerous for me.

CHAPTER 28
JUNE

think about Jake's kiss during the entire ride to the upscale restaurant in Melrose, where the party is taking place. I feel kind of naughty for kissing him the day after I slept with Lachlan. It almost felt like cheating, even though I don't regret any of it. This is all new territory to me, and I'm way out of my depth.

But once we arrive and I see the photographers outside the venue, snapping pictures of the guests arriving, my love-life complications take a backseat in my mind. My hands become clammy, and my stomach ties into knots.

Jake enters the line for the valet and turns to me. "You good?"

"There are so many photographers."

He chuckles. "This is LA, and there are probably quite a few celebrities on the guest list."

Grimacing, I glance at my Nordstrom Rack dress, which is probably from three seasons ago. I don't know why it didn't occur to me that there would be celebrities here. Hell, Jake *is* one. He's a pro athlete, after all.

"Do I look okay?"

He glances at my dress cursorily before looking into my eyes. "More than okay. You're a knockout, sweetheart. I'll have trouble keeping my hands to myself."

His green eyes are pure fire, and it sets me ablaze. I lean across the space separating us and kiss him. What is it about these men that gives me so much confidence? It can't be all the praise. It's the way they treat me, as if I'm a queen in their world.

Jake's hand is in my hair, and his tongue brushes mine, making me unravel. Every nerve ending in my body is alive.

The car behind us honks, shattering the spell. Jake pulls back but doesn't break eye contact right away. The car honks again.

"You'd better go," I say.

"Right." He drives a couple feet forward before shifting into Park. "Ready?"

"Yeah."

The valet opens my door and helps me out. I wait for Jake to circle the car, hoping my nerves don't get the better of me. I'm on pins and needles, and more nervous than when I attended the Titans party a few days ago. I don't make eye contact with anyone in front of me, but they aren't looking in my direction anyway. I'm not famous. I'm invisible to the photographers until Jake puts his hand on my lower back. Then the flashes go off.

"Here goes nothing," I mutter.

Jake keeps his expression shut off and ignores the questions thrown at him. They ask about the fight, then about me. God. Will our pictures end up in the tabloids tomorrow? I hope not. I'm sure my mother will be calling to ask what I'm doing dating another man two days after my fiasco of a proposal. And this isn't a date. I'm just Jake's plus one.

Only when we're inside the restaurant and insulated from the paparazzi do I release the breath I was holding. "Wow. That was intense."

"More so than usual."

"Oh no. Because of me?"

"Don't worry about it. Let's get a drink." He takes my hand and steers me deeper into the restaurant. This place is bigger than the venue from two nights ago, and much darker too. I try to find Lachlan and Ryan, but I don't see them anywhere.

Even though the lights are dim, I can sense multiple stares in my direction. Why didn't it occur to me that being Jake's date would draw attention to me?

"Everyone is staring," I say.

"They're wondering who the gorgeous woman next to me is."

I feel the blush spread across my cheeks, but mercifully, no one can see.

The crowd parts ahead to let us through, revealing a group of three tall men.

"T-man is in the house!" one of them says, raising his palm.

Smirking, Jake high-fives him. "Looking good, Banksy. Nice to see you in a grown-up suit."

"Melissa made him do it." The ginger guy with a full beard laughs.

"Ballbuster, that one," Banksy grumbles.

"Man, that fucker got you good," Ginger man pipes up.

Jake shrugs. "Lucky hit."

"You mean sneaky hit," I butt in, getting as angry as I did when it happened.

My outburst draws their attention to me, making me wish I hadn't spoken.

"Are you going to introduce your beautiful friend to us, T-man?" the shortest of the trio asks, staring at me intensely.

"I was getting to it. June, meet Simon Banks, Robert Anderson, and Ian Hurst."

I wave at them. "Nice to meet you. Why do you call Jake T-man?"

"Because he's the Terminator." Simon grins, then squints. "Hey, you're Jumbotron girl."

Damn. Someone had to mention it. To be fair, it's been only a couple days, even though it feels like much longer. Jake moves closer to me, and his hand returns to the small of my back. I love the protectiveness of that gesture, but I don't want him to bite his teammate's head off.

"Dude! Think before you speak." Ian bumps his elbow against his teammate's arm.

"It's fine," I reply quickly. "Yes, I'm Jumbotron girl. I'm also the one who kicked Jake's and Ryan's butts playing pool a couple days ago."

"I saw that. It was awesome!" Robert grins from ear to ear. "Too bad there isn't a pool table here. I'd love to witness their decimation again."

"Speaking of Ryan, have you seen him or Lachy?" Jake asks.

"Melissa cornered Lachy a while back. Poor guy." Simon laughs.

"And Ryan went off somewhere with a hot chick," Robert adds.

My spine goes taut in an instant. It's an involuntary reaction. Ryan is free to do whatever he wants. I'm unsure why I'm reacting as if he's betraying me.

"Are you okay?" Jake asks, frowning.

Crap on toast. He noticed my reaction. "Yeah. I'm fine. Why wouldn't I be?"

He stares at me in his intense way without saying a

word. Is he jealous? Annoyed? Shit. There I go again, fucking things up.

"No reason," he finally replies.

"Oh, here comes Melissa with Mr. Hollywood," Ian pipes up.

Now I'm really tense. Mr. Hollywood must be Melissa's fiancé. I turn and confirm my suspicion. I can't believe I'm about to meet Elijah Foreman without an ounce of liquid courage coursing through my veins. I'm shaking already.

Jake leans closer and whispers in my ear, "He's just a man, June. Relax."

"That's easy for you to say. Elijah Foreman is a god in Hollywood."

"No one is a god."

Melissa is smiling brightly when she reaches us. "Hi June, you look stunning as always."

"Thank you, Melissa. So do you."

She looks at Jake and shakes her head. "Jake... no comment."

"Good," he grumbles.

"June, I'd like you to meet my fiancé, Elijah Foreman. I told him all about you."

Face. Burn. "Oh my. I'm not sure if that's a good thing."

Elijah extends his hand. "Nice to meet you, June. I look forward to reading one of your screenplays one day."

I open my mouth to reply, but he fishes out his phone from his jacket pocket and says, "Excuse me. I need to get this."

He walks away with his phone glued to his ear before anyone else can say a word. Melissa glares at his retreating back, then turns to me. "I'm sorry about that. Elijah doesn't have an off button. It's always work, work, work."

I'm a little disappointed that I barely had a chance to talk to him, but I try to hide it. "Don't worry about it. He's a busy man. I understand."

"Jake, you were looking for Ryan and Lachy. There they are," Simon points with his head.

I turn and spot them, plus a young and attractive woman. I can't see her face well, but her shoulders are hunched forward, and she's hugging her middle. She looks dejected. Lachlan and Ryan seem to be arguing. What the hell is going on?

"Are they fighting over some random girl?" Simon asks.

"I'd better go find out what that's about." Jake steps forward, but Melissa reaches for his arm and stops him.

"Let them be. I need you somewhere else."

Jake frowns at Melissa, and while he's paying attention to her, he misses the girl who was with Lachlan and Ryan walking away. Lachlan says something to Ryan, but he shakes his head and then walks away too.

"Where do you want me to be?" Jake asks Melissa.

"It's time to play nice with your father."

I whip my face toward Jake. I didn't know his father would be here. Jake's expression has turned as hard as a stone. This can't be good.

CHAPTER 29
JAKE

As much as I want to find out what's happening with Lachy and Ryan, Melissa is right to stop me. My father never hid he's a Bobcats fan, but if I ignore him tonight, the media vultures will spin whatever story they want, and it won't benefit me. I don't get along with the asshole, but I don't want lies about my family to spread like a disease.

It's time to do what I came here for—deal with the jackass.

June looks at me with a deer-in-the-headlights glint in her eyes. On top of the edginess, guilt enters my chest. It was a dick move not to warn her about my father. But there was a chance she wouldn't have agreed to come, and I needed her with me tonight.

"Let me get drinks first," I tell Melissa, then turn to June. "What would you like, sweetheart?"

"Nothing too strong."

"Champagne?"

The last time we drank champagne was right before our first time. The memory is at the forefront of my mind, and I wonder if she's thinking about it too.

"Yes, that'd be great."

"Oh, nothing like bubbles to get you in the party mood." Melissa jokes.

I almost say this isn't a party, but it wouldn't be fair to June. I dragged her here, knowing what I had to face. I get the drinks, and then, with her hand in mine, I look for my father. I might as well get this over with. I'm focused on not bumping into anyone when I hear my name called.

"Jake?"

I turn and find my brother standing beside a beautiful blonde who isn't his wife. Typical. I haven't seen Gregory in three years, and if he hadn't spoken my name, I wouldn't have recognized him. He looks ten years older than he is. It's not only the weight gain but also the bags under his eyes. Gregory might be our father's favorite, but living under his thumb has taken a toll on him. I'd pity him if he weren't a despicable human being. Growing up, he followed in my father's footsteps to make my life miserable.

"Gregory. I barely recognized you." I turn to his companion. "And you're definitely not his wife."

The woman winces. Maybe I shouldn't have put her

on the spot, but I doubt she was unaware that Gregory is married. If she hadn't known, she'd be making a scene.

"She's a friend," Gregory replies in a clipped tone. "And who is your date? Do I even need to know her name, or is she another flavor of the week?"

I bristle in an instant. My entire body is poised to fight, but June squeezes my hand and replies, "My name is June Summers. And I'm not food."

Gregory's head snaps back, and I smile. He wasn't expecting that sassy response from June. Still grinning, I look at her. Gregory ruffled her feathers, and her expression of defiance is hot as hell. Pride swells in my chest, making my heart speed up.

"June is my guest, and if you can't treat her with respect, this catching-up convo is over."

Gregory narrows his eyes and clenches his jaw tightly. He never got used to me talking back. He forgets it's been a long time since I was a young kid looking for his older brother's approval and affection.

"Jake, I wondered when you would find us," my father says from behind me, making the small hairs on the back of my neck stand on end.

My entire body tenses, especially my shoulders and neck. His preferred method of punishment, when I was a kid, was to grab me from behind whenever I did something that displeased him. I guess I still have PTSD from that. I finish the champagne, hoping the drink will help me relax. In hindsight, I should have gotten something stronger.

I turn, forcing a smug grin to my lips. "I didn't. Greg found me. Did you enjoy the game?"

His shrewd eyes narrow. "I was enjoying myself until my youngest son decided to act like a thug."

I laugh derisively. "If you don't want to see fights, I suggest you stick to golf."

He switches his attention to June, but it's fleeting. He doesn't acknowledge her. No surprise. He believes all women are beneath him. He's a chauvinist pig. It pains me that we share DNA.

"I head back to New York late tomorrow. My secretary made reservations at Providence. Be there at seven-thirty sharp. *Alone.*"

Unreal. I'm an adult who hasn't depended on this man's money in over a decade, but he still believes I'm at his beck and call.

"Sorry, Father. You'll have to enjoy your dinner without me. I already have plans."

His eyes flash with anger. "Cancel them. Whatever you have planned isn't more important than spending time with your family."

"Picking up trash would rank higher on my list of priorities," I retort.

He grabs my arm and yanks me closer to whisper in my ear. "Don't fuck with me, boy. You might think you don't need me now, but remember, I can take your career away in the blink of an eye. I bet the press would love to know how you almost killed someone and never paid for your crime."

My entire body goes stiff, and my blood runs cold. My father hasn't mentioned that incident since he made it disappear, and I did my best to put it behind me. I don't regret what I did. The scum I almost killed deserved what he got. Even though charges weren't pressed against me, if the media finds out, my career will be over.

I pull my arm free from his grasp. "If the truth comes out, your reputation will also take a blow."

"I can survive the scandal. Can you?"

Every fiber of my being is urging me to tell my father to go to hell. I don't want to give in and obey his orders, but hockey is everything to me. I'm not ready to give it up. I worked too hard to be where I am now. Plus, I'd be letting my teammates down too.

"I'll be at Providence tomorrow," I grit out.

He pats my shoulder. "Good boy. Come on, Greg. There's someone I'd like you to meet."

Gregory's eyes glint with satisfaction. He always loves to witness my father humiliating me. My entire body shakes with barely contained rage as I watch them walk away.

"Jake, are you okay?" June touches my arm, and I flinch.

I forgot she was next to me, witnessing everything. Shit. What does she think of me now?

"No."

"Anything I can do to help?"

I hold her stare. "Yes. Let's get out of here."

CHAPTER 30
JUNE

We left the party nearly an hour ago, and my stomach is still tied in knots and my heart consumed with worry for Jake. He hasn't said much during the drive to I don't know where. He only said that he was taking me somewhere peaceful after he texted Lachlan asking him to check on the pets.

The radio is on, but the songs that have played since we got on the road haven't registered. I keep thinking about how awful Jake's father and brother were to him. I can't imagine growing up in that type of toxic environment. It makes me appreciate my parents more. They can be a pain in my butt, but I know they love me.

I sneak a peek at Jake for the umpteenth time and find him frowning. "A penny for your thoughts," I say.

"What?" He turns to me.

"You looked like you were concentrating really hard on something."

He gives me a half smile, then returns his attention to the road. "It's nothing. We're almost there."

"And where is *there* exactly?" I glance out the window, trying to guess where we are. We left the freeway some time ago, but I didn't notice the signs.

"Hermosa Beach. I have a beachfront condo."

My eyes widen. "You do?"

"Yeah. I usually rent it short-term, but it's vacant now."

He turns onto a quiet street that leads to the beach, then pulls up the driveway of a sleek two-story modern construction. I can't see all the details in the dark, but it has a lot of windows. The garage door opens, and the lights inside turn on automatically, revealing a spacious three-car garage. It's empty besides some storage units and a large fridge.

If I owned a condo by the beach, I'd live there full-time. But I get why Jake doesn't. It's far from the arena, and with LA traffic, he'd spent most of his time stuck on the road.

I get out of the car and wait for him. Instead of circling around the front, he walks to the rear, opens the trunk, and pulls out a duffel bag. I stare at it but don't say anything. I don't want to assume he planned to come here and didn't tell me to pack an overnight bag.

"This is my gym bag. I always have it in my trunk," he says as if reading my mind.

"Okay."

He loops his free arm around my waist and pulls me closer. "I don't want you to think I planned this and didn't tell you."

"I know you wouldn't do that."

His brows furrow ever so slightly. "I'm sorry I didn't warn you about my father though. I should have."

I touch his face. "After meeting the man, I can see why you didn't."

He covers my hand with his, but instead of leaning down to kiss me as I thought he would, he laces our fingers together and steers me toward the garage door. "Let's go inside."

The door opens to a short and narrow corridor, which gives way to an open kitchen space, as well as the living room. The lights are still off, but the curtains in the living room are partially open, allowing the street-light illumination to flow inside.

"Are you hungry?" he asks.

I'm alone with Jake in a dream location. The last thing on my mind is a late-night snack. I look into his eyes, then drop my gaze to his lips. "Yes, but not for food."

In the blink of an eye, Jake's hands frame my face, and his lips cover mine. I open them, welcoming the invasion of his sweet and demanding tongue. My body is already plastered to his, and my arms are around his waist. His lips are soft, but his mouth is hungry and possessive. When he grabs my ass, squeezing it, I don't think; I jump into his arms, crossing my legs behind him. I'm glad my skirt is flowy, not form-fitting, or I'd have ripped the seams.

He pulls back and smiles. "I guess you want a tour of the house later."

I capture his face between my hands, mindful of his swollen eye. "I'll settle for a tour of the bedroom."

"It's upstairs."

I try to slide down, not expecting him to carry me up the stairs, but he holds me tighter. "Where do you think you're going, sweetheart?"

"I can walk."

"I know, but I like the feel of your wet pussy rubbing against my cock."

On cue, my clit throbs, and I gyrate my hips, causing more friction between our bodies.

Jake's eyes narrow, then he pivots. "Fuck the bedroom."

He sets me down on the couch and drops into a crouch in front of me. Holding my stare, he parts my legs. "I never got to taste you last time. It's time to fix that."

He rolls my panties down my legs slowly, keeping his heated gaze on mine. That action alone is making me breathless. He touches my clit with the tip of a finger and swipes left and right, sending shivers down my back.

"You're so wet already, babe."

My chest rises and falls faster. I'm panting as if I just came home from a run. "That's what your kisses do to me."

His lips curl into a crooked smile. "Is that so? I wonder what's going to happen when I kiss you here?" He leans forward and kisses my inner thigh, a few inches away from the spot where I desperately need him to be.

Sighing, I grab a fistful of his hair. "Why do you want to torture me?"

"Because I enjoy your moans, kitten."

"I'll moan louder if you eat me out."

"Is that so?" He licks my clit in a long and glorious stroke, making me arch my back.

"Oh *yes*."

He chuckles against my pussy, and his hot breath teases my sensitive skin. Every nerve in my body is tingling with pleasure.

"I love your taste. Peaches is a very appropriate nickname for you, gorgeous."

He runs lazy circles around my nub, driving me crazy with need. "Oh Jake. This feels so good. Fuck."

"I can make it feel even better." He stands up and takes off his clothes.

I watch, hoping my galloping heart doesn't jump

out of my chest. It's beating so fast, I can almost hear it. Or maybe that's just my pulse, drumming in my ears. All I know is that I'm horny as hell, and I might come just from watching this beautiful man undress in front of me. And when his piercing comes into view, I let out a whimper. His jewelry felt so good inside of me.

He jerks off slowly, rubbing his thumb over the Apadravya. "Lie down and keep those legs wide for me."

I do as he says, bunching up my skirt to give him unrestricted access to my pussy. I'm burning with desire, aching for Jake's touch.

"You're so beautiful, June. A masterpiece." He leans down, resting his left forearm next to my body while pressing the head of his cock against my clit.

I close my eyes, melting against the couch. The contrast of warm and cold and soft and hard overloads my senses. "Jake..."

He kisses the corner of my mouth. "Do you like that, June?"

"Yes, so, so much."

Slanting his lips over mine, he rubs his cock against my clit, up, down, and sideways, making me so slick, he could easily penetrate me in one swift move. I'm unraveling, spinning out of control. It's not only his teasing that's making me lightheaded; it's his kiss too. Everything he's doing is scrambling my thoughts. I'm ready to forget protection and guide his cock to my entrance. I need him inside of me like I need air.

But I don't take that step. Maybe I do have a shred of self-control left. Jake leaves my mouth to kiss my neck, giving me delicious goose bumps. I moan loudly and say his name as if in prayer. I can feel my orgasm building, making me tingle. God, how I love this moment, the seconds before the climax hits. My toes curl, and I'm almost there, but suddenly, Jake stands, taking with him my source of pleasure.

"Wha—"

"I need to be inside you, June. Right. The. Fuck. Now."

He pulls a condom from his duffel bag, and it makes me wonder why he needs a condom at the gym. Maybe the guys just stash condoms everywhere, which is smart, considering how hot they are. They probably have women hitting on them all the time. It's hard to believe they want to be with me. They want to *share* me.

Lost in my thoughts, I don't see Jake put the condom on, but when he returns to the couch, he's ready.

"I've been dreaming about your hot and tight pussy milking my cock since the last time, gorgeous." He rubs his Apadravya against my clit again, then slides to my entrance and sheathes himself in me to the hilt.

I whimper and shake, trying to hold off the orgasm just a bit longer. It's like swimming against a riptide. The way his piercing rubs against my special spot makes me delirious. He cuts off my moans with his tongue, kissing me deep while he pounds into me, his pace increasing with each thrust. My body convulses in the next moment, and a vortex of pleasure engulfs me. I scratch his back and scream against his lips. That makes Jake move faster, fuck me harder than before. I've barely recovered from my orgasm's onslaught when a new wave crashes over me. I'm coming again, and this time, I might disintegrate.

Jake groans against my lips, a deep and guttural sound that I can feel in my bones. I feel the vibrations coming from him as he chases his release. It seems to go on forever. Finally, with one last jerky movement, he stops, and his body relaxes as he hides his face in the crook of my neck.

We don't move for seconds, maybe minutes. I'm busy trying to catch my breath. I keep my eyes closed while basking in the weight of Jake's body on mine. I feel serene and complete, same as with Lachlan. It's a sensation I never had before, and that tells me something important. I want to keep them. All of them.

CHAPTER 31
JUNE

Spending the night with Jake at the beach house was a dream, but like all dreams, eventually, I had to wake up. No lazy Sunday in bed for us. We headed home soon after breakfast a little after seven. He ordered food, since I was still wearing last night's clothes and he didn't want to expose me to possible scrutiny by dining out. I wished we could have gone for a walk on the beach, but the last thing I needed was for someone to snap a picture of me with Jake.

I stare at his profile. The swelling around his eye is almost gone, but the bruise is darker now. Despite that, he's as handsome as ever, with messy hair and scruff on his face.

He turns to me and smiles. "What's up, boo?"

"Boo?" I laugh.

"Sorry, I'm still trying to figure out the best nickname for you."

"Last night, you said Peaches was a good nickname."

"It is, but that's Ryan's name for you. I want my own."

A warm and fuzzy feeling spreads across my chest. "I'm not fussy about nicknames. I'll like anything you call me."

He turns his attention to the road, but he reaches for my hand and laces our fingers together. "I'll figure it out. Do you have any plans for today?"

"Hopefully, I can get my car from the garage. Then, I have to take care of Mrs. Carpenter's pets, work on my weekly lesson plan, and read the notes the substitute teacher left for me. So, a light schedule."

"Make sure you get some R and R time as well. If I didn't have plans tonight, I'd take you out to dinner."

The butterflies in my stomach make their presence known. I'd love to spend more quality time with Jake, but then I remember where he needs to be tonight, and my giddiness disappears. I'm curious about his relationship with his father and brother, but that's a touchy subject for him, so I don't ask.

My phone rings, and I fish it out of my purse to see who's calling.

It's my mother. Normally, I'd let it go to voicemail,

but after witnessing Jake's horrible relationship with his father, I don't want to take my mother for granted.

I turn to Jake. "It's my mother. Do you mind if I answer it?"

His brows pinch together. "I don't mind at all."

"Thanks." I press the green button. "Hey, Mom."

"Hey, baby girl. How are you doing?"

"I'm great." I glance at Jake again with a smile. "How about you and Dad?"

"We're fine, considering what happened to you. But you don't need to pretend you're okay for our sake, hon."

"I'm not pretending, Mom. Being rejected and humiliated in public is the best thing that ever happened to me. I dodged a bullet."

"Well, that you did. That Bill is lower than a snake's belly in a wagon rut." Jake chuckles, and my mother hears it. "Who's with you?"

Shit.

"No one, Mom. It's just the radio. I'm driving."

I glance at Jake apologetically, hoping he didn't take offense that I lied about being with him. The corners of his lips are turned upward, though.

"Oh, all right. Anyhow, I called because I have some juicy gossip. Yesterday, we all went to a barn raising and bumped into none other than Primrose Larsson."

"What was Bill's great aunt doing at a barn raising? That's not her usual scene."

"Oh, I know. That woman is stuck up higher than a light pole. But that's a whole other story. She approached your father and me and profusely apologized for that good-for-nothing great-nephew of hers. You can imagine how surprised I was. I was ready to pitch a hissy fit with a tail on it."

And it would have been epic. No one pitches a hissy fit better than Mom.

"Oh, I bet. But Mom, I really don't want to hear stories about Bill or his family. I don't want to think about him at all."

"I understand, honey. I just thought you'd get a kick out of knowing he's on the shit list of his rich great-aunt. I wouldn't be surprised if she cuts him out of her will."

Bill would be furious. He never cared for his great-aunt, but the way he sucked up to her was embarrassing.

"That woman will outlive all of us."

Mom laughs. "Ain't that right?"

"Is everything good with you and Dad?"

"Yes, everything is good. Well... almost everything. Your father is losing sleep now that April has gotten herself a boyfriend."

"No. Not his sweet little girl," I tease.

"He just needs to get over it. Dash Wilkins is a good boy, despite his ridiculous name."

"Dash? But I thought he had a crush on May."

"Just a little boy crush. He got over that pretty

quickly when he saw April all dressed up at the Ferrero wedding."

As much as I want to hear more gossip about my siblings' love lives, I don't want to be rude to Jake.

"Mom, I have to go. I'll call you later, okay?"

"All right, peach pie. You drive safely."

"Okay. Bye, Mom."

I end the call and turn to Jake. "Sorry about that."

He grins. "Don't apologize. I enjoyed learning more about you. So, I take it May and April are your sisters?"

"Yeah, how did you know?"

His grin becomes broader. "Wild guess."

"Oh." I chuckle. "Yeah. My parents were into naming their kids after months. My older brother is August."

"So August, June, May, and April?"

"Yep."

"What happened to July?" he asks in an amused tone.

My smile wilts a fraction. "He was my brother. Stillborn."

"June, I'm so sorry."

I shake my head. "It's fine. It was a fair question. I get that a lot here in LA. Naturally, everyone in my hometown knows about him."

"You're close to your family, aren't you?"

"Yes, I am. They can be a pain in the butt and stubborn as mules, but I love them."

"I'd love to meet them one day."

My heart skips a beat. "Really?"

"Yeah. I'd like to know what it's like to have what you have."

Sadness rushes into my heart. I can't begin to imagine what his childhood was like. "Maybe we can visit my folks one day."

He smiles, but I see a hint of sadness in his eyes. "I'd like that."

God. What are we doing? I thought we were keeping things casual, but here we are, making plans as if we're a couple. And what about Lachy? There's a strong connection there too. I'd thought the same about Ryan, but after seeing him with that woman last night, I'm not so sure. Regardless, I can't show up in Baron, Texas, with two boyfriends in tow. I might give Mom a heart attack.

CHAPTER 32
RYAN

I drank way too fucking much last night, and I'm now regretting my life choices, especially when my alarm buzzes. It's not early. I'm not that much of a lunatic. It's already nine, but after drinking all that fucking booze, I could sleep until noon. A normal person would simply shut the alarm off and go back to sleep, but I'm not like other people. I have to get in a workout sesh now, as planned, or my brain will tell me the world is going to end.

Grunting, I get out of bed and go straight into the shower. It's counterintuitive to shower before heading to the gym, but I need a blast of cold water to wake up. I prefer to fast before lifting weights, and I can't stand black coffee, so I make a pre-workout drink and head out.

I don't hear a sound from behind Lachy's closed

bedroom door, and Jake didn't come home last night. Not sure if he's back yet. He must have taken June to his condo in Hermosa Beach. I'd have done that, too, if it were me. So far, both my friends have had alone time with the sexy teacher, and that usually wouldn't bother me; I'd have moved on to the next woman already. But now, there's a burning need inside me to create an opportunity to spend quality time with June, too. If only my life weren't on the verge of imploding. Mackenzie's ambush at the party last night was an unwelcome surprise. What the hell was she thinking? I was clear that I wanted nothing to do with her.

Hell. Thinking about that girl puts me in a foul mood again. In the elevator, I shove my AirPods into my ears, pick one of my favorite songs by Bad Omens, and let the loud music drown out my thoughts. My eyes are closed when the elevator stops again. That was fast. Or not. It stopped one floor down.

June walks in, looking like a vision. She's wearing the most basic clothes and no makeup, but I'm drawn to her like a moth to a flame. Maybe I'm already too into her. I smile, fucking happy about this pleasant surprise.

Her pretty eyes widen. "Ryan, hi."

I pause the song to reply, "Good morning, Peaches. When did you get back from Hermosa Beach?"

Her face becomes red. "Half an hour ago."

So easily flustered. I love it.

"And where are you off to now?"

"I need to get my car from the garage. They called when I was out with Winston."

"They're open on Sunday?"

"Yeah, just until noon."

Here's the opportunity I was looking for, delivered to me on a silver platter. *Thank you, providence.*

"Did you call an Uber?"

"Yeah. It'll be here in seven minutes."

"Cancel it. I'll take you."

"You don't have to."

"I know, but I want to." I give her my most dazzling smile, and it works like a charm. June's eyes drop to my lips, and I bet she's thinking about the last time we kissed. It's been too fucking long.

She looks into my eyes again, but her brows are furrowed. "But aren't you going somewhere?"

"Just the gym. I have time."

She clenches her jaw and looks away. "I don't want to impose."

Shit. Did I fuck up already with her?

"Do you not want to spend time with me?"

Hell, I sound pathetic and desperate.

"What?" She laughs nervously. "That's not it."

The elevator door opens at street level, and June steps forward, but I stop her and turn her to me. "I don't buy it. Did I do something, Peaches?"

She can't hold my stare for more than a second and drops her gaze to my chest. "You did nothing."

It finally occurs to me she might have seen me with Mackenzie at the party and drawn the wrong conclusion.

I pinch June's chin between my thumb and fore-finger and lift her face so I can look into her eyes. "Is this about the woman that was with me last night?"

"Ryan... you don't owe me any explanation."

I'll take her reply as a yes. I had no intention of ever talking to anyone about Mackenzie, least of all June. But thanks to that brat's ambush, I have no choice.

"I want to explain nonetheless." The elevator stops at the garage, and I tug June's hand. "Come on. I'll tell you on the way."

She lets me steer her to the car and remains quiet, waiting for me to speak. I drive out of the garage first to buy time.

"Did you change your mind about telling me?" June asks after a while.

"No. I'm sorry. It's not something I like to talk about." I run a hand through my hair. "The woman you saw last night is my mother's daughter."

There's a pause, and June says, "Your sister, then."

I swallow hard. "Technically, half-sister. But I never thought of her that way. My mother..." Fuck, this is harder than I thought it'd be. "She wasn't faithful to my dad, even though he worshipped her. I'm not sure when she started to cheat on him, but when I was old enough, I figured it out."

"Ryan, I'm so sorry. That must have been hard."

"Yeah. I confronted her when I found out. She begged me not to tell my father, said it was a one-time mistake, and I believed her. But she kept doing it, and I pretended I didn't know. My father would have been devastated if he found out. She left us a few years later and never came back."

My eyes burn, surprising me. I didn't think reliving those old memories would make me want to cry. I clench my jaw hard, trying to control my emotions.

"Was last night the first time you've met your half-sister?"

"Yes. She reached out a few months ago, but I blew her off. Cory—that's my younger brother—he must have told her where I'd be. He was too young when Mom left us to know what was going on. He doesn't get why I want nothing to do with that girl."

"I can't begin to imagine how painful it must have been for you, and I understand why you're angry at your mother, but your half-sister isn't at fault."

I hold the steering wheel tighter. "That's what Lachy said. I know it isn't logical, but Mackenzie is the reason my mother left and never came back. She got knocked up with Mackenzie, and there's zero chance Dad was the father. He was teaching abroad at the time."

June doesn't say anything, and I fear I lost my shot with her. "You must think I'm a jerk for taking out my anger on Mackenzie."

She shakes her head. "No, I don't think that at all. That's a deep wound, Ryan. It's understandable that you would see your half-sister as the reason for your mother's abandonment, and thus, transfer your anger to her. Thanks for trusting me with your story."

I blink fast, not quite believing this woman is real. "You're amazing, do you know that?"

She smiles. "Yes."

Laughter bubbles up my throat. "And here I thought I'd have to convince you of your awesomeness. It's good to see your confident side, Peaches."

She looks ahead. "It's good to *feel* confident. Being free of a toxic relationship did that."

At a red light, I stare at her profile for a bit. She looks serene and beautiful. I'm pleased her confidence boost has nothing to do with us. It needs to come from within to be real.

"I'm so fucking glad you came to the Titans party."

She looks at me, grinning wide. "Me too."

My heart skips a beat.

Hell and damn. When did it ever do that for any woman?

CHAPTER 33
JUNE

Before I walk into the garage, I tell Ryan he cannot offer to pay. No matter the cost, the car repair is my problem, and I'm not a mooch. Surprisingly, the repair doesn't cost an arm and a leg. When I see the invoice, I understand why. The owner charged only for the part replacement, not his labor. I glance at Ryan. I wouldn't put it past him to have sneakily tried to pay for part of the bill.

"What?" he asks innocently.

Instead of jumping to conclusions and accusing him, I ask the garage owner, "You didn't charge me for your services?"

"No, ma'am."

"Not that I don't appreciate it, but why not?"

"You're my grandson's teacher—Louis Miller."

Oh, Louis. He's having a tough year, thanks to his parents' divorce.

"That's right. I had no idea he was your grandson. He's a sweet kid."

The man nods. "He is. My daughter said you've helped him a lot this semester. With everything going on... you know, they've had it hard."

Sadness drops onto my shoulders. At the beginning of the semester, Louis's mom told me she had separated from her husband, and he was making things difficult. Divorces are hard, especially on children, but when it's not amicable, it's ten times worse.

"I do what I can to help," I reply.

From the corner of my eye, I sense Ryan watching me.

"And I appreciate it. Folks don't value what teachers do for their kids. But I do. I was happy to shave off the cost of labor for you."

My eyes prickle as gratitude overwhelms me. I'm not usually a crybaby, but I've been more sensitive to gestures of kindness these past few days. Maybe I'm not as healed emotionally as I thought. "Thank you."

I pay the bill, then head to my car.

Ryan follows me. "Nice guy. I'll make sure to send business his way."

"Yeah, I didn't expect that."

"What are you doing for the rest of the day? Maybe we can hang out after I come back from the gym."

My heart beats a little faster. I'd love to spend more time with Ryan. And after our conversation in the car, I feel more connected to him than before. If only I didn't have a million things to do today.

"Maybe we can have lunch together?"

He smiles broadly. "Sounds good. It's my turn to show off my cooking skills."

"It's a date then."

RYAN

For the first time since I moved in with the guys, I wish I lived alone. When I get home from the gym and the grocery store, I find Lachy sprawled on the couch, watching TV. I completely forgot about him and Jake when I made plans with June.

"Hey, what are you doing today?" I set the grocery bags on the kitchen counter.

"Nothing."

Fucking great.

"You should go outside and enjoy the weather. It's a perfect day for golfing."

"There's no bloody chance of me doing anything physical today. I'm beat."

"You're just going to sit on the couch all day?"

"Yep." He changes the channel.

I put things away, trying to keep my irritation at bay. It's my damn fault for not planning better. "Where's Jake?"

"Haven't seen him yet. I reckon he didn't sleep much last night."

I doubt asking Lachy and Jake to leave the apartment for a few hours so I can have June to myself will work. They'll not only stay, but they'll also tease me later, because we're grown men who act like teens. I resign myself that they'll be around when June comes over.

"June was up early."

Immediately, Lachy looks over his shoulder. "You saw her?"

"Yeah. Bumped into her on my way to the gym and ended up giving her a ride to the garage so she could pick up her car."

"I wonder what she's doing today."

"She's coming over for lunch." I try to sound as nonchalant as possible, but Lachy narrows his eyes.

"That's why you were trying to get me out of the apartment."

I give him a droll look. "Don't be ridiculous. I don't care if you and Jake are here when she comes. Unlike you two, I haven't fallen head over heels for her."

Lachy shakes his head. "You're so full of shite, it's not even funny."

"Believe what you want."

"I will. What are you making, by the way?"

"For you? Nothing," I grumble.

Lachy laughs. "I guess I'll have to use your sanctuary to fix myself some lunch then."

Over my dead body. "You can order food."

"Sure, I can do that. But June will probably wonder why you didn't cook enough for everyone."

His attention returns to the TV, so he doesn't see me glowering at him. Very rarely do I let Lachy irritate me, but this deal with June is throwing me off my game. I could cook something Lachy hates as retribution, but unfortunately, such food doesn't exist. He will eat anything.

CHAPTER 34
LACHLAN

could go out. It is a nice day, and I don't enjoy being a couch potato for too long. I get antsy. But knowing June is coming over for lunch—and Ryan would like nothing more than to get rid of Jake and me—is motivation enough for me to stay.

He's been busy in the kitchen since he got home, and the smell is already making my mouth water. If he didn't make enough food for everyone, I'll be seriously pissed off.

I get up from the couch to grab a piece of fruit, because my stomach is grumbling and who knows when lunch will be ready.

Ryan glares at me. "Where do you think you're going? You know the kitchen is off-limits when I'm cooking."

"I'm only grabbing a piece of watermelon from the fridge. Stop being so bloody anal."

Jake finally joins us in the kitchen after being holed up in his room this entire time. His bruise is still dark, but the swelling has gone down.

"Good morning," he says in a rough voice.

"Morning?" I arch a brow. "It's almost noon."

"Technically, it's still morning." He grabs a glass of water and drains it in large gulps.

Ryan turns around and tries to get to the fridge, but we're blocking his way. "Can you please get the fuck out of my kitchen?"

Jake's brows rise. "What's wrong with you?"

"He's angry 'cause June is coming for lunch, and he doesn't want us here."

Ryan scowls. "That's not it. I already told you I don't care."

Jake leans against the counter, crossing his arms. "Who was the woman with you last night?"

Ryan's expression turns as cold as ice. "I don't want to talk about her."

Jake looks at me with a question in his eyes. I reply, "Two words—family drama."

"Ah. So that was Mackenzie."

Ryan turns his attention back to the stove, and grits out, "I said I don't wanna talk about her."

"Fine. What time is June coming over?"

"When lunch is ready. She told me she has a busy

day."

Jake frowns. "When did you speak to her?"

"This morning. I gave her a lift to the garage."

"Oh, so she got her car back, then."

Someone's phone rings. It's not mine, and since Jake doesn't budge, it's probably not his either. Ryan pats his pockets, then searches for his phone in the vicinity. I spot the device before he does. It's about to vibrate itself off the counter.

I grab it before it takes a nosedive to the floor, and see June's name on the screen.

Instead of handing the phone over to Ryan, I answer it. "Hello, lass. We were just talking about you." I smile, loving Ryan's what-the-fuck expression.

"Hey, Lachy. I was calling to ask what time I should come over."

"Are you done with your chores?"

"Well, not all of them, but I could use a break. I just came back from walking Winston, and Admiral hasn't stopped talking since then."

I chuckle. "Really? What is he saying?"

Ryan stops in front of me with his hand outstretched. "Hello! Can I have my phone now? She called *me*."

I bat his hand away. "Bugger off."

"I had *Friends* on earlier, and now he keeps saying 'How *you* doin'?' It's driving me crazy."

I throw my head back and laugh.

Ryan uses my moment of distraction to snatch the

phone from my hand and put it on speaker. "Hey, Peaches. What did you tell Lachy that was so funny?"

"Admiral thinks he's Joey from *Friends*."

He snorts. "What?"

"I'll tell you in person. Can I come up now?"

"Of course. The food is almost ready."

"Okay. See you in a minute."

Ryan ends the call and shoves his phone into his pocket while glaring at me. "Don't answer my phone again."

I smirk. "You're only pissed cause it was June."

He narrows his eyes and clenches his jaw. I expect a retort, but he simply turns around and checks on the food.

A moment later, there's a knock on the door. Jake is closest to it and does the honors of opening it. "Hello, beautiful." He leans down and kisses June on the cheek.

"Hi," she replies shyly, and when she steps forward, I see the delicious blush on her cheeks. Damn it. Now I'm hungry for her, not food.

Unable to restrain myself, I walk over and pull her into a bear hug. "Hey, lass."

She laughs, hugging me back. "Hi, Lachy."

"Would you give Peaches room to breathe? Jesus," Ryan complains from the kitchen.

I step to the side but keep my arm around June's waist. "Stop being so grumpy. That's my thing."

"You aren't grumpy," June tells me.

Jake laughs, shaking his head. "Oh, you haven't seen Lachy's dark side."

I lean closer, and whisper in her ear, "Don't worry, lass. You'll never see it."

Before she can reply, Ryan clears his throat. "I want to know about Admiral."

June steps away from me and heads to the kitchen. I don't want to be a jerk, but my eyes have a will of their own, and they travel south. She's wearing jeans that hug her fine curves perfectly, and a simple loose-fit T-shirt. She could be wearing a potato sack and she'd be stunning.

"He kept saying "How *you* doin'?" It was funny at first, but it got old fast. I hope he stops doing that."

"It could be worse," Jake pipes up.

June turns. "Worse how?"

"He could be saying 'pivot' nonstop."

"Pivot! Pivot! Peevet!" Ryan yells, then shakes his head laughing. "Gotta love that bird."

"I'm glad you think so, because if he keeps this up, he'll be staying in your room," June tells him.

I wait for Ryan to follow with *I'd rather you stay in my room.* June totally teed that up for him. I can see in his eyes that the reply is on the tip of his tongue. But instead, he says, "No problem."

I narrow my eyes. Ryan isn't acting like himself. But I only waste a couple beats watching him before I turn my attention to June. "What are you doing after lunch?"

"I have to finish prepping my class schedule for the week and sort through all my boxes. What about you guys?"

"Nothing planned. Maybe I'll do some sketching or read a bit," I say.

Jake's expression is shut off again, and he doesn't answer June. What's gotten into him now?

"No plans for me. Just rest." Ryan replies. "I hope you're hungry. Lunch is ready."

She smiles brightly at him. "I am. What did you make?"

"Something simple. I hope you like red meat."

She rests her hands on her hips, and that sassy pose does my head in. "What kind of question is that? I'm from Texas. Of course I like red meat."

Ryan says something, but it's like background noise. I'm hyper-focused on June, and nothing else matters.

CHAPTER 35
JAKE

Lunch with June was a surprise. Being around her is turning into one of my favorite things, and Ryan outdid himself trying to show off his cooking skills. He didn't make anything fancy, but hell if his steak wasn't cooked to perfection, and the mashed potatoes the best I've ever eaten. Unfortunately, June had a busy day and didn't hang out long.

At seven o'clock sharp, I walk through the door of Providence and spot my father and brother sitting at a table. I make a beeline to them and, without a word of greeting, pull out the chair across from the old bastard.

"You're late," my father says.

I won't dignify him with an answer. He sets his watch five minutes ahead so he can be the first one in any meeting. He likes to start by bitching about other people's tardiness. Even knowing his trick, I make a point to arrive at the right time. Fuck him very much.

A waiter walks over, and I order a scotch, neat. My father and brother are both drinking something strong. Maybe I should have ordered vodka just to piss him off, since he considers it trash, but I went to my favorite drink automatically.

"I'm here," I start. "What do you want?"

"It's been a long time since we talked. I've let you run amok for too long in this godforsaken city. It's time to come home."

"Home?" I shake my head, and derisive laughter escapes my mouth.

The waiter arrives with my drink just in time. I need alcohol to survive this conversation without losing my temper.

"Yes, home, Jakey. Where you were born and raised," my brother pipes up.

"That means shit. Los Angeles is my home now."

My father narrows his eyes. "For now. Hockey players get traded all the time."

Dread licks the back of my neck. The asshole knows something. There have been rumors the Titans were looking to trade me thanks to my behavioral issues. But I'm at the top of my game, and if we keep winning, there's no fucking chance they'll get rid of me.

"True, but I have a no-trade clause in my contract. Guess which teams are on that list?"

Gregory grimaces. "You're a child."

I make a fist, dying to connect my knuckles with that condescending face. Instead, I take a large sip of my drink.

"That clause is a non-issue. I want you back in New York, and Miles is keen on bringing you to the Bobcats. He's prepared to make an offer your GM can't refuse." My father smiles smugly.

Miles, the owner of the Bobcats, is another asshole. A billionaire who owns several pro teams but doesn't give a damn about any of them. It's all about how many championships he can win.

"I'd rather retire than play for that egomaniac."

My father leans forward. "I don't think you understand, Jake. You have no say in this. It's a done deal. I'll have you back in New York whether you like it or not."

My spine becomes tense. "What's that supposed to mean?"

"You can accept your fate like a good boy, keep what's left of your reputation intact, and cash in, or I can let the world know about the mess I had to clean up eleven years ago."

I grind my teeth until my molars hurt. I should have known he'd keep blackmailing me. He was bluffing yesterday. If I hadn't come to dinner tonight, he wouldn't have revealed anything. He wanted to know if he had any leverage over me, and I gave it to him on a silver platter. I'm an idiot.

I drain the rest of my drink, then set it back on the table, hard. "Like I said, I'd rather give up hockey forever than play in New York. If you want to tell the world what I did, fucking do it."

I push my chair back and stand, taking great satisfaction in the look of surprise on my father's and brother's faces.

"Where do you think you're going?"

"I agreed to come, but I never said I'd stay for dinner."

"You might be willing to throw your career out the window, boy, but you're not the only one with skeletons in the closet. Would you risk your roommates' careers too?"

My nostrils flare. I should have known he'd have another nasty trick up his sleeve. But I won't make the same mistake and cave. He's a snake; there's a high chance he's lying through his teeth.

"You're grasping at straws, Father. You never cared about me. Why the fuck do you want me back in New York?"

"I might think little of you, but you still carry my name. I'm sick and tired of seeing you drag it through the mud."

My jaw drops. I've always known my father's ego was bigger than all of New York. I'm not even upset that he doesn't care about me. I accepted that reality many years ago. But to say I'm dragging his name through the mud is a whole new low for him.

"That's too fucking bad." I turn to leave.

"Don't you dare walk away from me," he grits out.

I ignore him and keep walking. My pulse is pounding in my ears as I stride toward the exit. I'm so fucking angry; the smartest thing to do is leave. I shove a healthy tip into the valet's hand so he can bring my car out as fast as possible. While I wait, Gregory finds me. Fucking hell.

"Go away, Greg."

"I will once you hear me out. You're making a huge mistake, Jake."

I glare at him. "Why do you care?"

"I don't. At least not about you. I'm looking out for myself."

I snort. "No surprise."

"If you disobey our father, he'll destroy your life and the lives of your friends. He's obsessed with getting you back home. God knows why."

"If he comes for my friends, I'll obliterate him and you. You can bet your life on it."

Gregory's eyes widen, but he quickly twists his face into a grimace. "What can you do to us? You're nothing but a glorified thug."

The rage burning hot through my veins is about to explode. Gregory obviously has a death wish, and he's lucky the valet returns with my car before I can make paté out of his face.

I force a chilling smile. "Watch me."

CHAPTER 36
JUNE

On Monday, I arrive at school a bit earlier than usual. Winston did his morning business quickly, and the other pets were easy to handle. Last night, I received an email from Principal Prescott asking me to see her before class starts. I get along with her well enough, so I'm pretty sure she just wants to check on me.

Principal Prescott is a short woman in her fifties, and many underestimate her due to her petite size, but when it comes to fighting for her school and students, she has the tenacity of a warrior.

"Good morning, Priscila," I greet her, addressing her by her first name when I'm not around students, per her preference.

"Good morning, June. How are you feeling?"

"Much better, thank you."

She studies me intensely for a couple beats. "You do look fantastic. I'd say glowing even."

My face becomes warm in an instant. She can't possibly know the number of orgasms I had over the weekend.

"It turns out getting rejected by Bill was the best thing that's ever happened to me."

Her expression becomes harder. "I'm glad you think so. What that man did... well, calling him a man isn't accurate, is it?"

I smirk. "Definitely not."

She rests her forearms on the desk, linking her hands together and leaning forward. "I asked you to come see me for two reasons. One, to make sure you were doing all right. And two, to ask for a favor."

"Of course. Name it."

"Do you think you can arrange for your new hockey player friends to visit the school and talk to the students?"

I don't answer for a moment. She caught me off guard. I wasn't expecting that question, but in hindsight, I should have. That's the kind of opportunity she wouldn't miss. If they come, it'll be great exposure for our school, which could result in more donations. But the idea of the guys coming to my place of work is a little unsettling.

"I can ask them. But I'm not sure they have the power to make that decision."

"Oh, the Titans' PR department will have to approve it, no doubt. But with your connection, we have a foot in the door."

I nod, forcing a smile. I don't want her to notice I'm freaking out. "That's true."

"Great. I'm counting on you, June. I'll let you get ready for class now."

"All right. I'll let you know."

I leave her office as fast as I can. I'm sure the guys will be more than happy to visit my school. But that's Melissa's territory, and I don't want to go over her head by asking them directly.

In my classroom, I shoot her a text asking if I can call her. I know Principal Prescott wants an answer as soon as possible. She likes things done quickly.

Melissa's reply comes a couple of minutes later.

> This is freaky. I was about to text you.
> Are you free now?

> Yeah.

She calls right away, and I answer on the first ring. "Hey, good morning."

"Hi, June. How was your weekend?" she asks in a cheery tone.

"It was great."

"Did you have fun at the party?"

"Honestly, no. But I did afterward."

I'm not sure why I'm being so candid with Melissa. I have to remember that she works with the guys, and if anything, her loyalty is to them.

"I bet. And I'm sorry the party was a bust. Anyway, I wanted to ask if you're free to have dinner with me tonight."

Melissa wants to have dinner with me? I'm shocked and a little worried too.

"Uh, yeah. I don't have anything planned."

"Great. I'll text you the address. Shoot, my boss is calling me. I have to go. See you later."

"Bye," I reply, but she's no longer on the line.

I stare at my phone for a moment and wonder what Melissa wants to talk about. Maybe she found out about my weekend adventures with the guys and wants me to stop. No, that doesn't make any sense. If anything, she encouraged me to be with them.

A knock on the door makes me jump in my chair. "Good morning, June."

"Jesus, Katrina. You scared me."

"Sorry. Why were you staring at your phone with such concentration?" She pulls up a chair from the front row and sits across from me.

"Melissa invited me to have dinner with her tonight. What do you think she wants?"

"Melissa is the Titans VP of Marketing, right?"

"Yeah."

Katrina smirks. "Maybe she wants to talk PR strategy, since you're banging her three star players."

"Katrina! Shush. Someone could hear you."

She laughs. "Who? Only the hard-working bees like ourselves and Prescott are around this early."

"You don't know that. But anyway, I'm a little nervous about having dinner with her. What if she wants the opposite?"

Katrina raises an eyebrow. "Like what?"

"Like she tells me I should stay away from the guys."

Katrina tilts her head. "Why would she do that? She's a boss lady, and I doubt she cares if her players are stuffing you like a Thanksgiving turkey."

I flatten a palm against my forehead. "Oh my God. The things that come out of your mouth."

She laughs. "That was a good visual, wasn't it?"

I wrinkle my nose. "No, it was awful. I'll never be able to look at turkey the same way now."

"Me neither. But I never liked turkey anyway." She shrugs. "Now tell me about your weekend. How was Jake?"

A fuzzy feeling spreads across my chest when I think about him. "Jake was great."

Katrina's smile broadens. "I bet he was. So what's going on? Are you dating them all at the same time?"

I frown. "I'm not sure. Jake told me they're cool with

sharing. And I had lunch with all three of them, and it was totally fine."

Katrina leans forward. "You had another tres leches fiesta?"

"What's a tres leches fiesta, Ms. Summers?" Louis Miller, the grandson of the garage owner, walks in.

Shit. I give Katrina the stink eye.

"It's a party where all they serve is tres leches cakes," Katrina replies.

Louis takes his seat and shrugs his backpack from his shoulder. "Oh. That sounds cool. Tres leches is my favorite dessert."

Katrina smirks at me. "June's too." She jumps to her feet and says, "I'd better go. Talk later, June."

CHAPTER 37
JUNE

Melissa wants to meet at seven at a restaurant not too far from the apartment, which gives me plenty of time to take care of Mrs. Carpenter's pets and get ready. Or so I thought. Nothing I own seems cute or fashion-forward enough. I don't want to look frumpy next to Melissa. In the end, I give up on wearing a dress and go with skinny jeans, a cute, corseted top with a sweetheart neckline and cap sleeves, and chunky high-heel sandals.

I stare at my reflection in the full-length mirror and strike a pose. Eros and Apollo are lounging on the bed, surrounded by Mrs. Carpenter's endless pillows, and staring at me. "What do you think, guys?"

If cats could roll their eyes, that's what Apollo would have done. He exudes an air of indifference while he licks his paw. Eros yawns.

"You guys suck." I glance at the mirror again. "Not bad, June. It almost looks like you know what you're doing."

A knock on the door sets the dog into a barking frenzy, and my heart skips a beat. Immediately, I assume one of the guys is outside. "One second."

I look through the peephole just to be safe and see Lachy standing on the other side. The butterflies in my stomach awaken.

Smiling, I open the door. "Hi, Lachy."

His eyes bug out as he looks at my ensemble. "Wow, lass. Where are you going looking like that?"

"Melissa invited me to dinner."

Looking sheepish, he rubs the back of his neck. "Oh, I came to ask if you wanted to hang out."

He could have texted me, but he chose to come down to ask. I don't know how I'm supposed to resist this man. He's too adorable and sexy for his own good.

"Rain check? How about tomorrow?"

He gives me a crooked smile. "Yeah, I can come over after the game. You're coming again, right?"

I arch my brows. "I didn't even know you were playing again. I really should look at your game schedule."

"You should." His gaze drops to my lips, but he doesn't make the first move.

I want a kiss from him though, so it's up to me. I step into his space, curling my fingers into the fabric of his shirt, and press my lips softly against his. He wraps his arms around my waist, pulling me flush against his body while he coaxes my lips open with his tongue. I didn't realize how much I was craving his touch. My heart is thumping hard inside my chest, pumping euphoria throughout my body. I relax into his arms, loving the feel of his scruff against my skin. My temperature is rising, and yet, goose bumps spread everywhere, and chills of desire run down my back. It's like I caught an ice-cold fever.

He leans back, biting my lower lip softly before releasing it. "If you don't want to be late, you'd better go back inside, lass."

"Right. Well, I'll see you later." I step back and close the door, still in a daze. Then I lean against the cold and hard surface and wait for my body to cool off.

Holy shit. Maybe I should avoid kissing Lachy when I don't have time for more.

I'm five minutes late thanks to Lachy's surprise visit, and Melissa is already waiting for me at the table. She waves at me from a distance, then stands to give me a hug. She looks like a rock star, as always. Tonight, she opted for jeans and a fancy top, paired with a cropped leather jacket. I'm glad I chose jeans too.

"Hi, June. You look so cute. I love your top."

"Thanks. You look stunning."

She flips her hair back and winks. "I try."

"I'm sorry I'm late. I got sidetracked a bit."

She smirks. "Sidetracked, huh? I wonder by who?"

I pick up the menu in front of me and lower my face to avoid her stare. "Lachy."

She laughs. "That's a nice distraction. I can't fault you for it."

The waitress walks over to take our drink orders. Melissa turns to her. "I'll have a spicy margarita."

"Oh, that sounds good. I'll have one too."

Melissa leans forward once we're alone again. "You must be wondering why I invited you to dinner."

"Yeah. A bit."

"I just want to check on you. Your life has gone through major changes, and now you're suddenly in the spotlight. I'm a little mad at Jake for bringing you as his date on Saturday night without thinking about the consequences to you."

Apprehension pierces my chest. "Oh? Did something happen?"

"Nothing terrible. But you're now linked to him. The press perceives you as his potential girlfriend. If you're caught being chummy with Lachy, for instance, that won't look good for you."

I sag against my chair. "Yeah, that's my biggest fear. But you can't blame Jake for it. I could have said no, but..."

"You wanted to go. I get it. Any woman would have a hard time saying no to him. He's a catch."

"They all are," I blurt out without thinking.

Melissa watches me closely. "June Summers, are you falling for all those boys?"

Cheeks. Flames. "What? No! That'd be crazy."

The waitress returns with our drinks, and am I glad to see her. I don't let her set the drink on the table. I take it from her hand and drink a couple of large sips, one right after another.

"I don't think it'd be that crazy," Melissa replies. "If it feels right, fuck what society says. Go for it."

Maybe the alcohol is already working because my tongue is loose. "I don't know what I feel. There's attraction, but also more. I enjoy spending time with them individually and as a group. It's doing my head in, to be honest. They're all cool with sharing, and I have a feeling that they're still happy when I spend time alone with one of them. I've never met any guys who behave like they do."

"There's a word for it. Compersion. They get a kick out of knowing you're having a good time with someone else."

I frown. "I'd get crazy jealous. I don't want to picture them with another woman. Does that make me selfish?"

Melissa's eyes harden. "No. I wouldn't be happy if Elijah was screwing someone else on the side. I'm not cut out to be in a non-monogamous relationship."

"Me neither." I drink some more, trying to drown the new anxiety swirling in my chest.

"You need to be honest with them."

"I know. God, maybe I should stop before it's too late."

She tilts her head. "I think it's already too late. Your eyes sparkle when you talk about them."

"Great," I mumble.

Our waitress returns. "Are you ready to order?"

"Shit. I didn't even look at the menu," I say in a panic as I scan the options quickly.

"I'll give you a couple more minutes," the waitress replies, and walks away again.

"The burgers here are really good," Melissa tells me.

I check the prices and almost gag. Twenty dollars for a burger?

"Get whatever you want. It's my treat," Melissa continues as if reading my mind.

"Okay, thank you."

"About the game tomorrow. Are you planning to come?"

I bite my lower lip. "Should I?"

Melissa shrugs. "I don't see why not? But I have to warn you, Wendy Wagner has been asking about you."

"Who is she?"

"Oh, that's right. You left the party on Saturday early and didn't meet her. She's Malcolm Wagner's wife.

Malcolm is one of our D-men. Wendy is the main WAG. She takes the lead on everything."

"WAG?"

"Short for wives and girlfriends. They have a group chat where they coordinate all kinds of social events, pick custom outfits for the playoffs, that kind of thing. Whenever a player gets an official girlfriend, they'll usually ask the WAG leader to add their girl to the group."

My pulse accelerates. That sounds like the moms on the PTA, but the rich and fabulous version. I've seen enough pictures of wives and girlfriends of pro athletes to know they're all gorgeous.

"But I'm not anyone's girlfriend."

"They don't know that. And after Jake brought you to the party on Saturday, they're all buzzing with curiosity. If you come tomorrow, Wendy will make sure to grill you with all the questions."

My stomach coils tightly. "Oh God. This is getting complicated."

"It doesn't need to be. Talk with the boys and figure out where you stand. Then make a decision. And if you do decide to stick around, I'll get you properly trained to deal with the media. Unlike Jake, I won't throw you to the wolves unprepared."

"Thanks."

"You said you wanted to talk to me about something. What is it?"

Crap. I already forgot about Principal Prescott's request.

"My boss asked if the guys could visit the school and speak to our students. I didn't make any promises. It's okay if you say no."

She frowns. "Why would I say no? I think it's an excellent idea. We're always looking for opportunities to connect with the community. I'll ask the PR manager to reach out to your principal. Just shoot me her details."

Relief and anxiety hit me at once. I'm relieved that I don't have to disappoint Principal Prescott, and anxious about spending time with the guys at my workplace. Sometimes, it's exhausting to be me.

When I get home from dinner with Melissa, I'm determined to skip tomorrow's game. I'm not ready to face the inquisition of a bunch of strangers when I don't know where I stand in my relationship with the boys. I could put my big girl pants on and ask them, but hell, what if I come across as needy?

I take my phone out to charge and notice a few messages from them. They added me to a group chat. My heart skips a beat, and I'm giddy like a schoolgirl.

JAKE: I already took Winston out for his evening walk.

LACHY: We're up if you want to
come by.

Oh, the temptation. If I go up to their apartment, I doubt I'll get much sleep.

I just got home, but it's late. I should
probably go to bed.

JAKE: Smart. I don't think you'd get
much sleep if you came over. 😉

It's ridiculous how hard I'm blushing right now.

Oh God. 😄

RYAN: Exactly what you'd be saying on
repeat.

😊

LACHY: Ryan made tres leches cake
but don't wanna share.

RYAN: I'll share with June, not you.

I love tres leches cake. Maybe I could stop by for a quick visit. It doesn't need to turn into anything. I'm grinning like a fool and read their messages a few times before I reply.

Okay. I guess I can make an appearance for cake. ☺

JAKE: I retract my previous message. Coming over IS the smartest choice.

RYAN:

LACHY: See you soon, lass.

I don't agree with Jake. Going to see them isn't the smartest choice, but it's the *best* choice.

CHAPTER 38
JUNE

take the stairs because I'm too anxious to wait for the elevator. When I reach their floor, I see they left their door partially open. My stomach is getting tight, and jittery energy is coursing through my veins. I wonder if I'll ever stop feeling nervous around them. It's fine when I know sex isn't likely to happen, but I know very well I'm not coming over for only cake. Or maybe I am. The song "Cake By The Ocean" by DNCE plays in my head.

I should have gone to bed. It's the sensible choice, but when it comes to these boys, I can't resist them.

"Hello?" I call out as I enter.

The main lights are off, but the TV is on, and there's some illumination coming from the kitchen counter lights. No sign of the boys though. What are they up to?

I keep walking when suddenly, Lachy jumps from a

dark corner and wraps his arms around my waist. "Boo!"

My heart jumps up to my throat, and naturally, I screech, "H-E-double hockey sticks!"

He laughs. "H-E-double hockey sticks?"

"You scared me to death." I press my hand over my chest. "Jesus."

"I couldn't resist."

"I told Lachy it was a stupid idea," Ryan says from behind us. "Sorry, Peaches."

Lachy is still holding me, so all I can do is look over my shoulder. Ryan and Jake are now standing near the kitchen.

"It's okay." I turn to Lachy. "But be warned, there *will* be payback."

His brows arch, followed by a slow and sensual grin that tugs the corners of his lips. "I can't wait."

He surprises me when he leans down and kisses me. It's the first time he's done so in front of Ryan and Jake after our hotel room adventure. My heart is thundering now for different reasons. I surrender to his kiss, and to the yearning that's been consuming me since these boys came into my life.

A throat clearing snaps me out of the haze, and heat spreads across my cheeks.

I pull back, stepping away from Lachy's warm embrace. "Where's the cake?"

"In the fridge." Ryan walks to the kitchen, and I

follow him, very much aware of Jake's and Lachy's gazes branding me.

Ryan sets the luscious cake on the counter, and my mouth waters. I'm glad I didn't order dessert at the restaurant.

"That looks so good," I say.

"Not as good as you," Jake whispers in my ear in a voice as smooth as whiskey poured over ice. He's behind me, and the proximity sends chills of desire down my spine.

"Thanks," I murmur.

Ryan is smiling like a fiend when he asks, "How big?"

I blink fast. "What?"

He has the cake cutter hovering over his creation. "How much cake do you want, Peaches?"

"Oh, a small piece, please. Too much sugar before bed will keep me up all night."

He chuckles, and I close my eyes for a second, realizing the double entendre.

"There you go." He slides the plate to me with a very large piece of cake on it.

My eyes widen. "You call this small?"

"Trust me. You'll lick the plate."

Jake moves away from me but doesn't go far. Lachy is also hovering nearby, and they're all watching me. "You're not going to eat?"

"We're fine watching you." Ryan smiles.

I put my hands on my hips and glower at the trio. "Oh heck no. There's no chance I'll eat cake alone while you watch. Now everyone get a piece and join me in the living room."

I grab my plate and stride away from the kitchen. I could have gone to the dining table, which would be more practical, but then I'd have to choose a chair, and I'd be far away from one of the boys. So the couch it is.

Belatedly, it dawns on me that maybe they don't like food in the living room, but then I remember they're guys. Of course they eat while watching TV.

"Don't you love when June is bossy, lads?" Lachy asks.

I look at them with my brow raised.

"Yes, very much so." Jake keeps his piercing eyes trained on me, and I feel the intensity of that heated gaze down to my core.

I can't eat cake alone for two reasons. One, I'd feel self-conscious stuffing my face while three gorgeous men watch me. And two, it'd be impossible to enjoy the dessert if desire is making me melt.

Ryan serves his roommates cake, then gets a plate for himself too before everyone joins me.

Jake and Lachy sit on either side of me, and Ryan, being the last to arrive, sits on the floor right in front of me. Now I'm surrounded by them, and it feels intimate and cozy like we've been doing this for years. The feeling is completely foreign to me. I thought I had that with Bill, but experiencing the real deal for the first time, I understand now that I'd been projecting.

Now would be a good time to ask what exactly we're doing, but fear makes me tongue-tied. I take a bite of the cake instead… and moan out loud.

Ryan looks at me. "Is that your seal of approval?"

I cover my half-full mouth so I can reply. "Are you kidding me? This is delicious. The best tres leches cake I've ever eaten."

He puffs up his chest and smiles proudly. "Thank you, Peaches."

I forget the boys for a moment and focus solely on the cake. It gets better with every bite. The sweetness is just enough, and combined with the moisture and the hint of coconut on my tongue, it's divine. Ryan was right, I could lick the plate.

When I look up, I find all of them staring. "What?"

"You really like cake." Jake laughs.

I notice none of them have touched theirs. In the end, I did stuff my face in front of them. My cheeks are so hot, I need to put ice on them. "Not fair. You just sat there and watched me eat."

"Och, and what sight it was, lass." Lachy reaches toward my face. "You have a little bit here." He wipes cake from the corner of my mouth, which should embarrass me more, but his blue eyes are pure fire, and all I can think about is the need to eat more cake, but off his body.

I grab his wrist and suck his thumb into my mouth. My plate disappears from my lap, and then Ryan's hands are on my thighs. Damn it. Why the hell didn't I change out of my jeans? Jake pushes my hair to the side and licks my neck. Goose bumps form everywhere.

I release Lachy's thumb and turn my face toward Jake. His mouth finds mine in an instant, and his tongue is hungry, as if *I'm* the dessert.

He pulls back, but his gaze remains glued to my lips. Lachy won't be denied though. He pinches my chin and turns me toward him so he can savor me too. Meanwhile, Ryan runs his fingers up my thigh and under my shirt. I'm still kissing Lachy when Ryan licks my stomach.

Breathing becomes difficult, all thanks to the way my heart is beating at a hundred miles per hour.

Lachy leans back and caresses the swell of my breasts with a feather-like touch. "Your shirt is lovely, lass, but your tits are better."

I sigh. "I know."

"Let's see them. I'm having withdrawals." Ryan unhooks every snap on the front, then parts the fabric. At least my top was a good choice.

"I know how I want to eat my dessert." Lachy breaks off a piece of the cake and smears it over my right breast.

The coldness makes my nipple as hard as a pebble. I gasp when he eats the cake off me. Ryan does the same, and now both are licking my breasts. I throw my head back, arching my neck, then Jake smears his cake over the sensitive skin. When all the cake is gone from me, they ease back.

"We need to get you out of your clothes, Peaches," Ryan says in a husky tone.

"Agreed."

I jump to my feet and shrug off my top, which was still hanging around my arms, and then unbutton my jeans. Ryan removes my shoes one by one, then peels my jeans off, along with my underwear. He looks up. "So stunning."

Smiling, I run my fingers through his hair. I should say something, but I can't find the words.

Jake runs his fingers across the base of my spine. "She *is* stunning. A masterpiece."

"You didn't finish your dessert yet," I reply.

God, why can't I say something sexy for a change?

Lachy grins. "No, we didn't."

He exchanges glances with Ryan and Jake, and it's like they share a secret message. My stomach coils in anticipation. Suddenly, Ryan bends his knee and lifts me in his arms.

"What are you doing?" I ask.

"Like you said, we didn't finish our dessert yet." He walks to the dining room, followed by Jake and Lachy.

Jake has all the plates of cake, and Lachy brings a

thick blanket and a couple pillows, which he uses to cover the dining table.

"What's going on?"

Ryan lays me on the table, sporting a cheeky grin. "It turns out the best way to eat tres leches cake is off you. Now spread wide, beautiful."

My chest is heaving. This is perhaps the hottest thing I'm about to do besides sleeping with three men at the same time. I do as he asks and spread my legs. With eyes blazing and locked on mine, he smears cake over my pubic bone. I'm glad I had a full Brazilian wax the other day.

My head is propped up by the pillows, and I hold his stare when he brings his mouth down and his tongue darts out to lick a piece of cake off me. My clit throbs, making me gasp. "Ryan..."

I'm so turned on that I could probably climax without being touched anywhere else.

"Peaches..." He digs his fingers into my inner thighs, spreading them farther apart, and runs his tongue down until he finds my clit. My hips would have buckled if Ryan wasn't holding me in place.

Jake holds his plate over my stomach, drawing my attention to him. As if daring me to stop him, he tilts it over slowly, and juices from the cake drip down on me, cool and sticky. He sets the plate aside before bending over to lick the sweetness off my skin. Ryan keeps working my clit, teasing it with side-to-side strokes. I'm completely losing my mind already. I never knew how many different types of pleasure I could feel.

"You look so delicious, lass." Lachy smears a little bit of cake over my lips, then leans down to kiss me. His tongue is slow and sensuous. He's really taking the time to savor me.

He covers my left breast with his big, calloused hand and kneads it carefully as he kisses me. I'm unraveling quickly, and when Jake moves up a bit and sucks my right nipple into his mouth, I lose it. My entire body quakes as wisps of desire spread through my body like wildfire. Lachy's kiss deepens, Jake sucks my nipple harder, and Ryan is fucking me now with his fingers. I'm not even sure I can keep track of all the delicious things they're doing to me.

I'm soaring high, uncaring what will happen to me when I come crashing down. That's tomorrow's problem. Tonight, all that matters is how happy these men make me.

CHAPTER 39
JUNE

My resolution to skip the boys' game tonight went up in flames after the cake-eating fiesta last night. I arrive at the arena late on purpose and miss the warm-up to avoid having a lot of idle time for conversation. But my seat is in the same row as the WAGs, so I don't escape the interrogation like I'd hoped.

"June, your life is like a fairytale," Maya, Banksy's wife, tells me. She's a petite and bubbly brunette, cute as a button. I liked her instantly.

"No, it's a romantic comedy," Fiona, Ian's fiancée, pipes up. "Jake, the bad boy captain, swooping in to save the day. I knew he had a romantic side to him."

"Uh, we're just friends," I remind them.

I don't want anyone thinking I'm Jake's girlfriend,

because I don't know if that's true. I'm not even sure if I want a boyfriend…or three.

"I was actually surprised," Wendy pipes up. "But I'm happy for you, even if you're only friends."

Somehow, I get the sense she doesn't mean it. I'm not sure why, but I don't get good vibes from her. Maybe it's because she's cold, and she stares at me as if trying to read my mind.

"Oh my God. You're not going to believe who was spotted making their way to the VIP area," Maya says while staring at her phone.

"Who?" Fiona leans closer to peek at Maya's screen.

"Lorena Pearson."

"No way!" Now Fiona scrolls through her phone as well.

Wendy chuckles. "That's ballsy."

"Who's Lorena Pearson?" I ask.

Maya looks at me, her eyes showing a glint of pity now. "Lachy's ex-fiancée."

My heart clenches painfully. Proverbial dagger, straight into it. Lachy was engaged?

"When was he engaged?" I ask, trying to sound nonchalant.

"Last year. They were only engaged for a few months before he broke things off," Fiona answers.

Wendy snorts. "Broke things off, my ass. Pictures of Lorena making out with one of her European fuck boys made it to the tabloids, and she wouldn't answer Lachy's calls. I say *she* ended things."

Oh no. Poor Lachy. What kind of vile human being would betray him like that?

"Yes, it was awful. And right in the middle of the playoffs," Maya adds. "Fucking bitch."

My brows shoot to the heavens, and she sees my reaction. "Sorry. I adore Lachy, and he didn't deserve to get his heart shredded to pieces like that."

"I agree," I say, and stare at the ice.

The game is about to start, but my mind is far away. I'm tempted to look up Lorena Pearson on my phone, but I sense Wendy watching me like a hawk. I'm trying my best to keep my emotions bottled up, but I'm terrible at it. I hope she can't tell I'm consumed with retroactive jealousy. We all have a past, but why does Lachy's hurt so much?

LACHLAN

The first period ended with no goal for either team. The Miami Lions are one of the best, and we're evenly matched. But I'm feeling good about our defense. We just need our playmakers to do their magic. I'm the last one to make my way into the tunnel but stop in my tracks when I hear someone mention Lorena. I'm tense in an instant. I haven't thought about her in a while, but for months after I discovered her betrayal, I could barely function outside the crease. The fact that it happened during playoffs saved me from spiraling into a dark place. Hockey kept me distracted.

I turn, looking for the person who said her name out loud. I spot two of Melissa's interns. They're both glued to their phones and don't realize I'm nearby. I should ignore them, but I walk over instead.

"What did you say?" I ask.

Both look up from their phones and widen their eyes.

"Oh, nothing," the lad replies.

"Nothing my arse. Go on, out with it already."

They trade a look, but it's the lass who replies, "Lorena Pearson is here with her new boyfriend."

I don't move. I don't even blink as I process the news.

"Lachy, what are you doing standing there like a statue?" Ryan asks.

"Nothing. Not a bloody thing." I turn around and stride to the dressing room.

Ryan runs after me. "You heard, didn't you?"

I grunt in response.

"Are you gonna be all right?"

I stop suddenly and glare at him. "What are you implying?"

He steps back. "It was just a question. Don't need to bite my head off."

"I'm not going to fucking crumble, if that's what yer worried about." I push the dressing room door open and find my seat.

I'm surprised that Lorena would come to a Titans game after what she did. There isn't a Titans fan that doesn't hate her guts. I also had my phase of loathing her, and it was a shock to hear her name after so long. I expected the anger to resurface, and that's why I walked away from the interns. I didn't want them to see my reaction. But I feel nothing, and it's freeing. I can move on without fear that I'm doing it only to get over that snake.

June's image comes to the forefront of my mind. I've known her for only a few days, but it doesn't matter. She's already left her mark on me. Now, I can't screw up.

CHAPTER 40
RYAN

Things in hockey happen so fast that you never know when a hit will fuck you up good. I know it this time as if it's happening in slow motion. I'm chasing the puck to a corner in the offensive zone, when Alex Kaminski, the Lions rookie D-man, comes barreling toward me as I'm turning. I don't have time to protect myself before I'm slammed hard against the boards on my right shoulder. I wind up on the ice.

The hit stuns me, and I don't get up right away. Honestly, I'm trying not to pass out from the pain. Motherfucker. From the corner of my eye, I see Malcolm is already on top of Kaminski, but the rookie looks like fucking Thor and is giving our veteran enforcer a run for his money. Soon it turns into an all-hands-on-deck brawl.

One of the referees checks on me. He's speaking, but

I can't hear a word he's saying over the buzzing in my ears. Hell. Did I hit my head too?

"Are you all right, son?" he asks, and I guess he's repeating the question.

"I'm not sure."

He helps me get up, and—slowly—I skate to the bench and go straight to the dressing room to get checked by the medical staff.

The pain is less intense, but it's still too much, and I can't move my right arm. I need assistance getting out of my jersey and protective gear.

"On a scale of one to ten, how badly does it hurt?"

"Seven." He touches my shoulder, and I wince. "Fuck. Eight or nine."

"Yeah. You aren't going back into the game tonight."

Hell. I know that look on his face. It's not only the rest of this game I'm missing. I'll be benched for the foreseeable future.

***

JUNE

I let out a loud gasp and jump from my seat when Ryan goes down. "Oh my God."

"Ouch. That was a hard one," Maya chimes in.

"There goes my man," Wendy says with a smile

when her husband shoves the Lions player back, then throws a punch.

I don't know how she can be amused when Ryan is still down, and we don't know how badly hurt he is. The Lions guy locks Malcolm in a tight grip and punches his middle a few times. It's clear to me who's winning that fight. Wendy's smug grin turns into a grimace. I should feel bad about it, but I don't. I like most people, but when I don't vibe with someone, I really don't.

"Ryan's getting up now," Fiona pipes up.

The crowd claps, but I remain frozen like a statue as I watch Ryan skate toward the bench with his chin dipped low. I can't see his face thanks to the helmet, and I hope he's not in too much pain.

"Jesus, now everyone wants to fight." Maya takes a large sip of her drink.

I spot her husband in the scrum, throwing punches, and I wonder how she can remain so calm. I hated seeing Jake get sucker punched the other night, and now I'm consumed with worry about Ryan. Maybe I'm not cut out to date hockey players.

"They need to eject that Lions brute," Wendy seethes.

The referees finally manage to separate her husband from the Lions' D-man, but they still trade insults. It takes another minute before all the fights end, and then the referee goes to the middle of the ice to dole out penalties.

Surprisingly, Kaminski doesn't get one, but Malcolm does for roughing.

"That's fucking bullshit!" Wendy shouts.

"As hard it was to watch, it was a clean hit," Fiona replies.

Wendy whips her face to her. "Shut up, Fiona. No one asked you."

Fiona arches her brows. "Jesus, take a chill pill."

Wendy gives her another scathing glance before exiting the row.

"You shouldn't have said anything," Maya chimes in. "You know how Wendy gets when her *man* doesn't win a fight."

"It's hard to watch though," I say, remembering how angry I got about Jake's fight in the last game.

"You'll get used to it." Fiona shrugs. "The boys love it."

"I'm not sure I'll come to a lot of games."

Both look at me as if I spoke sacrilege. "If you and Jake decide to be more than friends, you have to be here."

"Why?"

"First of all, to show your support, and second of all, to mark your territory. There are so many girls who would do anything to be in your shoes," Maya replies.

"For real. The ice girls for instance." Fiona wrinkles

her nose. "A bunch of whores just waiting for the opportunity to get in bed with a player regardless of their relationship status."

I don't like how this conversation turned into woman-on-woman bashing. Surely not all women who work for the team are interested in hooking up with a player.

"If my presence is needed all the time to prevent a boyfriend from cheating, then that relationship is not worth keeping."

"Shit. Sorry, June," Maya apologizes. "I forgot about your cheating ex."

I wait for the reminder of Bill's infidelity to hit me like a ton of bricks. But I feel nothing but annoyance at myself that he fooled me for so long.

"That's okay. I forgot about him too." I smile.

"You're right to keep Jake in the friend zone," Fiona adds. "He and his buddy Ryan can't be trusted."

I swallow the sudden lump in my throat. Fiona's comment was shitty, but I can't fault her for it. I don't know the guys, so perhaps she's not wrong. Maybe I'm just getting all their attention because I'm a shiny new toy. Once the novelty wears off, they'll move on, leaving me more broken than when they found me.

Despite the new dark cloud hanging over my head thanks to Fiona's comment, I still need to know how Ryan is doing. He didn't return to the game, which means, his injury must be serious. When the girls are distracted gossiping about someone I don't know, I text Melissa.

> Do you have news about Ryan?

Mercifully, it doesn't take long for her to reply.

> They don't want to make an official statement yet, so I can't give you details. But he's okay.

I let out a breath of relief, then decide to be bold and text him. I mean, he ate cake off my pussy last night. I don't expect him to get back to me until later, though.

> Hey, I hope you're doing okay. That was tough to watch.

I'm about to put my phone away, when it pings with his reply, making me giddy beyond measure.

"Who put that smile on your face, June?" Fiona asks, stretching her neck to try to read what's on my screen.

God, why is she so nosey?

I put the phone away, lest she sees Ryan's reply. I can't let any of the WAGs suspect I'm involved with three players. With the way there were bad-mouthing the girls that clean up the ice during the breaks, I'm pretty sure they'll call me a whore if they find out.

"No one." I get up from my seat. "I need to use the restroom."

"I can come with you if you want?" Maya offers.

Shit. I don't need to pee. I just want privacy to read Ryan's message for crying out loud. "Oh no. If you don't need to go, stay and watch the game."

She frowns. "Are you sure?"

"Gee, Maya. June is a big girl," Wendy retorts.

Ignoring the queen bee, I reply to Maya, "Yes. I'm sure."

I get out of the row and up the steps as fast as I can before Maya decides to follow me. I pull my phone from my purse only when I find a quiet spot.

I'm good, Peaches. Thanks for checking on me.

I was so worried.

I'm happy you were.

Butterfly rave happening in my stomach right now.

Meany. 😄

Not trying to be. I gotta go. Talk later?

You betcha.

I'm still smiling when I turn and come face to face with Wendy. I wince, spooked by her presence. Then I start to worry she was there the whole time and read my messages. "Shoot, you scared me."

"I thought you were going to the restroom."

"I was. I am."

She narrows her eyes. "Were you texting a new boyfriend?"

My cheeks warm in an instant. Fuck my open-book face. "What? No. I don't have a boyfriend."

"Uh. You had a new-love-smile on your face just now. I'd suspect you were texting Jake, but he's playing." She shrugs. "I guess I just imagined it. I'm getting a drink. Do you want anything?"

"No. I'm good. I still need to pee." I pivot and walk away quickly. My pulse is pounding in my ears.

Wendy is way too observant. I need to be careful around her.

CHAPTER 41
RYAN

"June's not replying to my texts." I stare at the phone as if it'll magically make her reply.

"She must have put it on silent, you eejit," Lachy grumbles from the shotgun seat. "It's late, and she didn't sleep much last night."

I frown. "Hey, there's no need to be aggressive."

"I'm not." Lachy turns to Jake. "How many painkillers did they give him?"

"Fuck if I know."

"I'm not high," I argue. "I feel fine." I shake my head, and the world spins. "Shit. Stop driving like a maniac, Jakey."

"Oh God. I won't bloody survive the evening," Lachy groans.

I ignore him and send another message to June.

> We're almost home. I can bake another tres leches cake.

"For fuck's sake. They turned Ryan into a horny teenager." Lachy shows his phone to Jake. "Look at all the emojis he sent June."

"Why are you reading my messages?" I retort. "They're private."

Jake laughs. "You've been using the group chat, dumbass."

"Oops." I chuckle. "Maybe that's why she's not answering. She's mad at one of you, not me."

"Why would she be angry with us? We've done nothing wrong." Lachy turns to me.

"I bet you never told June you were engaged before, and Jake let June hang out with the WAGs. God knows what those women told her."

Jake groans. "Fuck. I hate to admit it, but Ryan is right. That wasn't a smart move."

"I didn't tell June I was engaged before because it never came up," Lachy grumbles.

"I'm the only one who has come clean to her," I say proudly.

"About what?" Jake asks.

"Probably that he's a neat freak who pre-selects his outfits for the week." Lachy snickers.

"Laugh all you want. I don't see that as a flaw. Besides, that wasn't my confession." I put the phone away before I tell June I love her, which would be insane and not true, right?

Oh Jesus. Maybe I *am* a bit high.

"What was your confession then?" Jake looks at me through the rearview mirror.

"I told her about Mackenzie." My statement is followed by silence supreme. "Wow. I stunned both of you."

"You did. You must like June a lot," Jake finally replies.

"Like you and Lachy do?" I arch a brow that neither can see because it's fucking dark in the back seat.

They don't reply, and their silence makes me chuckle. "Who knew we would all fall for the hot middle-school teacher."

"That's not what's happening here," Jake retorts. "She's just different and exciting."

"You sound like me—in complete denial. Only Lachy has the balls to put himself out there. Too bad he did it first with that conniving bitch. Honestly, what did you ever see in Lorena Pearson?"

Lachy looks out the window. "We're not talking about her."

I shrug, forgetting that my shoulder is busted. "Ouch."

"Are you okay there?" Jake asks, concerned.

"I'll live. Man, that Kaminski is a menace on the ice. And they got two of them! I can't tell those twins apart."

"Alex Kaminski came to me after the game to ask about you," Jake pipes up.

My brows shoot up. "He did? That was unexpected."

"He's a good kid, and the hit wasn't dirty. It was just bad luck." Jake sounds almost proud. It takes a lot to impress the guy. Alex Kaminski must be special.

"If he's that good, maybe we can steal him from the Lions in a couple years," I say.

"Or trade Malcolm for him," Lachy adds.

"Dude! He had my back," I retort.

"But he doesn't have mine. He hasn't for a while. The last three goals that I let through were assisted by him."

True. Malcolm's defense line has been shit in the past few games. And if Lachy is complaining, it's worse than I thought.

My phone vibrates, making me forget the convo in an instant. It's a reply from June.

> You can't possibly be offering all that when you're injured. Unless you just want to watch me eat DOS leches.

Lachy laughs. "Bloody hell. I love this girl."

It's hard to tell if Lachy's reaction is just a figure of speech or if he really means it. But in my current doped-up state, I think I love her too.

CHAPTER 42
JUNE

Last night, it was hard to resist Ryan's invitation to come up to their apartment again. But I'm exhausted after last night's activities. He also needs to rest. I don't want to be responsible for getting him in worse shape. Plus the conversation with Maya and Fiona gave me a lot to think about. If I was able to remain completely detached, having more gang bangs wouldn't be a problem. But the giddiness I feel every time I think about all three of them is enough to make me afraid of my feelings. I don't want to be that girl who falls in love with the next guy—or three—she meets immediately after getting dumped by her ex.

Winston woke me up me early, for which I was thankful. I forgot to set my alarm, and if it weren't for him, I'd be late. He was quick doing his morning business, allowing me to leave for work early.

After ten minutes on the road, I receive a message from Jake, asking if I left already. This week they have away games, and they're leaving in a couple hours. They wanted to say goodbye in person.

Disappointment and guilt lodge in my heart. I've been so caught up in my own fears and insecurities that I forgot to check their schedule. I'm an idiot.

ME: Sorry, I had to leave early.

JAKE: That's okay. We'll see you when we get back.

RYAN: Not me. You can see me today after work, Peaches. 😉

LACHY: FYI. Ryan turns into a needy baby when he's hurt.

RYAN: Don't be a hater.

I'm smiling from ear to ear when I reply.

I don't mind playing nurse.

RYAN: In your face, Lachy.

LACHY: Don't laugh just yet, bawbag. This will be your doom.

I teach middle school. I'll survive needy Ryan.

JAKE: Ryan is Sheldon Cooper level.

Driving. Gotta go. Have a safe trip, boys.

I put the phone away before I get into a car wreck. I'm behaving badly by texting and driving. Proof that I can't make smart choices when it comes to those boys. The only way to avoid temptation is to find a new place to live, but that would be a dumb move financially. I need to save up, and these three months living rent free is the best way to do it.

Come on, June. You're a strong woman. You can have mind-blowing sex with the three yummy hockey players without falling in love.

I obsess about my predicament the entire way to work, and I'm still thinking about it as I head to the teacher's lounge to grab coffee. Katrina's already there. "Good morning. You're here early."

"Yeah. I like beating traffic whenever I can, and our morning routine ran as smooth as silk today." She blows on her coffee and watches me over the rim. "How's Ryan?"

"He's okay."

"I read he's benched and won't go to the away

games this week. Does that mean you'll be taking care of him?" She wiggles her eyebrows up and down.

Avoiding eye contact, I sit across from her with my coffee in hand. "Maybe. But... I'm a little worried."

"What's up, buttercup? Trouble in paradise already?"

"Not exactly. I met some of the WAGs last night, and they said something that's been bothering me."

Katrina sits straighter. "You'd better tell me if I have to come to the next game and put some bitches in their place."

The visual makes me laugh. Katrina would absolutely hate Wendy. "They didn't treat me badly. It's just... they said it's a good thing I'm only friends with Jake because he and Ryan can't be trusted."

She raises an eyebrow. "You told them you're only friends with Jake? Why?"

"Because that's what we are... sort of. Friends with benefits."

She rolls her eyes. "Whatever you say. Anyway, I wouldn't worry about their comment. It was bitchy, and I don't think they were looking out for you."

Frowning, I stare at my coffee. "Why would they diss the boys?"

"I don't know. Maybe there's bad blood between their partners and your guys, or they have a thing for Jake or Ryan."

"I didn't think about that."

Katrina smirks. "Of course you didn't. You're too innocent and pure. That's why you have me."

"I'm definitely not pure anymore," I reply, making Katrina laugh.

"Amen to that. But seriously, even if Jake and Ryan were players in the past, it doesn't mean they'll screw you over. Besides, those women didn't mention the goalie. Worst case scenario, you keep one."

I grimace. "Riiight. I found out Lachy was engaged last year."

Katrina's brows shoot up. "Oh. That's right. I remember reading something about it in a gossip magazine."

"You knew and you didn't tell me?" I shriek.

"It was a small article about someone I didn't know." She shrugs. "I glanced at it briefly last year, and immediately forgot. Sorry."

My shoulders slump. "It's okay. I don't know why it bothered me, finding out about his ex-fiancée. Everyone has a past."

"It bothered you because he didn't tell you, and you already have feelings for him."

I rest my forehead against the table. "Ugh. Don't tell me that. I can't have feelings for him. It's too soon."

"Girly, if I had been treated like a queen by three hunky hockey players, you bet your pretty face that I'd be head over heels in love right now."

I sit up straighter again. "I can't allow that to happen. You know how this is all going to end."

She frowns. "Why are you being so pessimistic? Don't let a bunch of strangers scare you from pursuing something that could be wonderful. Trust your gut and trust your guys."

I'm able to put my love-life troubles on ice during the day. My students deserve my full attention, and it's a busy day. On the way home, I'm beat, dying for a hot shower, but I'm also eager to see Ryan. I texted him when I had a moment during lunch, but he still hasn't replied. I hope he's okay. Unfortunately, I have to bake for our school's fundraiser, which is in two days. If I don't start tonight, I'll never finish in time.

Taped to the front door, I find a note from Ryan.

Hey, Peaches. Judging by your radio silence, I figured you were busy today, and probably the last thing you want is to take the doggo out for a walk. I took care of that for you. Come over if you feel like having a yummy dinner. I made more tres leches cake.

Your friendly neighbor,

Ryan.

I frown at first. What does he mean by radio silence? On cue, my phone pings several times. Hell. I bet he replied, but his messages didn't come through. I really need to change my cell phone network.

A slow grin unfurls on my lips, and my heart does somersaults inside my chest. If Ryan was still the player he was before, he wouldn't have gone to all this trouble, nor would he have shared something so personal with me. And I've already slept with him! I really shouldn't let the comments of people I just met get to me.

I walk into the apartment, and immediately, Winston comes running to greet me. Eros jumps on the kitchen counter and stares at me judgmentally.

"Come on. I don't look that bad." I set my bag on the dining room table and check my messages.

There are a few texts in the group chat from Jake and Lachy saying they've landed in Chicago, and a few messages from Ryan that he sent separately throughout the day.

> I'd love to cook dinner for you, Peaches.

> Come save me from my boredom.

> You must be busy. I'll talk to you when you get home.

I feel like an ass now for not replying to him sooner, not that it was my fault.

> Sorry. My messages didn't come through until now. Just got home. Thanks for walking Winston. I'll take a quick shower and come over.

I set the phone down, not expecting an immediate reply, but when my phone chimes, my heart skips a beat.

> Awesome. See you soon.

The butterflies in my stomach act as if they just drank an entire case of Red Bull. I forget all about baking those damn cupcakes and run to the shower. Not even when I was in high school and falling in love for the first time did I feel like this. Katrina was right. I never had a chance against these boys.

CHAPTER 43
RYAN

The pasta is cooking, and the porcini sauce is almost ready when June knocks on the door.

I try to ignore how my pulse seems to accelerate. "Come in."

"Hi, it smells fantastic in here. What are you cooking?"

Her voice is as sweet as her taste. Not hearing from her all day did a number on me. I've never experienced feeling insecure about a girl before. But the way she sounds so open and warm puts me at ease instantly.

"Fettuccini ai funghi. I hope you like mushrooms."

"Love them." She walks over holding two bottles of wine—red and white. "I didn't know what you were cooking, so I brought both options."

"You didn't need to bring anything, Peaches."

She sets the bottles on the kitchen island. "Nonsense.

I can't show up for dinner empty-handed, and you already have dessert covered."

I smile. "You have no idea."

Her cheeks turn bright red. "Do you need any help?"

"Nah, I'm good."

Her gaze focuses on the sling I have to wear. "How's your arm?"

"My arm is fine. The problem is my shoulder. I pulled a muscle."

"I'm not sure how all the WAGs can stand watching their partners getting hit like that. My heart stopped beating for a second."

I've had women say shit like that to me before, but only June sounds genuine. I can't help grinning. "Aw. You truly were worried about me."

"Of course I was. You didn't believe me?"

"Honestly, I was already medicated when you texted. My memory is a bit fuzzy. But I'm happy you care." I reply sincerely. I *am* happy, and it's a damn strange feeling when it's caused by a woman. "Come here. I want you to try this." I hold the spoon out and wait for her to walk over.

She stops next to me, smelling like the first day of spring. Her scent is fresh and floral without being sickly sweet. I feed her the sauce, not taking my eyes from hers. She holds my stare, and the moment becomes charged with electricity. If the food wasn't the type that demands to be consumed immediately, I'd fuck her right here over the counter.

"It's delicious," she breathes out.

"Good." My gaze drops to her lips, and I lean closer, but she steps away before I can kiss her.

"I can't stay long," she blurts out.

"Why not?" Disappointment laces my question. Maybe she *was* avoiding me earlier.

"I have to bake a million cupcakes for a school fundraiser."

Disappointment turns into delight. I beam, not believing my luck. There's nothing sexier than baking with someone you desperately want to fuck. "You've come to the right person. I'll help you."

Her brows arch. "Oh, no. I couldn't ask you to do that."

"You aren't. I'm offering. You know I love to bake. You don't want to deny an injured man, do you?"

Chuckling, she shakes her head. "Lay on the guilt trip, why don't you?"

"Hey, I gotta use all the arsenal at my disposal."

The sound of a text message chimes in the room. I glance at my phone quickly, but it wasn't mine. June is looking at her phone now with her brows furrowed.

"What's wrong, Peaches?"

She puts the phone back in her pocket. "Nothing."

Bullshit. One thing June can't do is lie. "I can tell it wasn't nothing. Is someone bothering you?"

Immediately I think that her ex is harassing her. It's a damn shame that scumbag wasn't around when we went to June's apartment.

She hunches her shoulders. "It was a text from Danika, the woman Bill was cheating on me with."

"What did she want? Please don't tell me she's begging you to take that piece of shit back."

"No. She's mad at me for going to the party with Jake, and then attending last night's game. I'm not even sure how she knows I was there last night."

"If you were hanging out with the WAGs, it was posted on their social media accounts. But how is that her damn business?"

June runs her fingers through her hair. "I think she's mad that I'm not crying in a dark room, moaning about losing Bill."

I narrow my eyes. "And you said that woman was your friend?"

She laughs in derision. "I know. Stupid, right?'

I turn off the stove and move closer. June swivels in her chair, tilting her face up. She's damn beautiful, but her looks aren't what's pulling me to her. It's her heart. She's the only woman who has ever truly wanted to know me. I'm unraveling, and I don't care.

Carefully, I run my fingers over her cheek. "Not stupid. Some people hide their true nature well."

"I guess." She looks at my mouth, and hell, I'm not letting her escape again.

Cupping her face, I shorten the distance between us and claim her sweet lips. June parts them with a sigh, setting my body aflame. I step closer, moving my hand to the back of her head and deepening the kiss. She wraps her arms around my waist, caging me in her space. Not that I ever want to leave.

The timer goes off, cutting our fun short. Reluctantly, I lean back. "Pasta is ready."

JUNE

"Are you sure you don't want my help cleaning up?"

"I'm sure." Ryan carries our dishes to the sink with one hand. "This should be quick. Then, we can start on your cupcakes."

I get up from my chair. "I'll go grab the ingredients."

He curls his lips into a crooked grin. "I have ingredients."

Oh, he's being sassy. So can I. With my hands on my lips, I ask, "Really? Do you also have baking cups and rainbow sprinkles?"

He rubs the back of his neck, looking adorably sheepish. "Eh... no."

I laugh. "All right, then. I'll be right back."

I zoom out of his apartment before I succumb to Ryan's charms and forget baking all together. He's been acting sweeter and more relaxed since he opened up to me. Maybe he's beginning to trust me. I don't take the elevator, instead opting for the stairs. I'm eager to get this chore over with so I can move on to sexy times. It's funny how I could go for weeks, even months, without thinking about sex when I was dating Bill. Now, I'm turned on every time I think about the guys, which is often.

I left the dry ingredients on the counter. I just need to pack everything and grab stuff from the fridge. I notice that Winston's water bowl is empty, so I grab it to fill it up first. But when I turn on the faucet, water sprays in all directions, drenching me in seconds.

"What the hell!"

I try to shut it off, but the damn thing is broken. I try to contain the spray with a dish towel, but it barely does a thing. I should have known something would go wrong. I went too long without any disasters in my life.

Winston runs over, and jumps excitedly, thinking this is all play. But all he's doing is making more of a mess. "No, Winston." I pick him up and put him in his crate. "I'll let you out soon. Promise."

I run back to the kitchen and drop into a crouch to check under the sink. The first order of business is to shut off the water supply. I locate the valve, but it's old and rusty, and it doesn't budge.

"Oh come *on*."

The hissing from the water jet gets louder. That

towel is about to give. I probably didn't tie it hard enough.

"Peaches, I came to ask—" Ryan says from the front door.

"Help!"

"Oh shit." He runs over and drops next to me. "Scooch. Let me shut off the water."

"I was trying, but it's stuck."

Naturally, Ryan and his bulging muscles have no problem turning the valve. "There. Done."

I spring to my feet. "What a mess. I need to clean this up."

He unfurls from his crouch and stares at me, sporting a grin.

"What?" I ask.

Holding my stare, he runs his fingertips across my collarbone, eliciting a throaty moan from me. "Your clothes are soaked through."

I'm wearing a white button-down shirt that's now see-through. Okay. I'm no longer thinking about mopping the floor. "My clothes aren't the only things that are wet."

He reaches for the back of my head and twists a lock of my hair around his fist. But instead of kissing me as I thought he would, he tilts my head back and runs his hot tongue over the column of my neck.

"Ryan..."

He keeps going south over the fabric until he finds

my nipple and sucks it into his mouth, hard. My legs turn into jelly, and my knees almost buckle. Carefully, I grab his arms, needing the support to stay upright. Ryan takes my hand and guides it to his rock-hard erection while giving attention to my nipple.

"Feel how hard I am for you already, Peaches," he whispers against my feverish skin.

"I want to taste you, Ryan." I step back and, keeping eye contact, drop to my knees.

I unzip his pants, loving how smoldering his gaze is. He grabs my hair again, and when I suck his cock into my mouth, he tugs a little.

"Peaches, I love your mouth on me."

I take my time savoring Ryan, sucking his length until it hits the back of my throat, and toying with the sensitive head. He grunts, pulling my hair harder until it hurts. The pain spurs me on. He starts to move, thrusting his hips forward.

"Fuck, Peaches. You suck me so good."

I'm lost in the moment, getting more and more aroused by watching Ryan lose control. His lips are parted, and his eyes are hooded.

"Fuck, Peaches," Mrs. Carpenter's parrot says suddenly, and I freeze.

Ryan whips his face to the parrot's cage. "Oh no."

I release his cock and turn, remembering the how-*you*-doin' incident. "Is he going to start repeating that nonstop too?"

"Well, he's a parrot." He laughs.

"Fuck, Peaches," the parrot repeats, making Ryan laugh harder.

I get up. "Don't laugh. This is mortifying."

Ryan walks to the kitchen counter and grabs something from my ingredient bag. He turns, holding a container of icing and smiling like a fiend. "I have an idea."

My brows shoot to the heavens. "What? Kill the bird by feeding it icing?"

He shakes his head. "*Tsk.* No, I'm the one who's in the mood for something sweet again."

"Oh."

His cock is still hard despite the interruption, and suddenly I want to lick icing from it. "Not here. Let's go back to your apartment."

"Too far." He takes my hand and steers me into the master bedroom. "I've never been in Mrs. Carpenter's room."

"Thank fuck you haven't." I laugh.

He turns me around, bringing me flat against his body to kiss me deeply. I melt against his hard frame, loving how powerful and possessive he is. I consider myself a feminist, but in this moment, I don't care about any of that.

Ryan steps back, his eyes burning with desire, then he removes his sling. "Time to get you out of these wet clothes."

Unexpectedly, he yanks the sides apart, popping several buttons off. "Ryan!"

"Sorry, Peaches. I'm hungry."

He kisses me hard, leaning forward till we both fall on the mattress. His mouth is ravenous, and his tongue is relentless, trailing a fiery path over my body, burning me, branding me. The same frenzy sweeps over me, and all I want is to rip off his clothes and feel his skin against mine. But I'm worried about his shoulder. Now that the sling is off, I have to be even more careful. Our clothes finally come off, and then Ryan's cock is pressing against my clit.

I grab a fistful of his hair and yank it back, forcing him to look at me. "I need you now."

"Do you have a condom, Peaches?"

I arch a brow. "You don't have one in your pocket?"

He chuckles. "I wasn't expecting to find you wet and ready for me."

"Oh my God." I laugh.

He kisses the crook of my neck, then whispers in my ear. "I love the sound of your laughter, beautiful."

Goose bumps spread over my skin, and my heart pumps at breakneck speed, propelled by an insatiable craving. I'm already addicted to this man even though this is only our third time together. I'm addicted to all of them, like a sexually deprived deviant.

"Condoms are in the bathroom under the sink."

Ryan jumps out of bed like a ninja, and while he's

getting a condom, I open the can of icing and scoop a dollop onto my fingers.

"You got into the icing without me?" He returns to the bed with the whole box of condoms.

"I couldn't resist." I smear some over his chest, then lick it off.

He groans. "Peaches..."

With icing coating my tongue, I kiss him hard. He grabs my ass, digging his fingers into my skin possessively. His erection presses against my belly, hard and smooth. Ryan matches my passion stroke for stroke before pulling back and gripping my wrist. He keeps his heated gaze glued to mine while he sucks my fingers into his mouth. I hold his stare, lost in his eyes. My heart is overflowing with emotion, and it isn't only lust. Trying to stop what's happening to me would be like trying to stop the tide. Impossible.

I reach for the box of condoms and take one out while maintaining eye contact.

"Put it on, Peaches."

I rip the packet with my teeth and then lean back to roll the condom down his dick. The moment protection is in place, he lies down and makes me sit astride him. "You're riding me tonight, gorgeous. I want to see your lovely tits bounce as you move."

I bet the visual is hot as hell for him, but with me on top, it's probably easier on his shoulder too. "I always wanted to be a cowgirl."

He rewards me with a crooked grin. "Is that so?"

I press my palm over his chest, so I don't fall off. That would be embarrassing. My pussy is slick with arousal, making it easy to impale myself on Ryan's cock. The stretch and the sensation of being filled by him is glorious.

Closing my eyes, I let out a throaty moan, "Ryan..."

Ryan hisses. "Peaches... you're so fucking tight."

I open my eyes and begin to move, slowly at first. I want to get used to his girth. I can't believe he fucked my ass and I survived. His fingers dig into my hips, and he begins to move as well, pistoning into me every time I come down. The synchronized movements make me see stars when he hits my special spot. Ryan not having a piercing like Jake isn't making a damn bit of difference. He's more than capable of destroying my pussy.

"God, you're beautiful." He sits up suddenly and sucks one of my nipples into his mouth.

I gasp, loving this new layer of pleasure. We're moving faster now. Ryan keeps one arm looped around my waist while I ride his cock as hard as I can. I can feel him getting harder inside of me, and I'm winding up tighter and tighter, ready to explode.

He releases my nipple to kiss me as if he's dying and I'm his only salvation. I grab his hair, pulling at the strands. I'm gasping for air when the orgasm hits like a hurricane, sending me spinning out of control.

Ryan keeps moving faster and faster, and maybe it's

another minute before he groans against my mouth, and his dick pulses inside of me. His entire body shakes, joining mine in the frisson.

Breathing hard, he says, "I'm never happy when I have to sit out games. But I am now."

My heart overflows with emotion. I'm still flying high, caught in post-orgasm bliss. No one could fault me if I mistake my reaction for falling in love.

CHAPTER 44
JUNE

hanks to Ryan's help, we were able to bake all the cupcakes I needed last night, and all that's left for me to do today is add the frosting.

By the time the end of the school day rolls around, I'm begging for mercy. I got my period, and the first day is always brutal. I'm not sure how I was able to drive home, but as I trudge out of the elevator, the pain is so intense that I'm afraid I might pass out.

Feeling woozy, I stick my hand in my purse, searching for the apartment key. But the bugger isn't in the small pocket, which means I have to empty the whole purse to find it. I press my back against the wall and slide down until my butt meets the floor.

As all the contents spill out of my purse, I wince in disgust. There's so much crap in there that I don't need, such as old receipts that have already faded, pens that probably don't work, and an assortment of hair ties that I can never find when I need them.

My phone rings, and when I see Bill's name flashing on the screen, it makes me even sicker. Usually, I'd reject the call, but I don't have the energy to do that. I let it ring until it goes to voicemail. Nothing good will come of that conversation. Maybe he wants to complain about my social life like his new girlfriend did. Fuckers. They deserve each other.

The elevator door opens again, and Ryan steps out, looking like a male model who just came off the runway. "Peaches! What are you doing on the floor?"

I tilt my head back, resting it against the wall. "I'm trying to find my key."

"You look pale. Are you sick?" He crouches in front of me and touches my forehead.

"I don't have a fever. I got my period, and it's usually rough on the first day."

I expect Ryan to make a face—Bill hated when I mentioned anything related to what he called women's problems. But Ryan looks concerned.

"What can I do?"

"Help me find the key?"

He glances at the mess I created in front of me and fishes out the key from under my small notebook. "Here. Do you wanna come to my place instead? I can make you chicken soup."

I laugh despite the pain. "I don't think I can eat anything right now."

"Okay."

The idea of being in my apartment alone and in misery doesn't appeal to me though. I hate feeling weak and needy, but he offered.

"I'll come to your place. But I need to check on the pets first. Also, the cupcakes are in your fridge, and we need to decorate them."

"Don't worry about the pets or the cupcakes. I'll take care of them." Ryan puts all my things back in my purse, then helps me to my feet. "Can you walk?"

"Yeah. Why? Did you want to carry me?" I smirk, trying to distract myself from how awful I feel.

"It wouldn't be a chore if it weren't for my shoulder." He smiles back, keeping my hand firmly clasped in his.

I shake my head. "You're sweet, Ryan."

He chuckles. "That's new."

"What is?"

"I've never been called sweet before."

I tilt my head, narrowing my eyes. "Never?"

He shrugs with his good shoulder. "No. Maybe because I'm an ass to most people."

"I don't believe that."

He toys with a strand of my hair. "Believe me, Peaches. I'm only sweet with you."

Be still my heart. Not even my current wretched state can prevent me from feeling all warm and fuzzy inside.

"Why?" I look into his eyes. I'm not looking for a declaration of eternal love. I'm not insane enough to expect that from any of them. But I'm curious.

He holds my stare for a moment, then grins. "You bring out the best in me, I guess."

I don't know how to respond to that. I always believed the core of every successful relationship was the ability to bring out the best in the other person. Ryan might not realize how romantic he sounds.

I'm still tongue tied when we arrive at his apartment, but now it has more to do with excruciating cramps than anything else. I make a beeline for the couch and collapse there as if this were my place. I suppose I've achieved a new level of intimacy with him, now that I've fucked his brains out a few times.

"How are you feeling?" He walks over.

"Lousy. I'm in a lot of pain."

"Do you take anything?"

"I already did, but it barely makes a difference. I'm used to suffering through."

"I don't accept that. Hold on."

I watch him leave until I can't see him anymore. I'd have to lean up on my elbows to find out where he's going, but I don't have the strength. I just close my eyes and try to think of something nice.

A few minutes later, I sense Ryan's return and open

my eyes again. He has a hot water bottle and a steamy mug in his hands.

"What's in the mug?"

"Chamomile tea. I read online that it can help. This too." He lifts the bottle.

Maybe it's the hormones screwing with my emotions, but tears fill my eyes. "Thank you."

"Can I?" He motions to help me with the bottle.

Even though we've slept together already, this gesture feels more intimate. "Yes," I croak.

Ryan unbuttons my jeans and pulls the zipper down before placing the hot water bottle on my belly. I sigh.

"Is it too hot?"

"No. It's perfect."

"You should drink the tea while it's hot."

"In a moment. I'm quite comfortable right now."

"Okay, Peaches. I'll go check on the pets, then start on the cupcake decorating. Any instructions?"

"No. I trust you."

I don't mean only with the cupcakes. I know now I can trust him with my heart too.

I fell asleep on Ryan's couch last night, but when I wake up in the morning, I'm in a satin-sheet-covered bed. I vaguely remember stumbling here with him. It's pitch black in the room, and that gives me a mini panic attack. I roll onto my back and collide with a warm body.

"Good morning, Peaches," Ryan whispers in a raspy voice, curling his arm around my waist.

I'm hyperventilating. I can't think straight with him so close to me. "How do you know it's morning?"

"My body knows." He presses his hard-on against my leg, making my entire being buzz with desire.

I'm not feeling in the least bit sexy though, and I need to get ready for work. "What time is it?"

"Probably before six." He moves, and a moment later there's a humming in the room, and a bit of light penetrates the darkness. He opened the shades.

"I should get going or I'll be late for work."

He holds me tighter, bringing his nose to the crook of my neck. "Don't go yet."

I melt against his body, but my mind is far from relaxed. "You know there's no chance we'll have sex right now."

"Do you think that's what I have in mind?"

"Uh... your hard cock pressed against my leg tells me that."

He snickers. "I can't help my body's reaction to you, beautiful. But don't worry, I respect your boundaries. I just want to snuggle for a little bit."

Oh God. Now my heart and the butterflies in my stomach are having a contest to see who can move faster.

"Okay." I close my eyes and enjoy the heat coming from Ryan's body, and the sense of peace that washes over me. "This feels nice."

"I know. I never understood why people like it."

"You never snuggled with anyone before?"

"Nope. I never felt the desire to do so before you."

As much as I want to bask in his words, the dark seed of doubt sprouts in my head. Instead of melting into Ryan's arms, I tense. I curse those WAGS for making me doubt my relationship with my guys.

"What's wrong, Peaches?"

"It's nothing."

He rolls on top of me and looks into my eyes. "You can tell me."

"Why are you being so sweet to me?"

Ryan's brows scrunch together. "You don't want me to be?"

"Of course I do, but... why? When we first met, I thought you were a one-night-stand kind of guy."

He caresses my cheek, giving me goose bumps. "I thought I was too."

I can't help how my heart takes off at breakneck speed.

"But I like spending time with you. You are... easy."

"What?"

His eyes widen, then he shakes his head. "No! I didn't mean it in a bad way. I meant..." He rolls off me and stares at the ceiling. "God, I'm fucking it up already."

"Did you mean it like the Lionel Richie song?"

He looks at me. "Well, sort of. I know that song is about a dude's relief over a break-up, but the sentiment is the same, only caused by the opposite. Being with you is easy."

My heart is fluttering, pumping giddiness through my body. "'Easy' is one of my favorite songs."

A slow smile unfurls on his handsome face. "Mine too, even though it's bittersweet. My dad used to play it on the guitar all the time. I think he secretly wished he could end his unhappy marriage and feel okay about it. He tried to teach me how to play, but I wasn't very good at it."

"Nonsense. I'm sure you could be very good."

Ryan's eyes seem to twinkle with amusement. "Once a teacher, always a teacher."

"That's right." I grin.

He watches me for a moment, then rolls out of bed. I lean on my forearms to see what he's up to. He retrieves an acoustic guitar from a mount in the corner of his room and returns to bed.

"You know how Lachy's most treasured possession is his blankie? Well, this is mine. My dad's old guitar. He gave it to me a month before he passed." He stares affectionately at the instrument and then strums the cords.

I throw my legs off the bed and sit up next to him. "If you want, I could teach you."

He whips his face to mine, then offers me the guitar. "I think I'd rather listen to you play."

"What? Now?"

He nods. "Yeah. Any song you'd like."

I take the guitar from his hands and adjust the strings. There are so many songs I could play for him, but now I have "Easy" on my mind. As I start the song, it's a like a weight is lifted off my shoulders. My decade-long relationship has ended in the most spectacular way, and I feel as light as a feather. I never knew what I was missing until I met Ryan, Lachy, and Jake. My boys.

CHAPTER 45
JUNE

I honestly didn't think I'd hear much from Lachy and Jake while they were away, but the influx of messages in the group chat kicks up a notch when I'm already at work. Class starts in fifteen minutes, so I have time to check them.

LACHY: Good morning, lass. Did you sleep well?

I slept like a baby.

RYAN: I can vouch for that 😁

Oh my God. He's so bad. But I can't help smiling. He's bad in the best possible way.

JAKE: Taking advantage of our absence, I see.

RYAN: No, keeping our girl satisfied.

I can't believe he said that. I'm blushing furiously, and some of my students are starting to arrive. Let's see if I can rescue this conversation from the gutter.

I'm sure I'll gain a few pounds if you keep it up.

JAKE: You'd still be gorgeous.

RYAN: Does that mean no more tres leches cake? 😊

I rest my forehead in my hand. I should have known better. Of course food will always bring sex to the fore-front of our minds after the tres leches fiesta.

I'll never say no to that.

JAKE: Now I want cake.

LACHY: Me too.

I'm distracted, reliving that hot evening, when Louis approaches my desk. "Are you okay, Ms. Summers?"

I lift my face quickly, turning my phone so the screen isn't visible. "Yes, I'm fine."

"Oh, okay. I thought you had a headache or something. My mom always has those, especially after she fights with my dad."

I frown, forgetting my embarrassment. "Does that still happen a lot?"

He nods. "Yeah. He comes by the house often, even though he's not supposed to. I think he wants to move back. I'm not sure why she won't let him. I want to be a family again."

"Oh sweety, I'm sure you do. But sometimes things aren't as simple as we want them to be."

He looks down. "I know. That's what my grandpa says."

The first bell rings, ending the conversation. Louis slumps his shoulders and returns to his seat. It breaks my heart to see him like that.

My phone vibrates with another incoming message. Oops. I forgot about the boys.

RYAN: Are you still with us, Peaches?

Sorry. A student needed me. Class is about to start. Talk later.

I want to include a heart emoji, but in my hurry to type, I end up sending a cute sticker of a pussy cat saying *I love you*.

Shit. I spend precious seconds freaking out instead of trying to unsend the message, and then it's too late. They all read it.

Kill me now.

"Why didn't you unsend the text?" Katrina asks me after I tell her about the I-love-you sticker fiasco.

"What would be the point? They'd already seen it." I take a bite of my sandwich even though I'm not hungry.

We're having lunch in my classroom so we can talk freely about my love life.

"And they haven't texted you back?"

I grimace. "I was too afraid to check."

She narrows her eyes, then stretches out her hand. "Hand over the phone. Right now."

"Ugh. Fine. I'll check." A bubble of laughter goes up my throat when I see the messages from them. "They texted me back."

"See? You were worrying about nothing. What did they say?"

I turn my phone so she can see for herself all the emojis and cute stickers they used. Katrina laughs. "Boys."

"This probably means they didn't take my oops text seriously, right?"

She switches her attention to her plate and creates a

perfect bite of salad with her fork. "Obviously. It was clearly a case of fat thumb."

"Yeah. I should reply." I stare at my phone, biting my lower lip. When nothing witty comes to mind, I glance at Katrina. "What should I say?"

She shrugs. "I don't know. You seem to have a thing for food. Talk about that."

I frown. "It always ends up becoming dirty."

She smirks. "There's nothing wrong with that."

I shake my head. "You're such a bad influence."

She presses her hand against her chest. "*I'm* a bad influence? Says the girl getting railed by three hunky hockey players."

Ignoring her theatrics, I type a reply.

> I want to bake you my favorite dessert when you come back.

> LACHY: Oh, what is it?

> It'll be a surprise.

> JAKE: I love surprises, and from you, even better.

I smile, forgetting that Katrina is sitting across from me and watching me like a hawk.

"Aww, look at that face. You're so far gone for those boys, June."

I look up. "I know. And it terrifies me."

Jake and Lachy stopped messaging me after lunch. They were probably getting ready for their game tonight. But Ryan texted me a few times, first to give me an update on the pets—he volunteered to check on them, since he was bored. And then to invite me to watch the Titans game with him.

The game is early, so I don't have much time to get ready. I jump into the shower, make sure all the pets are good, and as I'm about to walk out of the apartment, I text him.

I'm coming over now. I'm bringing snacks.

Hey, something came up. Rain check?

I stop in my tracks and stare at my phone, waiting for him to say he's joking. But when no follow up text follows, my stomach dips. I'm disappointed, but I'm a bit worried too.

Is everything okay?

Yep. Talk tomorrow.

Wow, that was cold. A lump forms in my throat, and

my eyes prickle. I'm so confused. Did I freak him out with that accidental I-love-you sticker? No, that doesn't make any sense. All his messages afterward were normal. I have no idea what to think, but I can't remain rooted to the floor.

I turn around and put the bags with the snacks back on the counter. My first instinct is to call Katrina, but I know how busy it is at her house at this hour with four kids. I open the fridge and take out the bottle of white wine I bought the other day. As much as I want to watch the game, I need a moment to deal with the sadness swirling in my chest. It's crazy that a cold text from Ryan affects me this much. Maybe it's my hormones. I always get mopey during my period.

I fill the wine glass to the brim, grab the bag of potato chips, and head to the balcony. The weather is still nice. Mrs. Carpenter's balcony isn't as large as the one the boys have, but it's big enough to fit Humberto's little haven. Tortoises fare better outdoors.

The tension leaves me as the wine spreads through my body, but the sadness doesn't go away. I go back inside only when it starts to get chilly. I left my phone on the kitchen counter and, unable to control myself, I check to see if Ryan messaged me again.

He didn't.

I refill my glass and drink it in one gulp before I refill it again. I never drink this much during the week, but I'm making an exception tonight.

CHAPTER 46
JUNE

I wake up to the sound of loud knocking. I'm groggy —either from sleep, or I'm still drunk. My head is pounding, and it feels like I swallowed a desert. Winston barks, which only makes my headache worse. I left my phone in the kitchen, so I have no idea what time it is, but my body is telling me it's the middle of the night.

I get out of bed in a rush and stride to the living room. I'm going to kill whoever is at my door. In hindsight, whoever is knocking at this hour must either be having an emergency or have bad intentions. None of those thoughts are clear in my throbbing, cotton-candy-filled brain.

"Peaches.... let me in, please," Ryan says in a ragged voice, making my heart lurch.

Jesus. Why didn't I think it could be him? Blame the alcohol and lack of sleep.

I open the door and find Ryan leaning against the frame. He's wearing slacks and a button-down shirt, which means he went out. He canceled on me last minute to go somewhere, and that makes me beyond angry. Maybe I'd have controlled my emotions better if I wasn't so damn irritated already for getting woken up in the middle of the night.

"Where have you been?"

"To a bar... or a few. I don't remember."

"And you *drove*?" My voice rises in pitch, making him wince.

"I'm a very good driver." He leans forward. "Are you going to let me in?"

"I'm not sure yet. Why are you here?"

His lips curl into a crooked smile. "Because I missed you."

I know I shouldn't take the words of a drunk seriously, but my heart melts a little. Winston tries to escape, so I need to either let Ryan in or shut the door in his face. I bend over to grab Winston's collar so he won't take off, and open the door wider.

"You can come in for a little bit."

"Aww, only a little bit?" He shuts the door, then wraps his arms around my waist, pulling me closer. "Didn't you hear me when I said I missed you?"

I smell whiskey on his breath. It's not unpleasant, but I'm still annoyed and hurt over what he did, so I push him off me.

"I heard you, but I'm not super happy with you right now."

His brows shoot up. "Why not? Oh, is it because I didn't watch the game with you?"

I cross my arms. "No. It's because you waited until the last minute to cancel on me."

"I'm sorry. I'm not very good with appointments." He staggers into the living room and collapses on the couch.

What kind of lame-ass, half-baked excuse is that? I can't even bring myself to say so, because it wouldn't register. "What are you doing?"

"Resting."

"Go to your apartment and your satin sheets then."

"In a minute." He removes his sling, then covers his face with his good arm and, not much later, starts to snore.

My mouth hangs open as I watch him sleep for a couple beats. I'm so angry, I could throw a glass of cold water on his face. But I curl my hands into fists instead and count to ten in my head. The best I can do is to go back to bed and try to get some sleep. Unlike him, I have to wake up early and go to work.

RYAN

I don't know where I am at first, but I know I drank way too much last night. My memories are fuzzy, and my mouth tastes like something crawled inside and died. When my blurry vision adjusts, I realize I'm in Mrs. Carpenter's apartment. I slept on her couch.

Shit. Where's June?

I sit up too fast and regret it. My head is pounding. One of the cats—I can't tell if it's Eros or Apollo—glowers at me from the chair opposite the couch.

"What are you staring at?"

Upon hearing my voice, Winston comes over, wanting to play.

"Not now, boy." I get up and trudge into the kitchen. The clock on the microwave says it's past nine. June must be at work already. I look for a note, but I don't find anything. Maybe she texted me. I pat my pockets, trying to find my phone.

"Hell. Did I lose it last night?"

I return to the couch and find the sucker under the cushions. There's no text from June either, but there are a few from Jake, Lachy, and my other teammates. We won last night. I reply-all with a generic-as-fuck text, and then I massage my temples, regretting my life choices. I'm not one to lose control like I did last night, but the news I received from my brother ripped the rug from underneath my feet. Alcohol obviously didn't help. I feel as wretched as before, and now I have a hangover on top of it.

And I fucked up with June. I shouldn't have canceled on her like I did without giving her any explanation. Even though I've already shared so much of my past with her, I couldn't do it last night. As much as I hate not being with her, it's better this way. I'll never be the man she deserves.

JUNE

I could have been vindictive this morning and made a lot of noise to wake up Ryan. But I was no longer angry, just sad that I let myself get attached to him. To be fair, he warned me. It's my fault for being the dumb chick who thinks a man can change for her.

Jake and Lachy texted me earlier to ask if I watched the game. I lied and said yes, but I really caught only the highlights. They won, and I regretted being too tipsy to pay attention.

I don't see Katrina until lunch time, and only because she comes to my classroom.

"Why are you avoiding my texts, girlie?"

Resting my forehead in my hand, I groan. "I've been avoiding all messages."

She pulls up a chair. "What's wrong?"

"I drank too much white wine last night."

"Oh... with Ryan?"

I wince. "No. He bailed on me."

Her eyes widen. "Oh, fuck he didn't."

"And last minute, without any explanation. *He* was the one who invited me to watch the game at his place." I shake my head. "I can't even say I was blindsided. He told me on the night we met he wasn't Prince Charming."

"Don't you dare take responsibility for his douchery."

"I'm not. But I can't help feeling stupid for lowering my barriers around him. After he canceled on me, he came over at three in the morning, drunk as a skunk."

"No. Please tell me you didn't let him in."

I drop my gaze to my uneaten sandwich. "I did. I was tired and half drunk. It didn't do any good. He came in and passed out on the couch. He was still sleeping when I left this morning."

"You didn't wake him?"

"No."

"I'd have thrown a bucket of cold water on his head."

I crack a smile. "The idea crossed my mind, but then I'd have had to clean up the mess. Plus, I wasn't in the mood to deal with him."

Katrina shrugs. "It's his loss, baby girl. Don't forget

you still have two hunky players who are very much into you."

My grin broadens. "That's true. I can't wait to see them again."

CHAPTER 47
JAKE

This was a short trip; we had only two away games—one in Chicago yesterday, and one in Detroit tonight. We won both, and Lachy had a shutout in Detroit. But despite our achievements, I feel wretched on the flight back to LA, and not because it's late. The mood on the plane is celebratory. The guys are all laughing and horsing around, but I'm too anxious to join them. I can't wait to get home and see June.

But I haven't forgotten the conversation I had with my father prior to this trip. If the price to keep playing hockey is signing with the Bobcats, I'd rather retire. Still, I can't put Lachy's and Ryan's careers at risk too. Bluff or not, my father *will* find a way to ruin their lives as punishment for me not obeying him.

You'd think that a grown man wouldn't be bound by

his parents, but when you have a rich, narcissistic son of a bitch for a father, the chains are thick.

Lachy takes the empty seat next to mine, stretching his legs and crowding me. "What's on yer mind, lad? You've been brooding more than usual." His accent is thick thanks to all the beers he's had.

I shake my head. "It's nothing."

"Horse shite. Are you still thinking about yer father?"

At first, I clench my jaw and stare out the window. But I can't escape Lachy's intense stare, burning a hole through my face. "I don't want to drag you into my family drama."

He snorts. "Yer not dragging me into anything. Yer my brother, Jake. You and the other pest."

I chuckle. "That's right. You *are* my brothers. That's why I put up with you two."

"That's bloody right. When I was a kid, I always dreamed I'd get adopted by a family with lots of kids. I didn't care if they were boys or girls. I just wanted many siblings. I never got my wish then, but I got it now."

Lachy's voice is filled with emotion. When I glance at him, he seems far away. He's never tried to hide that he grew up in the foster system. The fraying blankie he still holds on to is the only thing he has left from his parents. My heart becomes small and heavy. I'd do everything for him and Ryan.

He turns to me, his blue eyes more intense than

usual. "Go on then. Tell me what that arsehole wanted with you."

I release a heavy sigh, knowing it's pointless to keep anything from him. "He wants me to play for the Bobcats."

Lachy snorts. "Is he delusional?"

"No, just an arrogant son of bitch who thinks he owns the world. I told him not a chance in hell."

"He's the royal admiral of arseholery," Lachy mutters.

"He's threatening to leak what he did for me to the press."

Knowing exactly what I'm talking about, Lachy furrows his brows. "I thought those records were sealed."

"They are, but that doesn't stop him from using them to blackmail me."

"You did nothing wrong. That piece of shite deserved what he got."

"It doesn't matter. It's all about perception, and with my current reputation of being a hothead, you know the media will eviscerate me. I might get fired."

"I won't let that happen. I'll walk if they let you go."

The barbed wire around my heart tightens. That's exactly what I can't allow to happen.

"I appreciate the sentiment, but you know I can't let you do that."

"Yes, cause you're a bloody martyr." He cracks a

smile. "Then we change the narrative before yer father has the chance to fuck things up."

"What do you mean?"

"You clean up your image."

I laugh without humor. "I don't know how I'll erase a reputation I cultivated for years in just a few weeks."

"We'll think of something. Don't worry. I got your back."

Arching my brow, I give him a double take. "Who are you and what have you done to Lachlan?"

His eyes widen. "What?"

"You're the most pessimistic person I know."

He focuses on the TV screen in front of his seat. "People can change."

"Yes, some people can. But you're not people. You're an immovable mountain."

He snickers. "Listen to yourself. You sound like Ryan."

I clench my jaw, trying to think of a retort, but nothing comes to me. "Whatever. What are you watching?"

"Castlevania."

I wrinkle my nose. "What is it? A cute cartoon about vampires?"

Smirking, Lachy puts his show on my TV screen as well. "Sure. Very cute. You'll love it."

It doesn't take long for me to realize this animated

series wasn't meant for kids. It's violent and gory, and I do love it.

I'm super into it when the plane drops suddenly, and my stomach goes with it.

"Bloody hell. What was that?" Lachy asks, his voice mixing with our teammates' murmurs.

The fasten-seatbelt light turns on.

"I don't know. Maybe we hit a patch of turbulence." I watch the flight attendant rush down the aisle toward the cockpit. She looks worried.

Then we all hear a loud *pop* before another drop lifts my ass from my seat. There are shouts and nervous cursing. My pulse accelerates. We've traveled through turbulence before, but this feels different.

A second later, the pilot makes an announcement that freezes the blood in my veins. We've lost one engine and need to prepare for an emergency landing.

"Motherfucker." Lachy glances at me, his eyes round with fear.

I grab his hand and squeeze it tight. "We're gonna be okay, buddy."

The front of the plane dips at a sharp angle. We're nosediving out of the sky.

I thought I had reached a point in my life that, if I died, I would have no regrets. But that was before June came along. I close my eyes and pray—something I've never done before. I want the chance to tell that sweet and sexy girl how much she means to me.

CHAPTER 48
JUNE

Jake and Lachy are coming home tonight. They've been gone for only three days, but I really miss them. They'll arrive in the middle of the night, and the sensible thing would be to see them tomorrow morning, but I doubt I'll get any sleep. I'm going to wait up to see them home safe.

But I have a plan to pass the time. Every year, Katrina and I knit sweaters, scarves, hats, and gloves to donate to homeless shelters across town. It's already October, and even though the weather is pleasant, it'll get cold soon.

I didn't hear from Ryan all day. A part of me was hoping he'd call, or even text to apologize, but his silence speaks louder than words. Our fling has reached its expiration date. Maybe he liked me only when he was sharing with his friends. My heart is bruised, but I won't let that sour my excitement about seeing his roommates.

I'm sorting through my knitting supplies when there's a knock on my door. For fuck's sake, if it's Ryan again dead drunk, he'll get a taste of a pissed-off Southern woman. Winston usually springs to his paws and barks whenever someone knocks, but it's already past one in the morning, and the poor guy is half asleep. All he does is lift his muzzle a little, then rest it on his paws again. Eros and Apollo don't move from their beds.

I get up and stride to the front door. I do find Ryan standing in the hallway, but he doesn't look drunk, he looks distressed.

My gut clenches. "Ryan? What happened." I step back so he can come in.

When the light hits his face, I see tear streaks on his cheeks. "Melissa called me just now. It's the team plane. It's vanished."

My heart constricts so tight, I can't breathe. "H-how can it vanish?"

"I don't know. What if Jake and Lachy are gone, June?" More tears run down his beautiful face. "What if they're gone?"

"They aren't gone." I'm crying, too, when I pull him into a hug.

He hides his face in the crook of my neck and sobs loudly. "I won't survive if they leave me too."

I lean back and capture his face between my hands. "They aren't leaving us."

He doesn't speak for a couple of beats, but he holds my stare. "I'm sorry I was a jackass to you, Peaches. I didn't want to hurt you."

Despite his ill-timed confession, his apology offers a balm to my heavy heart. "Don't worry about that." I drop my hands from his face and try to step back, but he holds me in place.

"I don't want to lose you too."

"You're not going to lose me." I rise on my tiptoes and kiss him hard, needing the connection so I don't spiral. His tongue is as savage as mine. I can taste his fear and desperation, and they match my own.

Jake and Lachy can't be gone.

They can't.

*** **TO BE CONTINUED** ***

ABOUT THE AUTHOR

USA Today Bestselling Author Michelle Hercules always knew creative arts were her calling but not in a million years did she think she would become an author. With a background in fashion design she thought she would follow that path. But one day, out of the blue, she had an idea for a book. One page turned into ten pages, ten pages turned into a hundred, and before she knew it, her first novel, The Prophecy of Arcadia, was born.

Michelle Hercules resides in Florida with her husband and daughter. She is currently working on the *Blueblood Vampires* series and the *Filthy Gods* series.

Sign-up for Michelle Hercules' Newsletter: